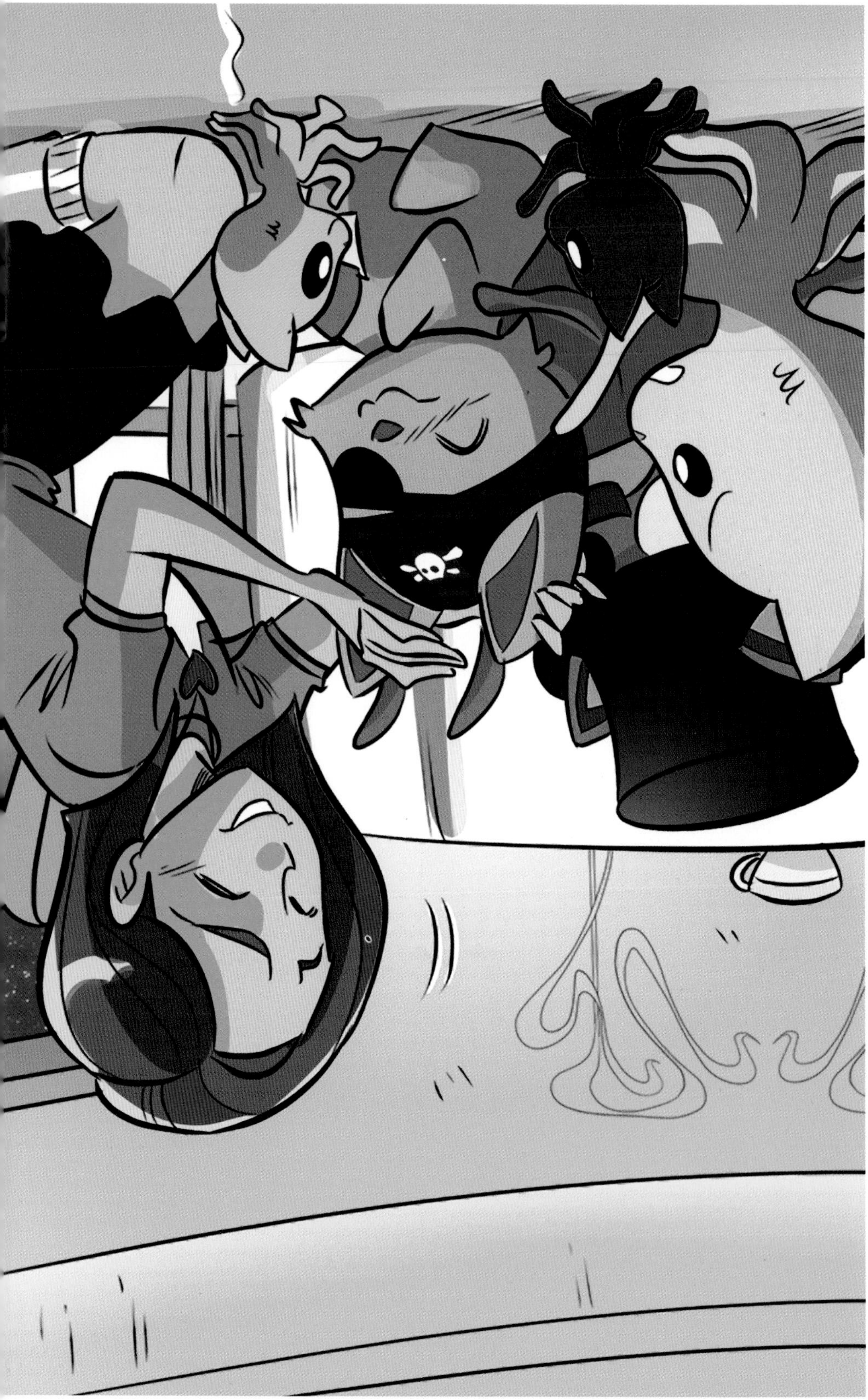

TENTACLE KITTY

Tales around the Teacup

Written by
John & Raena Merritt

Illustrated by
Jean Claudio Vinci

Lettered by
Taylor Esposito

Dark Horse Books

President and Publisher **Mike Richardson**

Editor **Shantel LaRocque**

Associate Editor **Brett Israel**

Assistant Editor **Sanjay Dharawat**

Designer **Diego Morales-Portillo**

Digital Art Technician **Samantha Hummer**

Neil Hankerson Executive Vice President • **Tom Weddle** Chief Financial Officer • **Dale LaFountain** Chief Information Officer • **Tim Wiesch** Vice President of Licensing • **Matt Parkinson** Vice President of Marketing • **Vanessa Todd-Holmes** Vice President of Production and Scheduling • **Mark Bernardi** Vice President of Book Trade and Digital Sales • **Randy Lahrman** Vice President of Product Development • **Ken Lizzi** General Counsel • **Dave Marshall** Editor in Chief • **Davey Estrada** Editorial Director • **Chris Warner** Senior Books Editor • **Cary Grazzini** Director of Specialty Projects • **Lia Ribacchi** Art Director • **Matt Dryer** Director of Digital Art and Prepress • **Michael Gombos** Senior Director of Licensed Publications • **Kari Yadro** Director of Custom Programs • **Kari Torson** Director of International Licensing

Published by Dark Horse Books
A division of Dark Horse Comics LLC
10956 SE Main Street
Milwaukie, OR 97222

TentacleKitty.com
DarkHorse.com

To find a comics shop in your area, visit comicshoplocator.com

First edition: April 2022
Ebook ISBN 978-1-50672-397-6 • Trade Paperback ISBN 978-1-50672-396-9

10 9 8 7 6 5 4 3 2 1
Printed in China

Library of Congress Cataloging-in-Publication Data

Names: Merritt, John, writer. | Merritt, Raena, writer. | Vinci, Jean-Claudio, illustrator. | Esposito, Taylor, letterer.
Title: Tentacle kitty : tales around the teacup / written by John Merritt & Raena Merritt ; illustrated by Jean-Claudio Vinci ; lettered by Taylor Esposito.
Description: First edition. | Milwaukie, OR : Dark Horse Books, 2022. | Audience: Ages 8+ | Audience: Grades 2-3 | Summary: Tentacle kitty and friends gather for tea and tell stories -- from hunting down cotton candy mice, to pirate hijinks.
Identifiers: LCCN 2021048185 | ISBN 9781506723969 (trade paperback) | ISBN 9781506723976
Subjects: CYAC: Graphic novels. | Storytelling--Fiction. | LCGFT: Graphic novels.
Classification: LCC PZ7.7.M465 Ten 2022 | DDC 741.5/973--dc23/eng/20211008
LC record available at https://lccn.loc.gov/2021048185

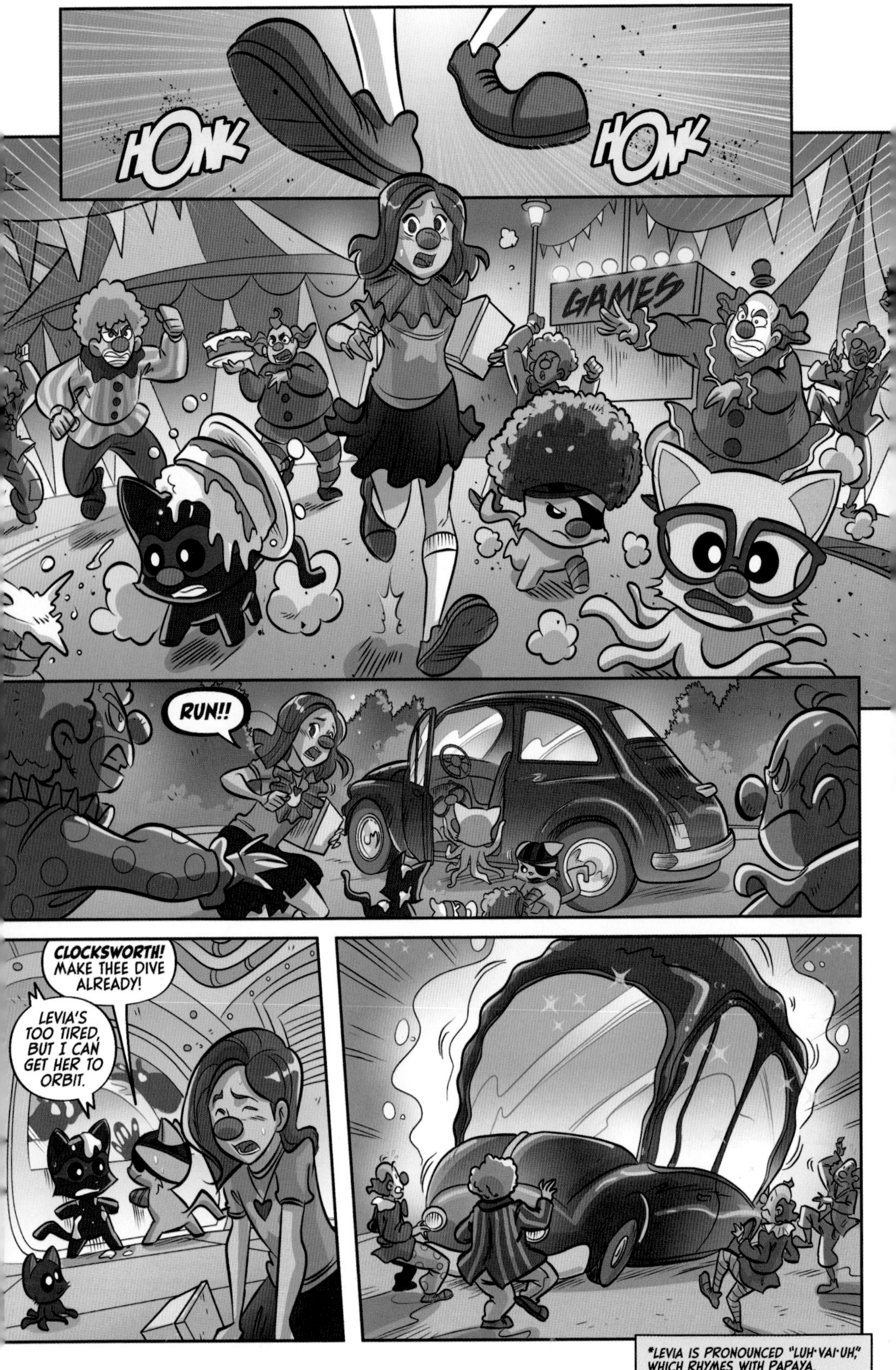
HONK
HONK
GAMES
RUN!!
CLOCKSWORTH! MAKE THEE DIVE ALREADY!
LEVIA'S TOO TIRED, BUT I CAN GET HER TO ORBIT.
*LEVIA IS PRONOUNCED "LUH·VAI·UH," WHICH RHYMES WITH PAPAYA.

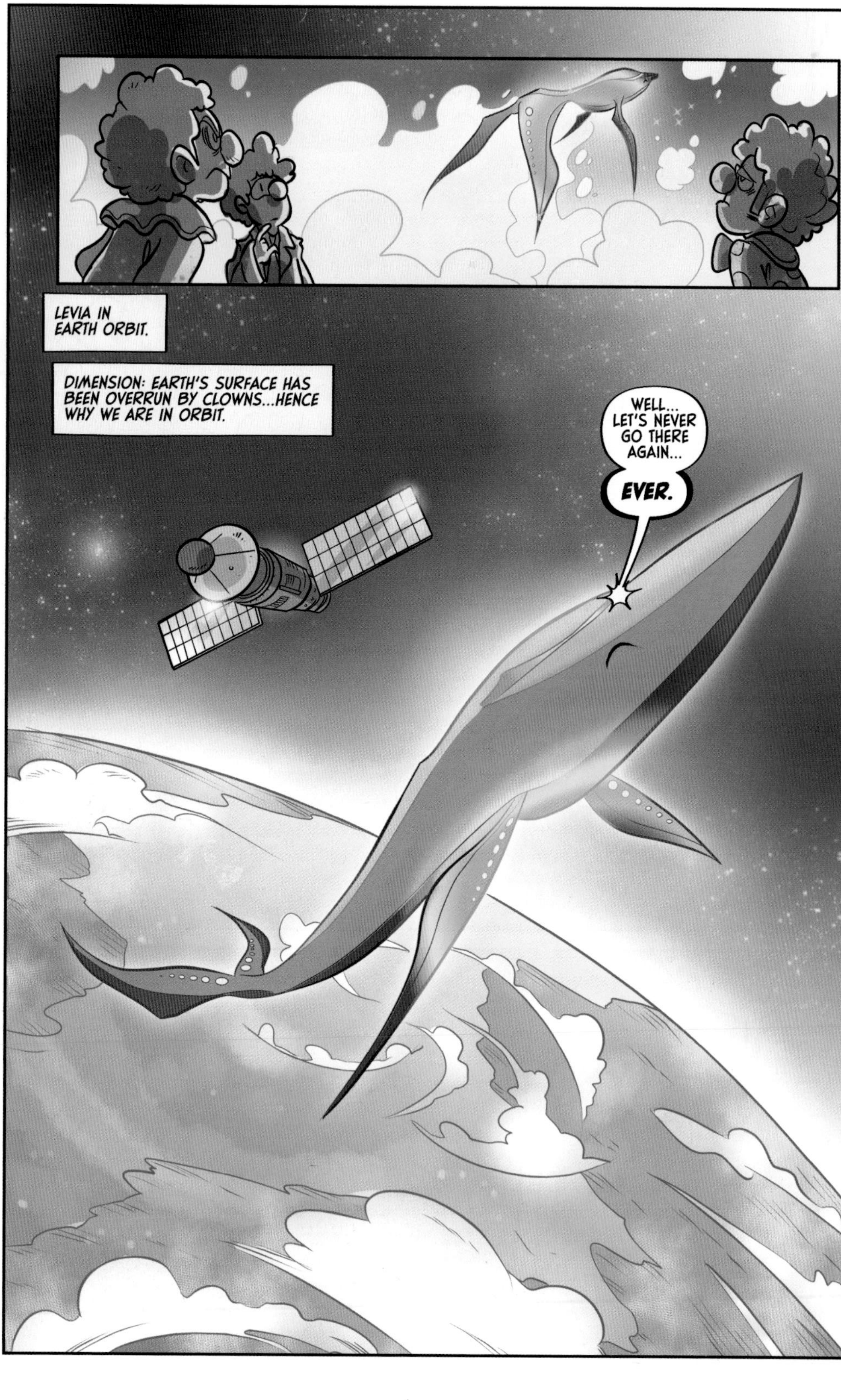
LEVIA IN EARTH ORBIT.
DIMENSION: EARTH'S SURFACE HAS BEEN OVERRUN BY CLOWNS...HENCE WHY WE ARE IN ORBIT.
WELL... LET'S NEVER GO THERE AGAIN...
EVER.

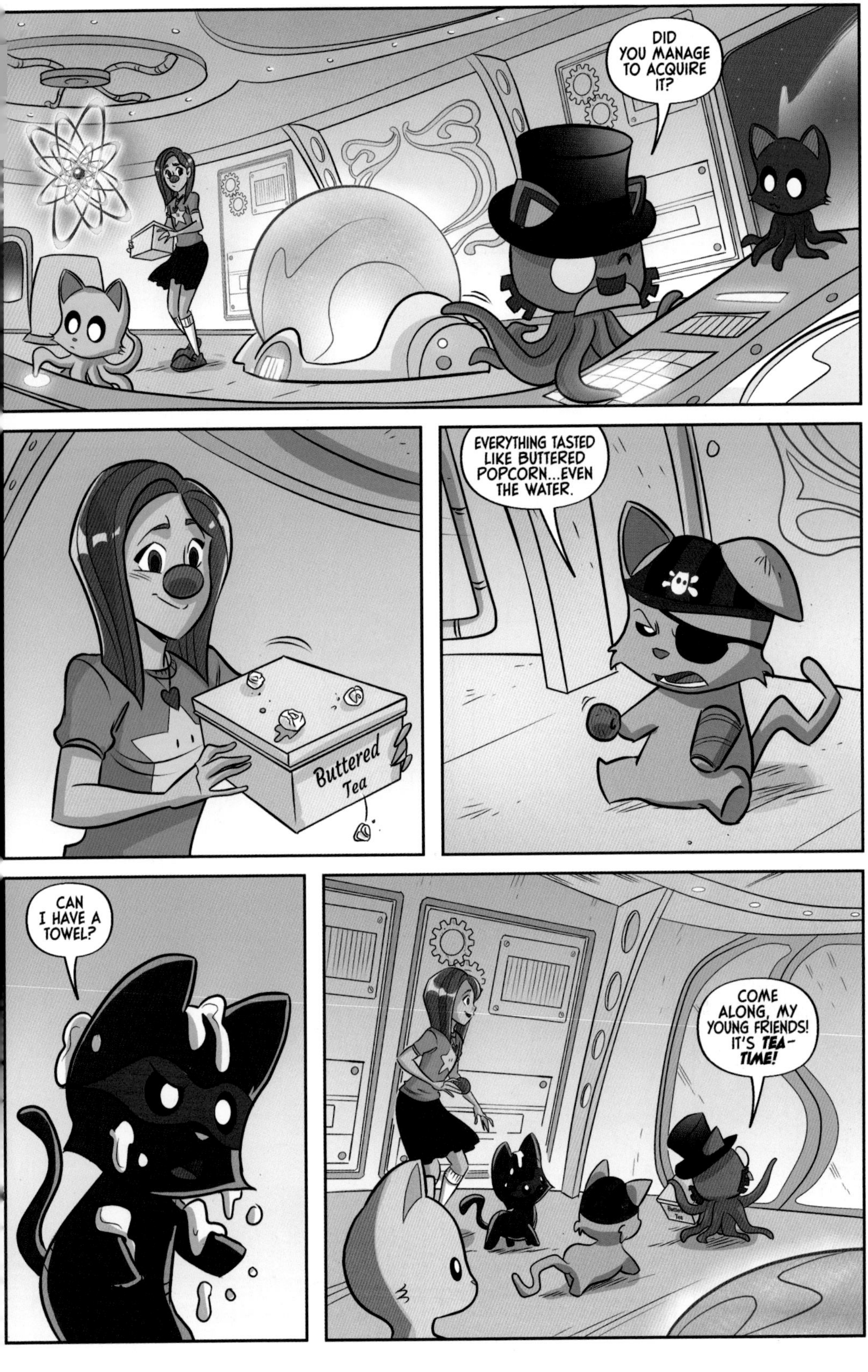
DID YOU MANAGE TO ACQUIRE IT?
Buttered Tea
EVERYTHING TASTED LIKE BUTTERED POPCORN...EVEN THE WATER.
CAN I HAVE A TOWEL?
COME ALONG, MY YOUNG FRIENDS! IT'S **TEA-TIME!**

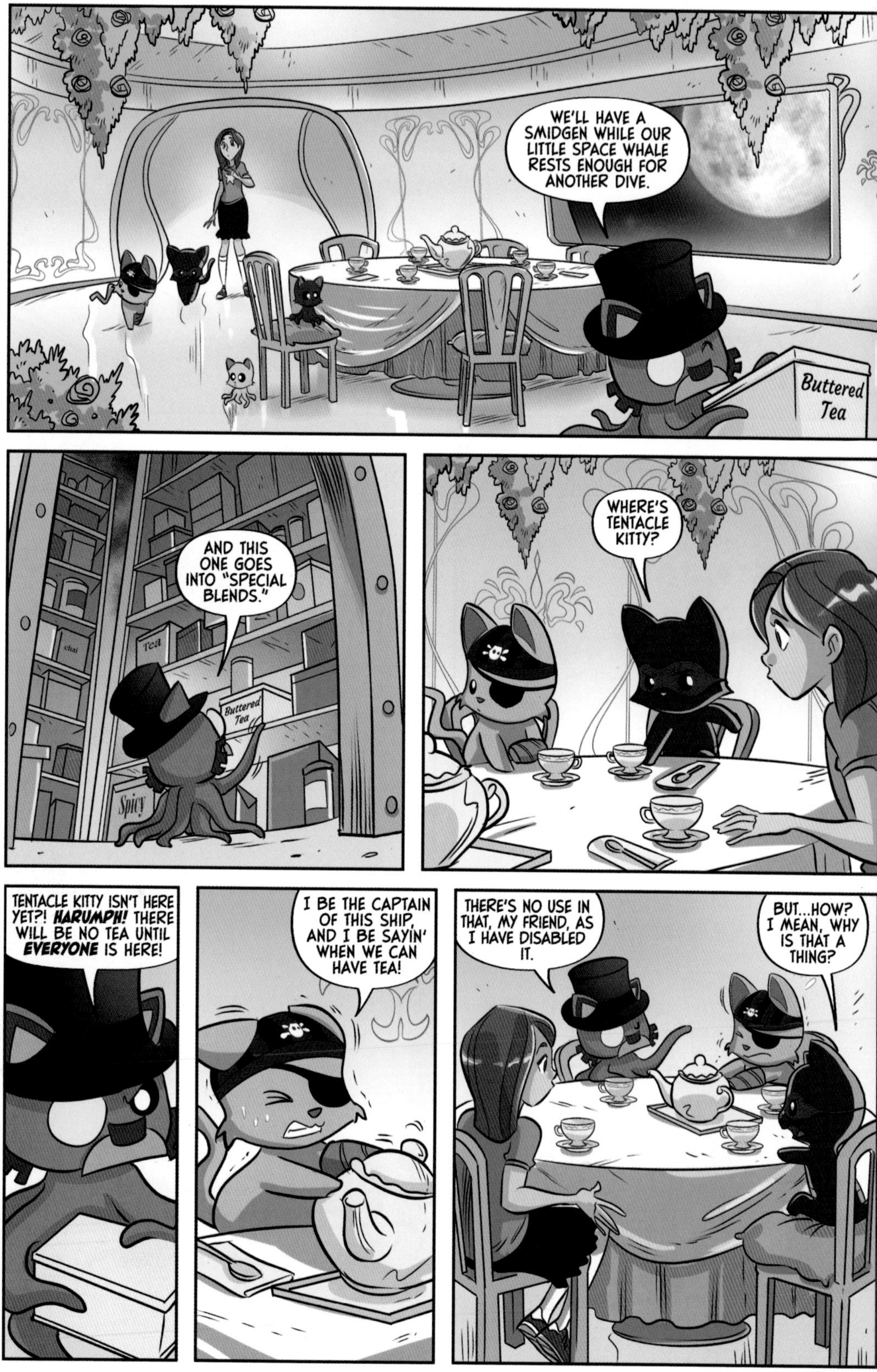
WE'LL HAVE A SMIDGEN WHILE OUR LITTLE SPACE WHALE RESTS ENOUGH FOR ANOTHER DIVE.
Buttered Tea
AND THIS ONE GOES INTO "SPECIAL BLENDS."
Tea
chai
Buttered Tea
Spicy
WHERE'S TENTACLE KITTY?
TENTACLE KITTY ISN'T HERE YET?! HARUMPH! THERE WILL BE NO TEA UNTIL EVERYONE IS HERE!
I BE THE CAPTAIN OF THIS SHIP, AND I BE SAYIN' WHEN WE CAN HAVE TEA!
THERE'S NO USE IN THAT, MY FRIEND, AS I HAVE DISABLED IT.
BUT...HOW? I MEAN, WHY IS THAT A THING?

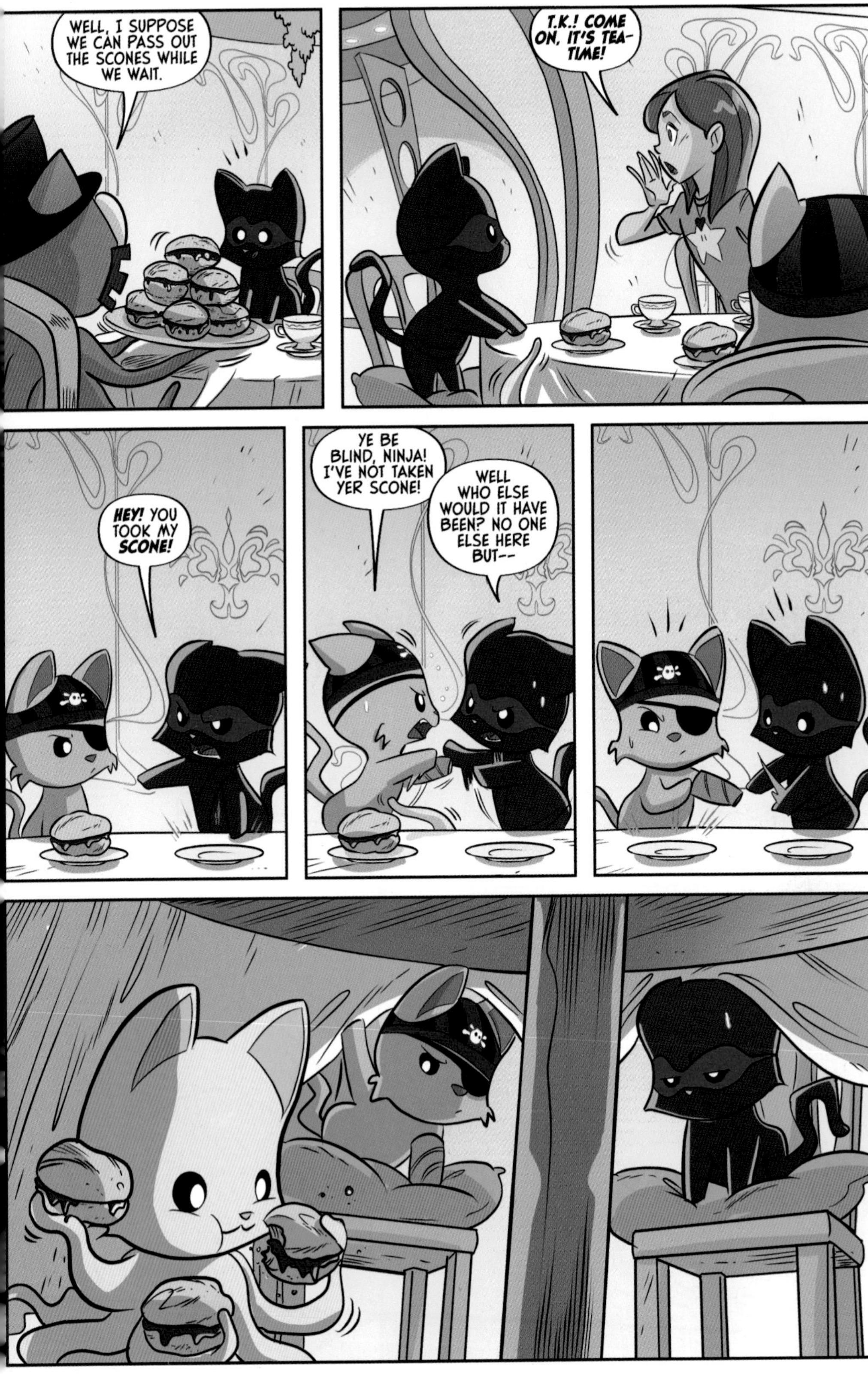
WELL, I SUPPOSE WE CAN PASS OUT THE SCONES WHILE WE WAIT.
T.K.! COME ON, IT'S TEA-TIME!
HEY! YOU TOOK MY SCONE!
YE BE BLIND, NINJA! I'VE NOT TAKEN YER SCONE!
WELL WHO ELSE WOULD IT HAVE BEEN? NO ONE ELSE HERE BUT--

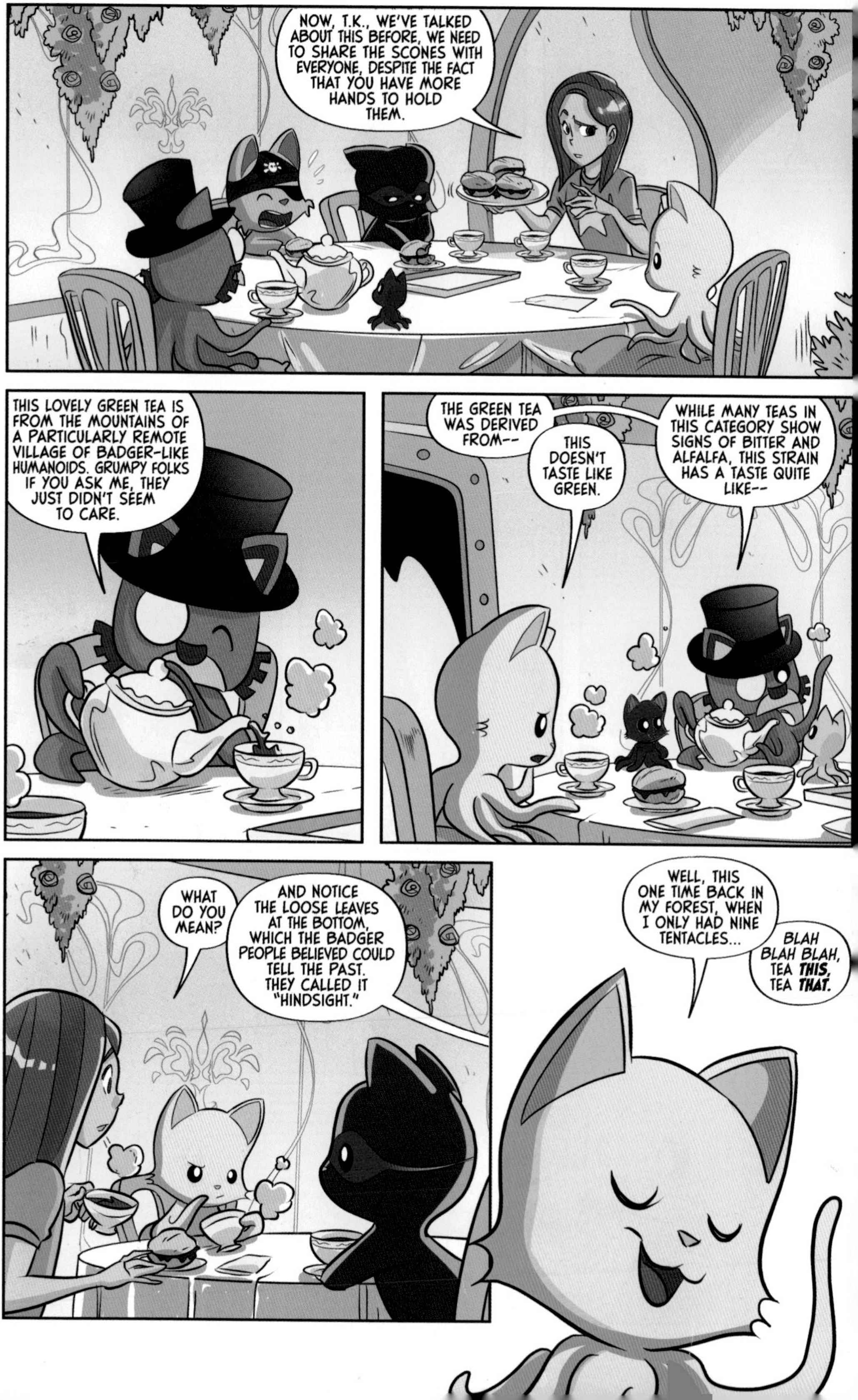
NOW, T.K., WE'VE TALKED ABOUT THIS BEFORE, WE NEED TO SHARE THE SCONES WITH EVERYONE, DESPITE THE FACT THAT YOU HAVE MORE HANDS TO HOLD THEM.
THIS LOVELY GREEN TEA IS FROM THE MOUNTAINS OF A PARTICULARLY REMOTE VILLAGE OF BADGER-LIKE HUMANOIDS. GRUMPY FOLKS IF YOU ASK ME, THEY JUST DIDN'T SEEM TO CARE.
THE GREEN TEA WAS DERIVED FROM--
THIS DOESN'T TASTE LIKE GREEN.
WHILE MANY TEAS IN THIS CATEGORY SHOW SIGNS OF BITTER AND ALFALFA, THIS STRAIN HAS A TASTE QUITE LIKE--
WHAT DO YOU MEAN?
AND NOTICE THE LOOSE LEAVES AT THE BOTTOM, WHICH THE BADGER PEOPLE BELIEVED COULD TELL THE PAST. THEY CALLED IT "HINDSIGHT."
WELL, THIS ONE TIME BACK IN MY FOREST, WHEN I ONLY HAD NINE TENTACLES...
BLAH BLAH BLAH, TEA **THIS,** TEA **THAT.**

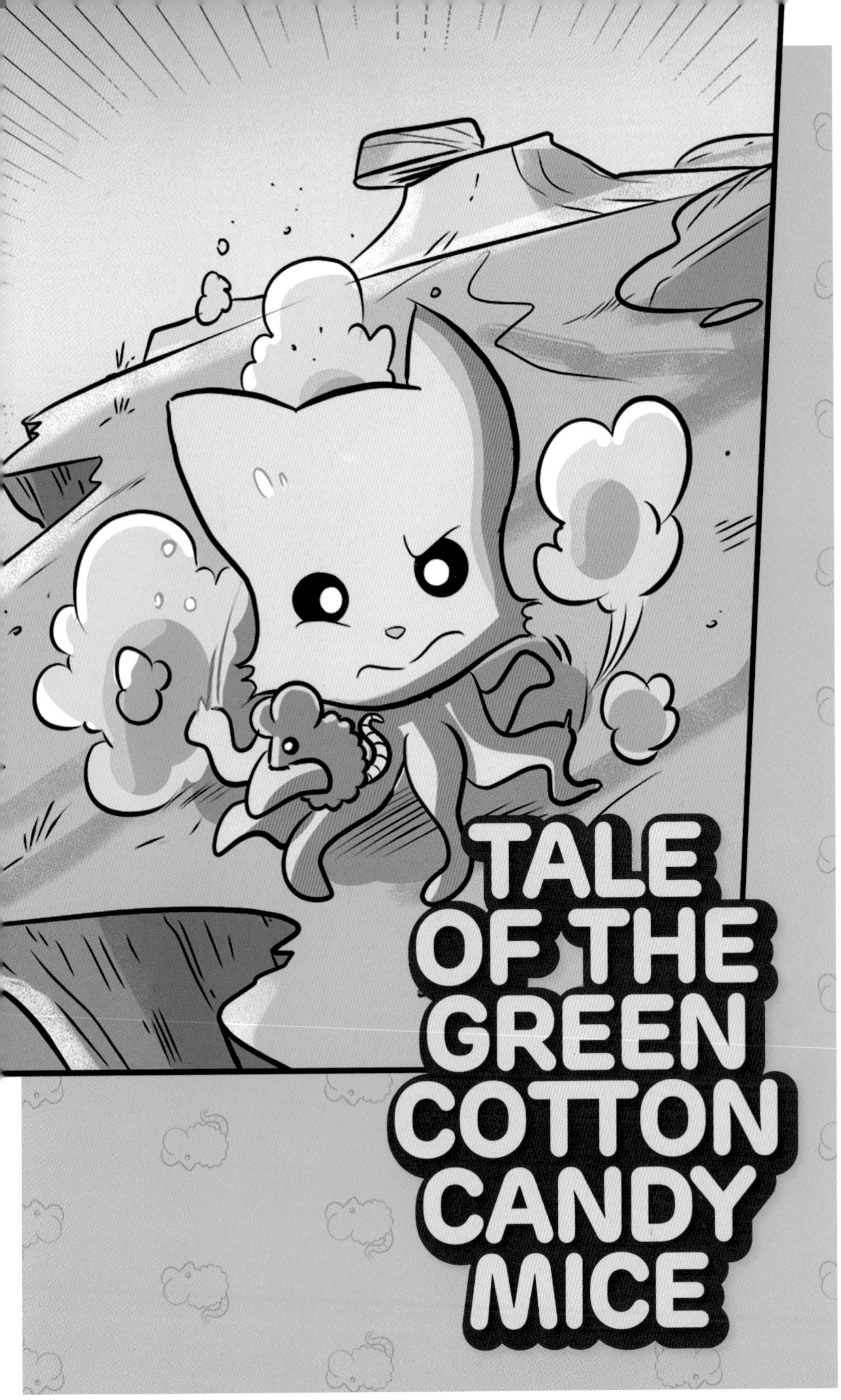

TALE OF THE GREEN COTTON CANDY MICE

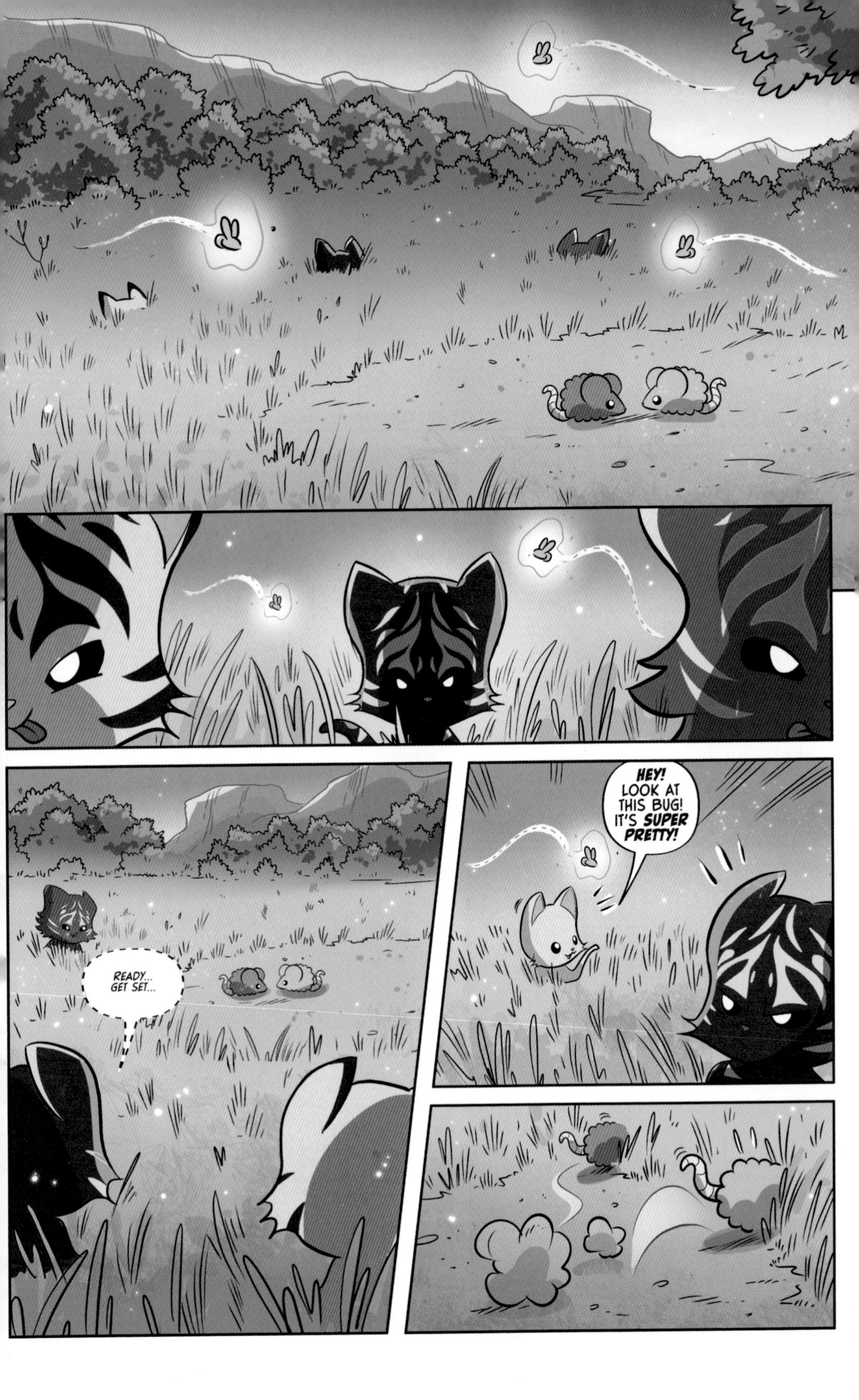
READY... GET SET...
HEY! LOOK AT THIS BUG! IT'S SUPER PRETTY!

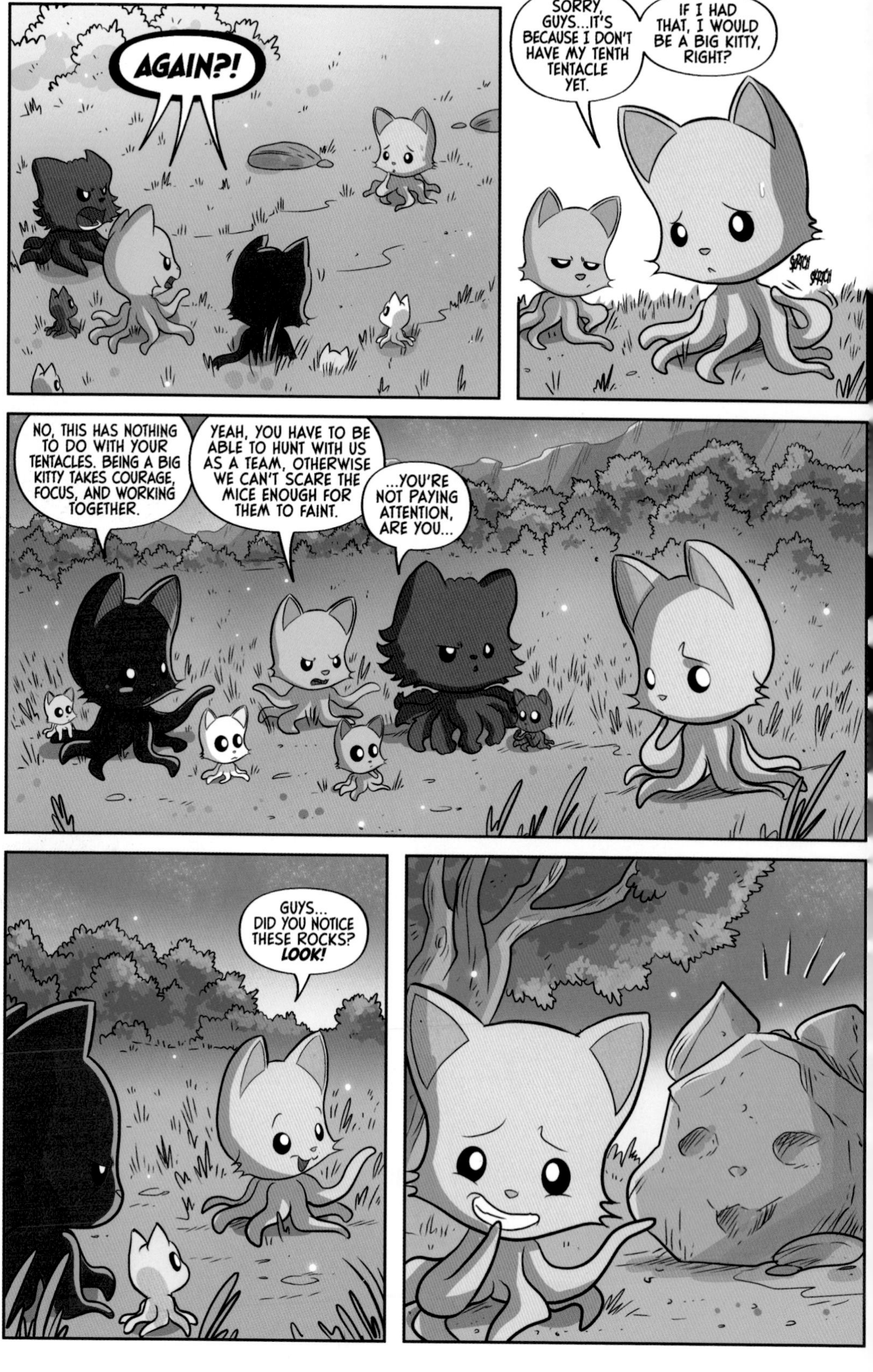
AGAIN?!
SORRY, GUYS...IT'S BECAUSE I DON'T HAVE MY TENTH TENTACLE YET.
IF I HAD THAT, I WOULD BE A BIG KITTY, RIGHT?
NO, THIS HAS NOTHING TO DO WITH YOUR TENTACLES. BEING A BIG KITTY TAKES COURAGE, FOCUS, AND WORKING TOGETHER.
YEAH, YOU HAVE TO BE ABLE TO HUNT WITH US AS A TEAM, OTHERWISE WE CAN'T SCARE THE MICE ENOUGH FOR THEM TO FAINT.
...YOU'RE NOT PAYING ATTENTION, ARE YOU...
GUYS... DID YOU NOTICE THESE ROCKS? LOOK!

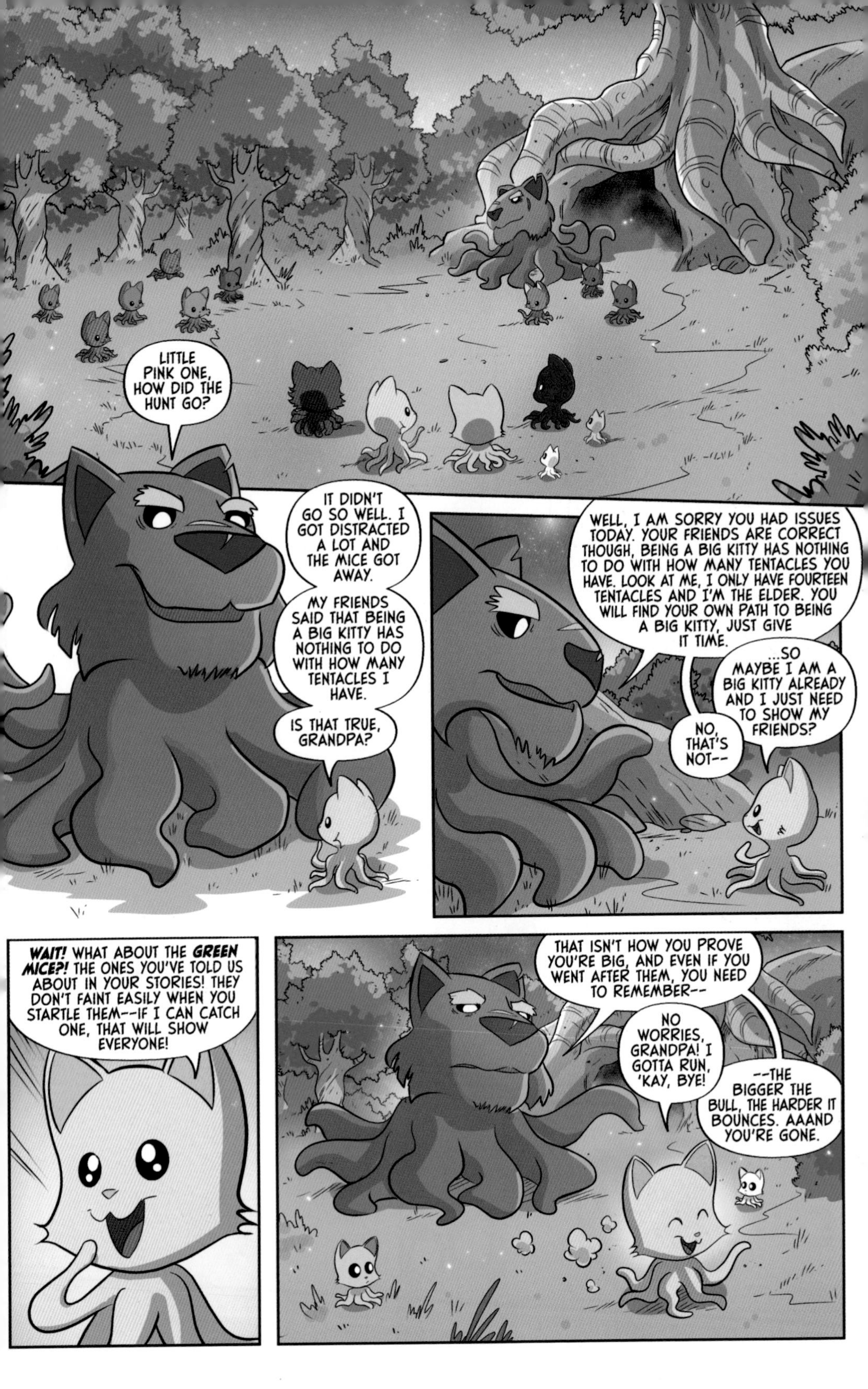
LITTLE PINK ONE, HOW DID THE HUNT GO?
IT DIDN'T GO SO WELL. I GOT DISTRACTED A LOT AND THE MICE GOT AWAY.
MY FRIENDS SAID THAT BEING A BIG KITTY HAS NOTHING TO DO WITH HOW MANY TENTACLES I HAVE.
IS THAT TRUE, GRANDPA?
WELL, I AM SORRY YOU HAD ISSUES TODAY. YOUR FRIENDS ARE CORRECT THOUGH, BEING A BIG KITTY HAS NOTHING TO DO WITH HOW MANY TENTACLES YOU HAVE. LOOK AT ME, I ONLY HAVE FOURTEEN TENTACLES AND I'M THE ELDER. YOU WILL FIND YOUR OWN PATH TO BEING A BIG KITTY, JUST GIVE IT TIME.
...SO MAYBE I AM A BIG KITTY ALREADY AND I JUST NEED TO SHOW MY FRIENDS?
NO, THAT'S NOT--
WAIT! WHAT ABOUT THE GREEN MICE?! THE ONES YOU'VE TOLD US ABOUT IN YOUR STORIES! THEY DON'T FAINT EASILY WHEN YOU STARTLE THEM--IF I CAN CATCH ONE, THAT WILL SHOW EVERYONE!
THAT ISN'T HOW YOU PROVE YOU'RE BIG, AND EVEN IF YOU WENT AFTER THEM, YOU NEED TO REMEMBER--
NO WORRIES, GRANDPA! I GOTTA RUN, 'KAY, BYE!
--THE BIGGER THE BULL, THE HARDER IT BOUNCES. AAAND YOU'RE GONE.

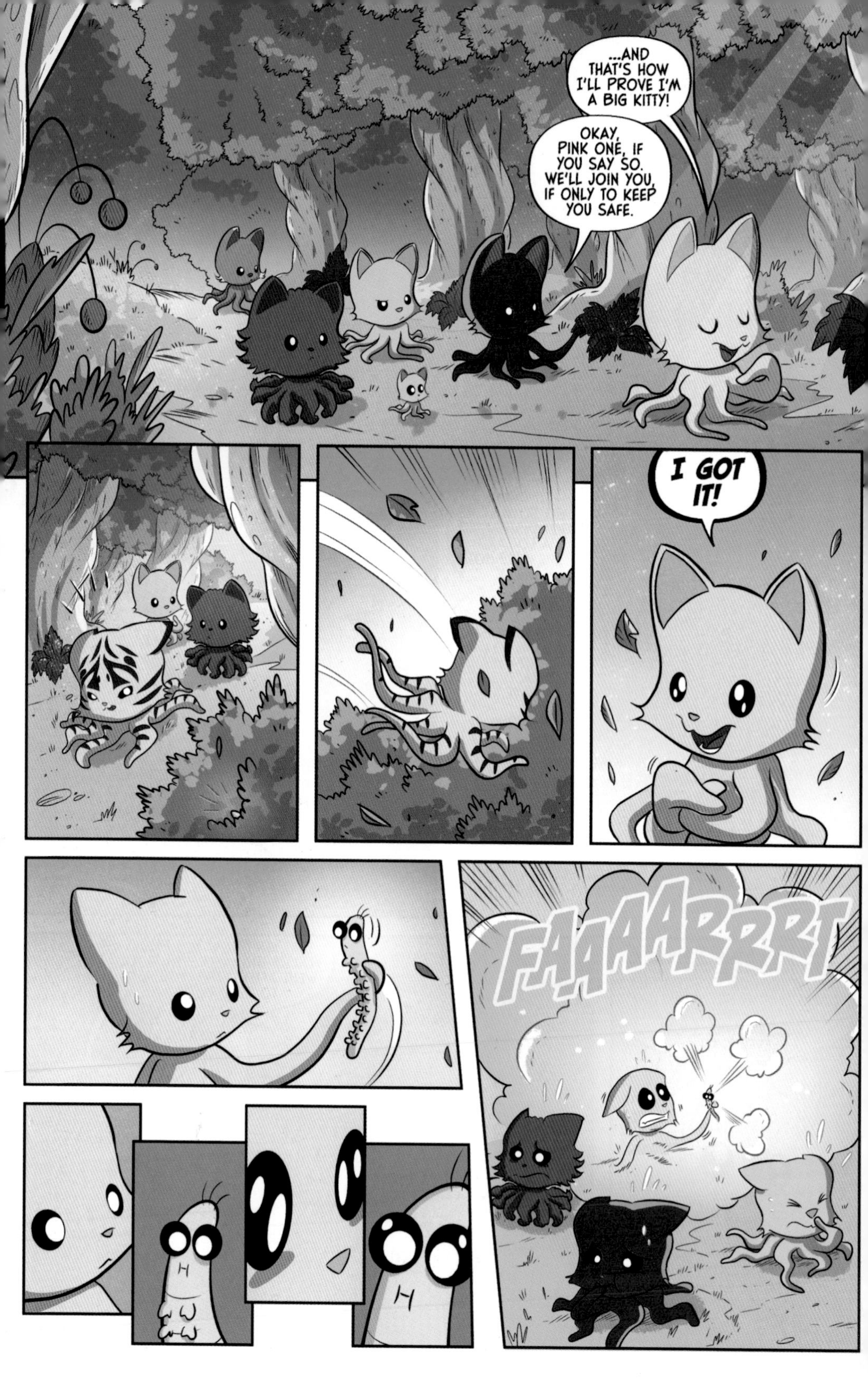
...AND THAT'S HOW I'LL PROVE I'M A BIG KITTY!
OKAY, PINK ONE, IF YOU SAY SO. WE'LL JOIN YOU, IF ONLY TO KEEP YOU SAFE.
I GOT IT!
FAAAARRRT

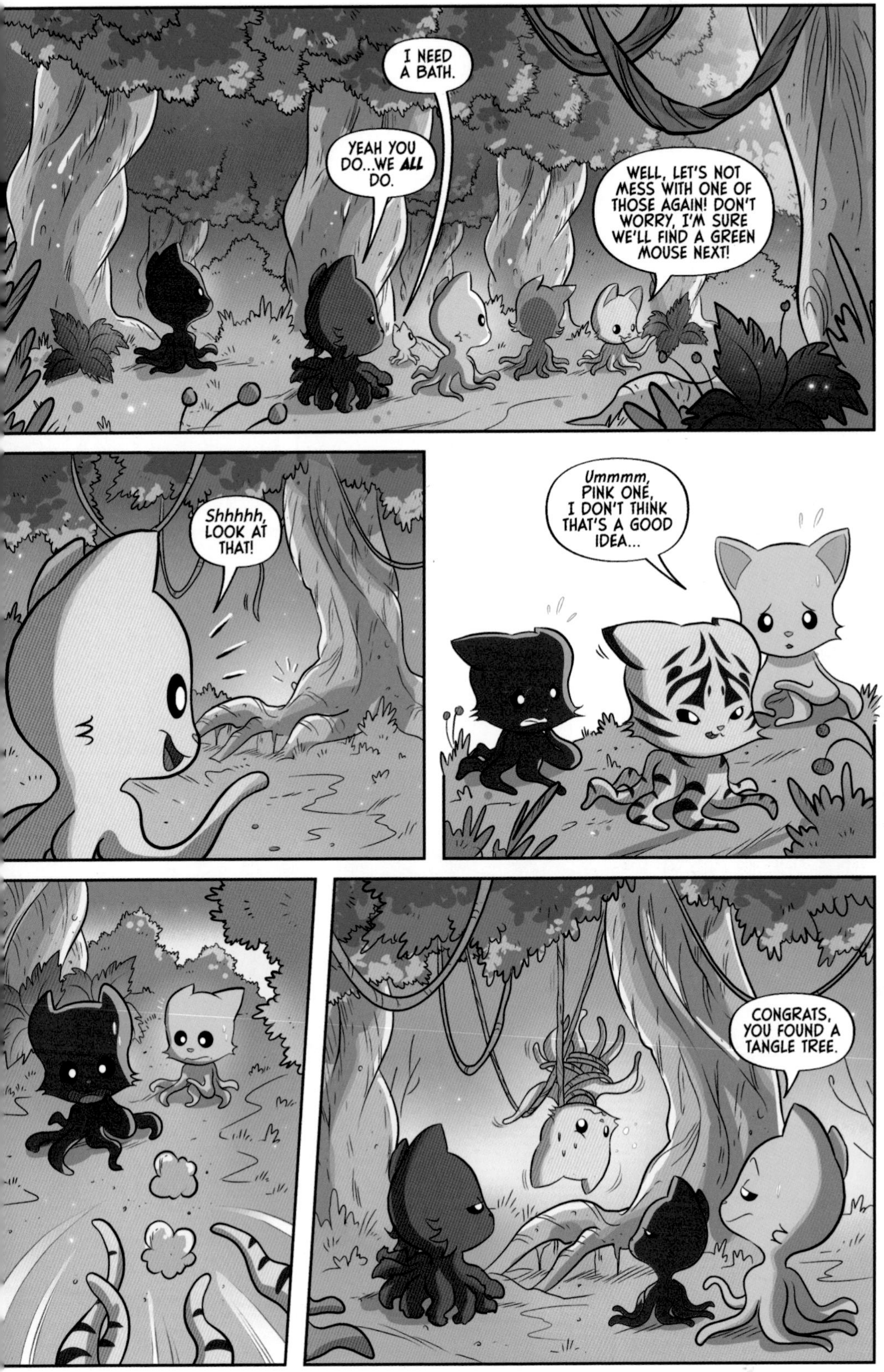
WELL, LET'S NOT MESS WITH ONE OF THOSE AGAIN! DON'T WORRY, I'M SURE WE'LL FIND A GREEN MOUSE NEXT!
YEAH YOU DO...WE ALL DO.
I NEED A BATH.
Shhhhh, LOOK AT THAT!
Ummmm, PINK ONE, I DON'T THINK THAT'S A GOOD IDEA...
CONGRATS, YOU FOUND A TANGLE TREE.

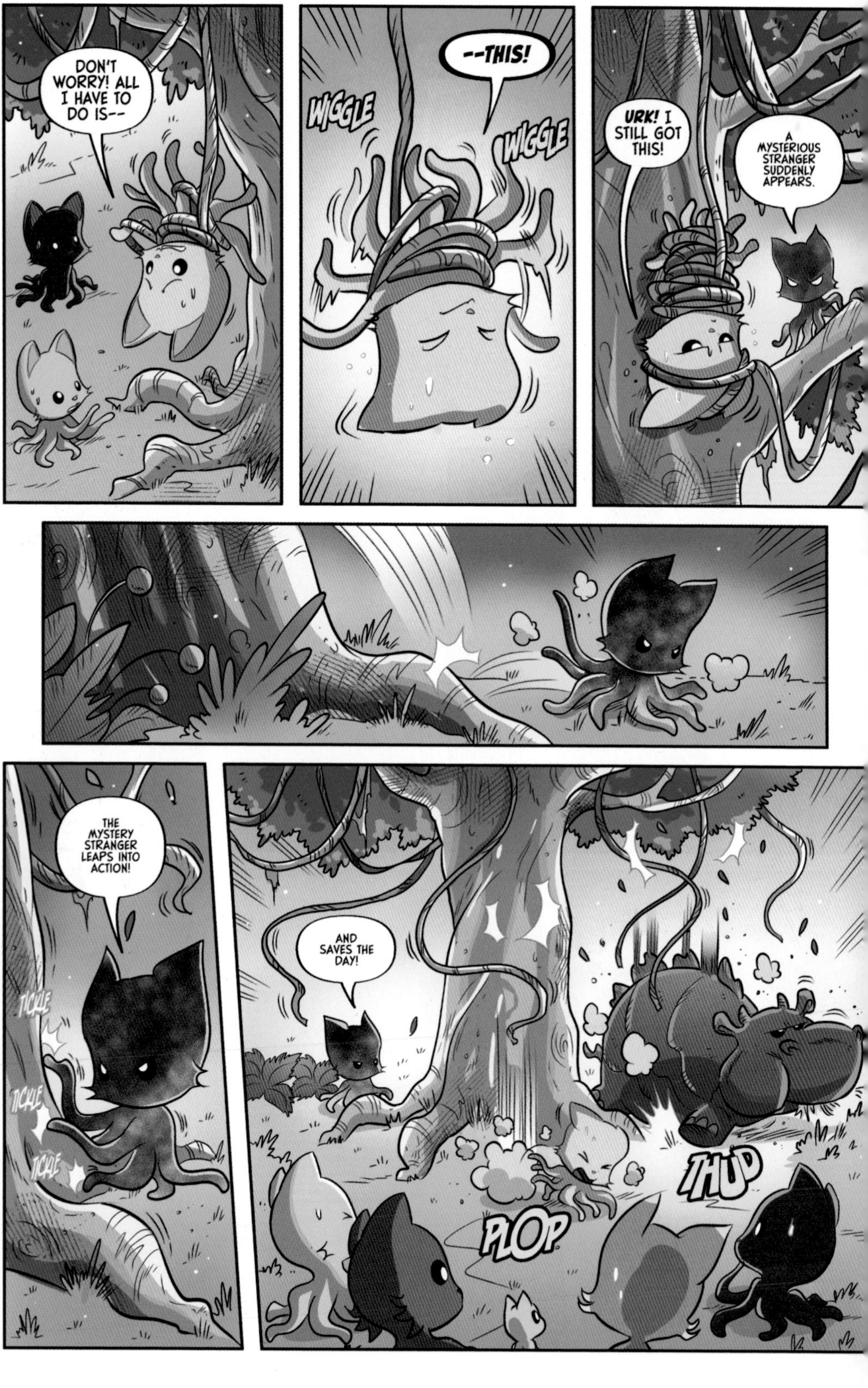
DON'T WORRY! ALL I HAVE TO DO IS--
WIGGLE
WIGGLE
--THIS!
URK! I STILL GOT THIS!
A MYSTERIOUS STRANGER SUDDENLY APPEARS.
THE MYSTERY STRANGER LEAPS INTO ACTION!
TICKLE
TICKLE
TICKLE
AND SAVES THE DAY!
THUD
PLOP

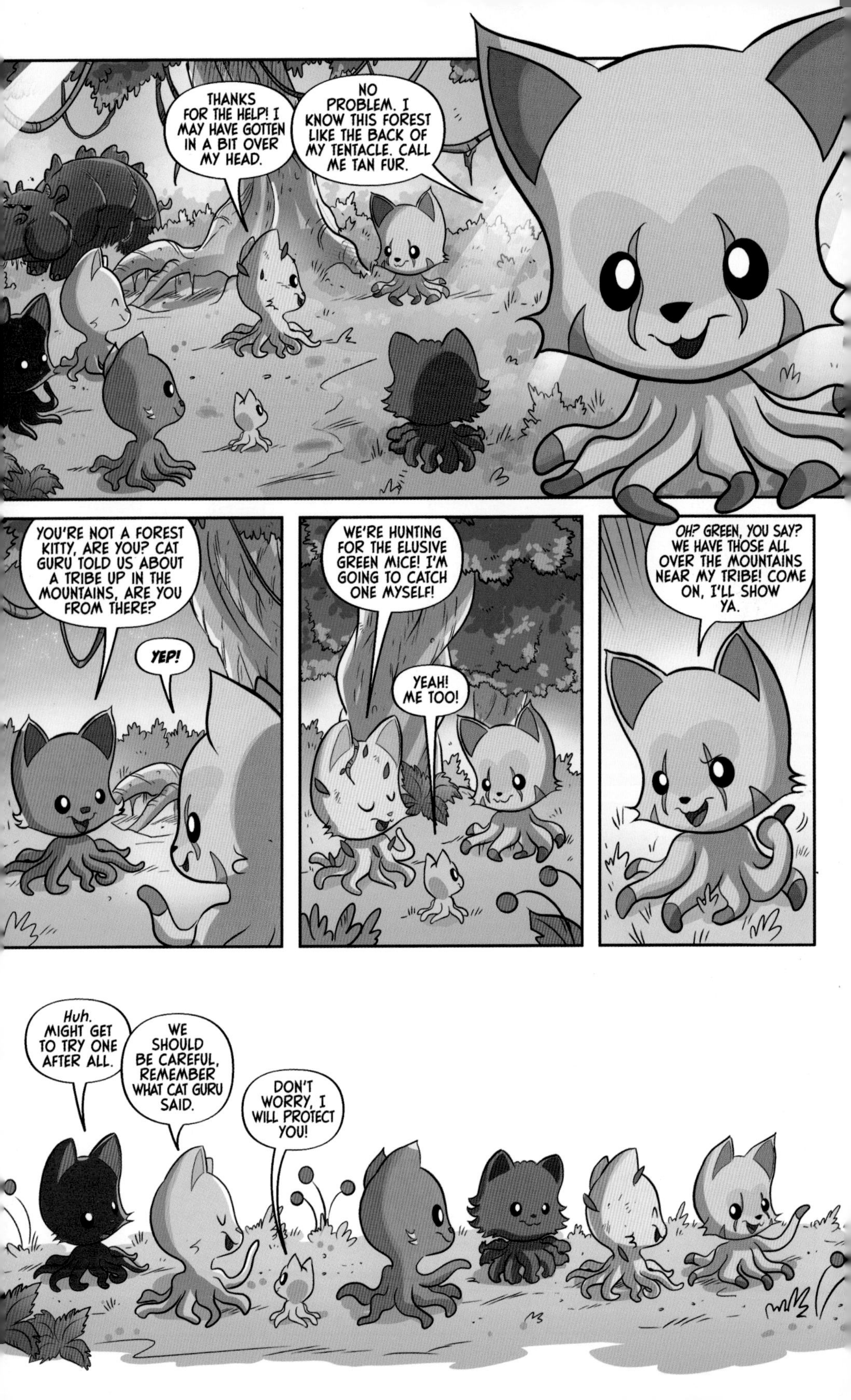
THANKS FOR THE HELP! I MAY HAVE GOTTEN IN A BIT OVER MY HEAD.
NO PROBLEM. I KNOW THIS FOREST LIKE THE BACK OF MY TENTACLE. CALL ME TAN FUR.
YOU'RE NOT A FOREST KITTY, ARE YOU? CAT GURU TOLD US ABOUT A TRIBE UP IN THE MOUNTAINS, ARE YOU FROM THERE?
YEP!
WE'RE HUNTING FOR THE ELUSIVE GREEN MICE! I'M GOING TO CATCH ONE MYSELF!
YEAH! ME TOO!
OH? GREEN, YOU SAY? WE HAVE THOSE ALL OVER THE MOUNTAINS NEAR MY TRIBE! COME ON, I'LL SHOW YA.
Huh. MIGHT GET TO TRY ONE AFTER ALL.
WE SHOULD BE CAREFUL, REMEMBER WHAT CAT GURU SAID.
DON'T WORRY, I WILL PROTECT YOU!

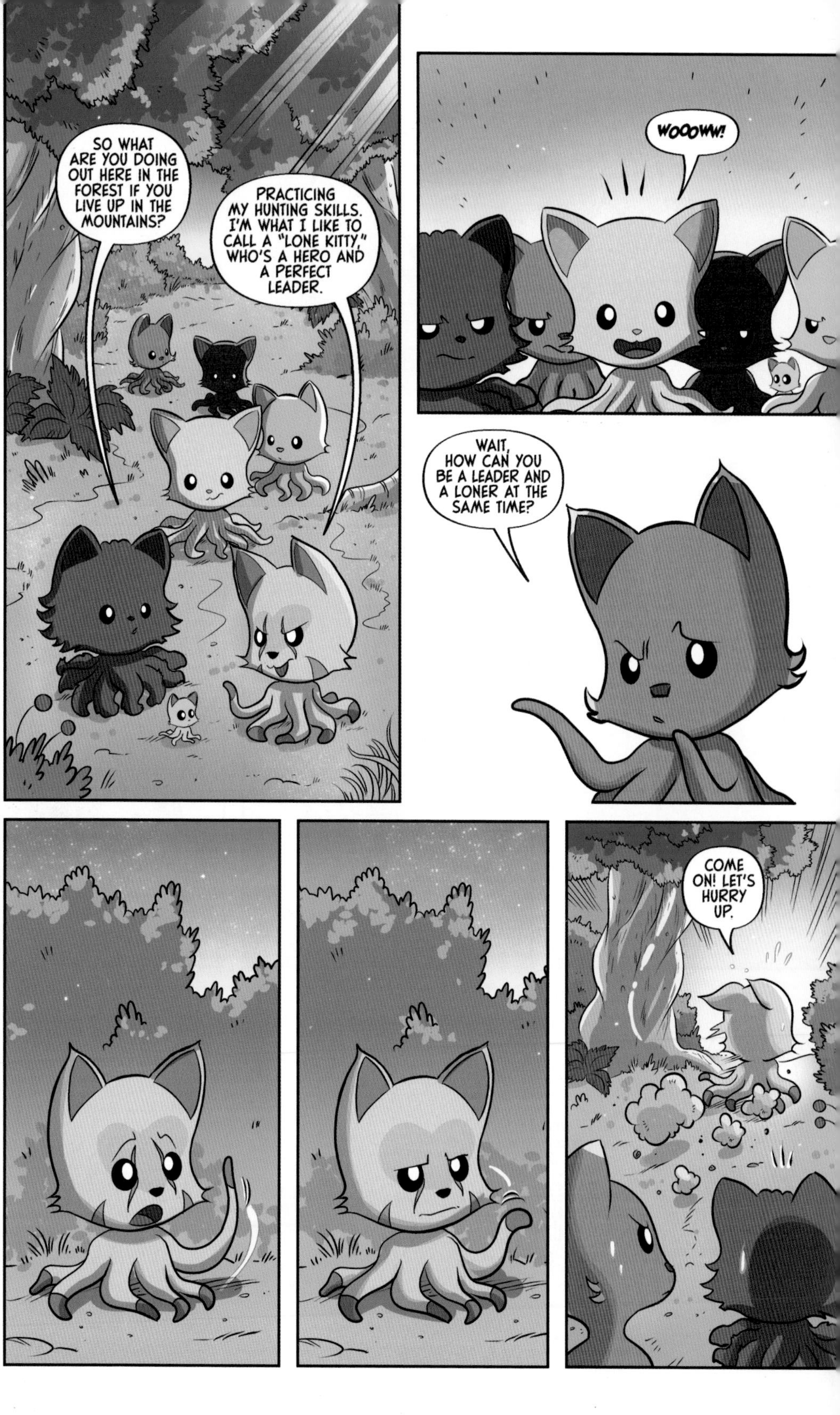
SO WHAT ARE YOU DOING OUT HERE IN THE FOREST IF YOU LIVE UP IN THE MOUNTAINS?
PRACTICING MY HUNTING SKILLS. I'M WHAT I LIKE TO CALL A "LONE KITTY," WHO'S A HERO AND A PERFECT LEADER.
WOOOWW!
WAIT, HOW CAN YOU BE A LEADER AND A LONER AT THE SAME TIME?
COME ON! LET'S HURRY UP.

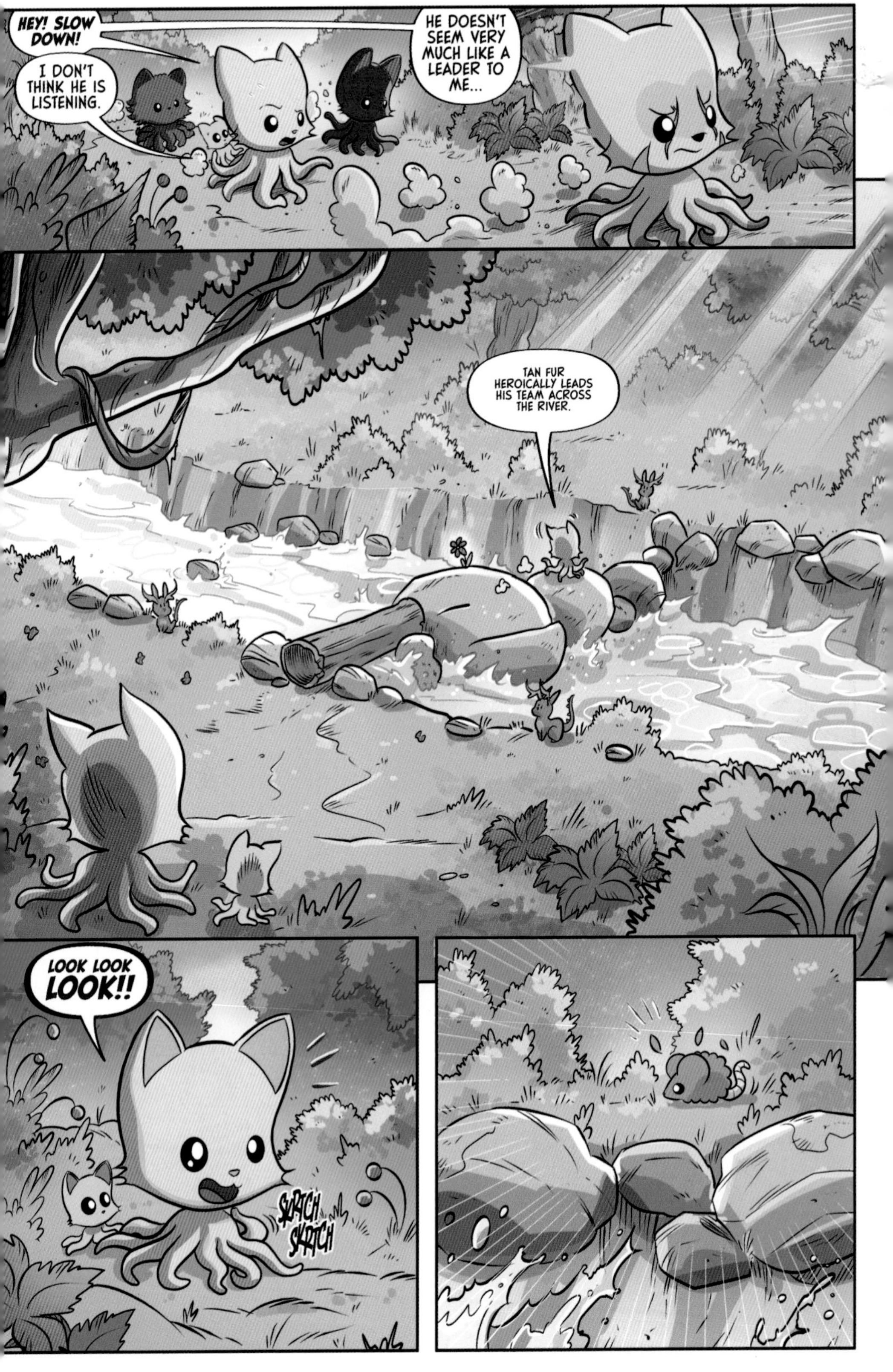
HEY! SLOW DOWN!
I DON'T THINK HE IS LISTENING.
HE DOESN'T SEEM VERY MUCH LIKE A LEADER TO ME...
TAN FUR HEROICALLY LEADS HIS TEAM ACROSS THE RIVER.
LOOK LOOK LOOK!!
SKRITCH SKRITCH

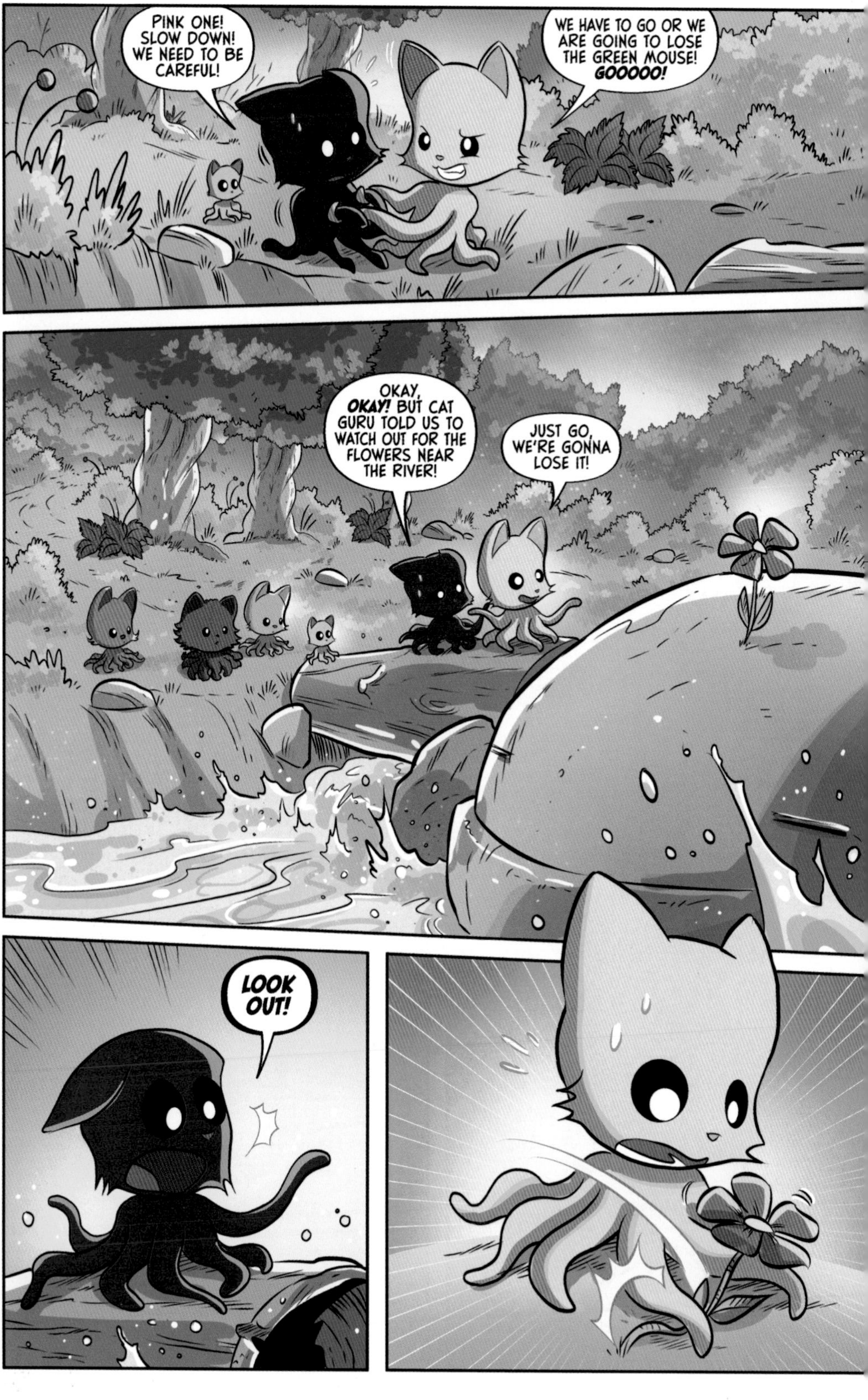
PINK ONE! SLOW DOWN! WE NEED TO BE CAREFUL!
WE HAVE TO GO OR WE ARE GOING TO LOSE THE GREEN MOUSE! **GOOOOO!**
OKAY, **OKAY!** BUT CAT GURU TOLD US TO WATCH OUT FOR THE FLOWERS NEAR THE RIVER!
JUST GO, WE'RE GONNA LOSE IT!
LOOK OUT!

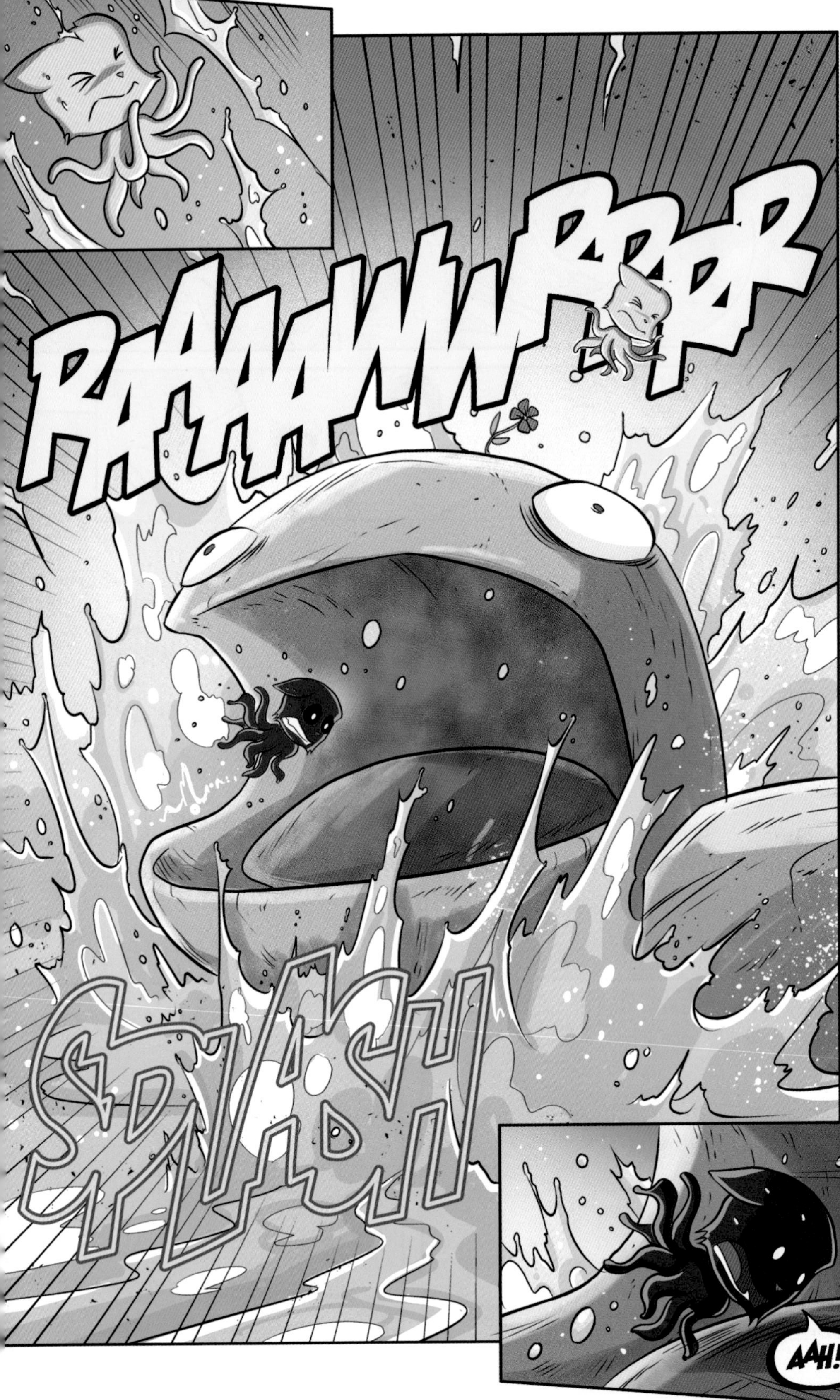
RAAAWWRRR
SPLASH
AAH!

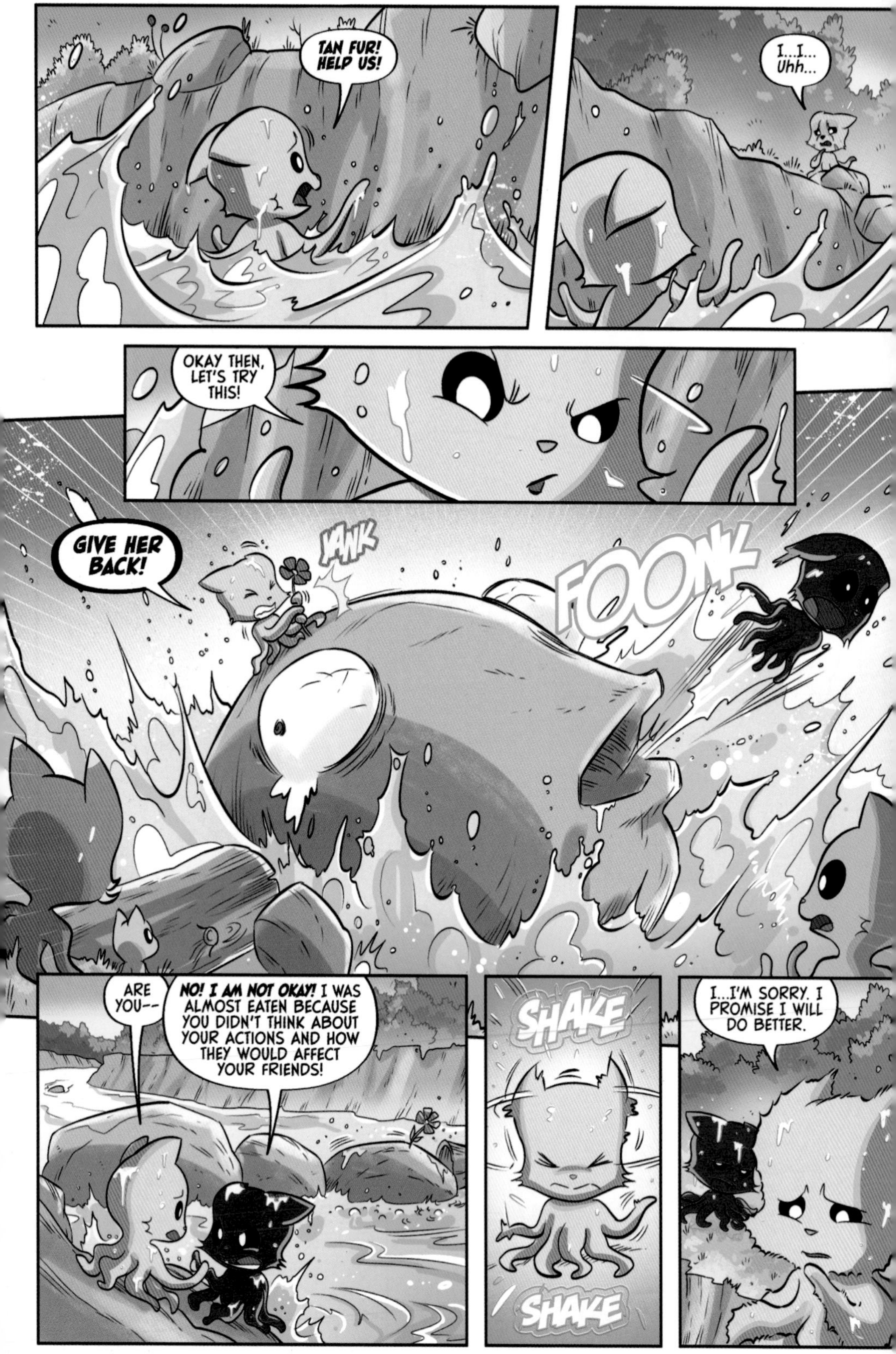
TAN FUR! HELP US!
I...I... Uhh...
OKAY THEN, LET'S TRY THIS!
GIVE HER BACK!
YANK
FOONK
ARE YOU--
NO! I AM NOT OKAY! I WAS ALMOST EATEN BECAUSE YOU DIDN'T THINK ABOUT YOUR ACTIONS AND HOW THEY WOULD AFFECT YOUR FRIENDS!
SHAKE
SHAKE
I...I'M SORRY. I PROMISE I WILL DO BETTER.

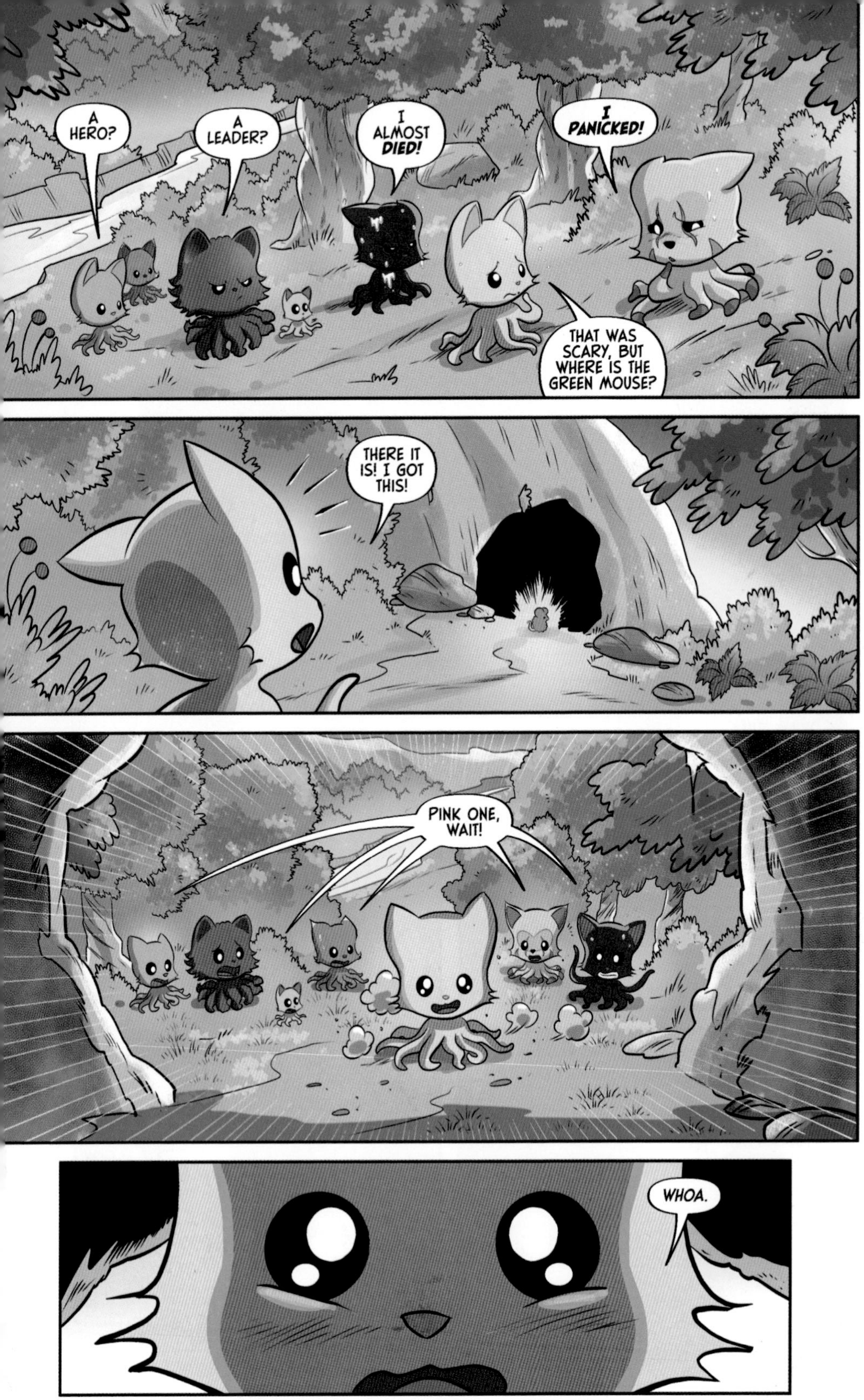
A HERO?
A LEADER?
I ALMOST **DIED!**
I PANICKED!
THAT WAS SCARY, BUT WHERE IS THE GREEN MOUSE?
THERE IT IS! I GOT THIS!
PINK ONE, WAIT!
WHOA.

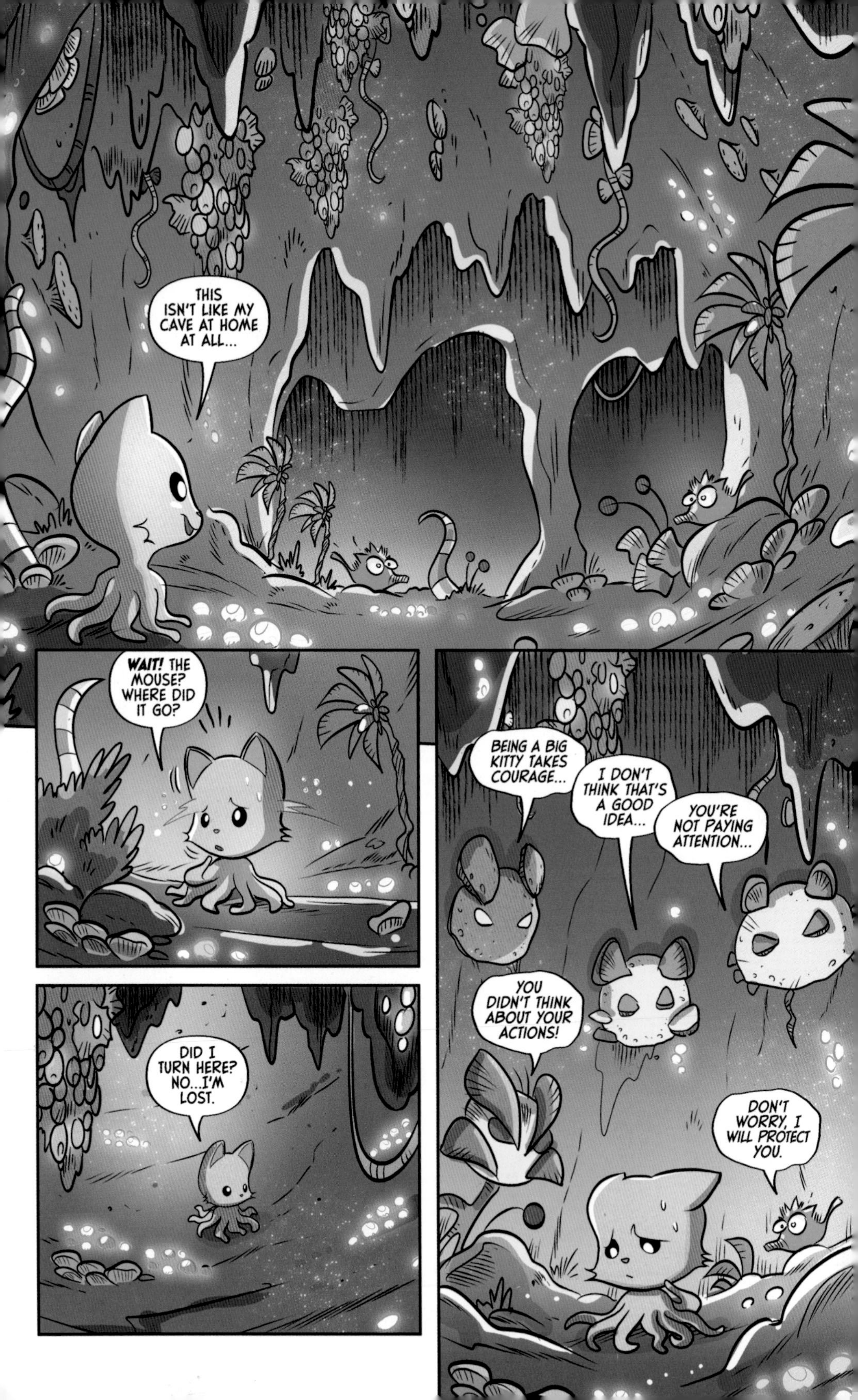
THIS ISN'T LIKE MY CAVE AT HOME AT ALL...
WAIT! THE MOUSE? WHERE DID IT GO?
DID I TURN HERE? NO...I'M LOST.
BEING A BIG KITTY TAKES COURAGE...
I DON'T THINK THAT'S A GOOD IDEA...
YOU'RE NOT PAYING ATTENTION...
YOU DIDN'T THINK ABOUT YOUR ACTIONS!
DON'T WORRY, I WILL PROTECT YOU.

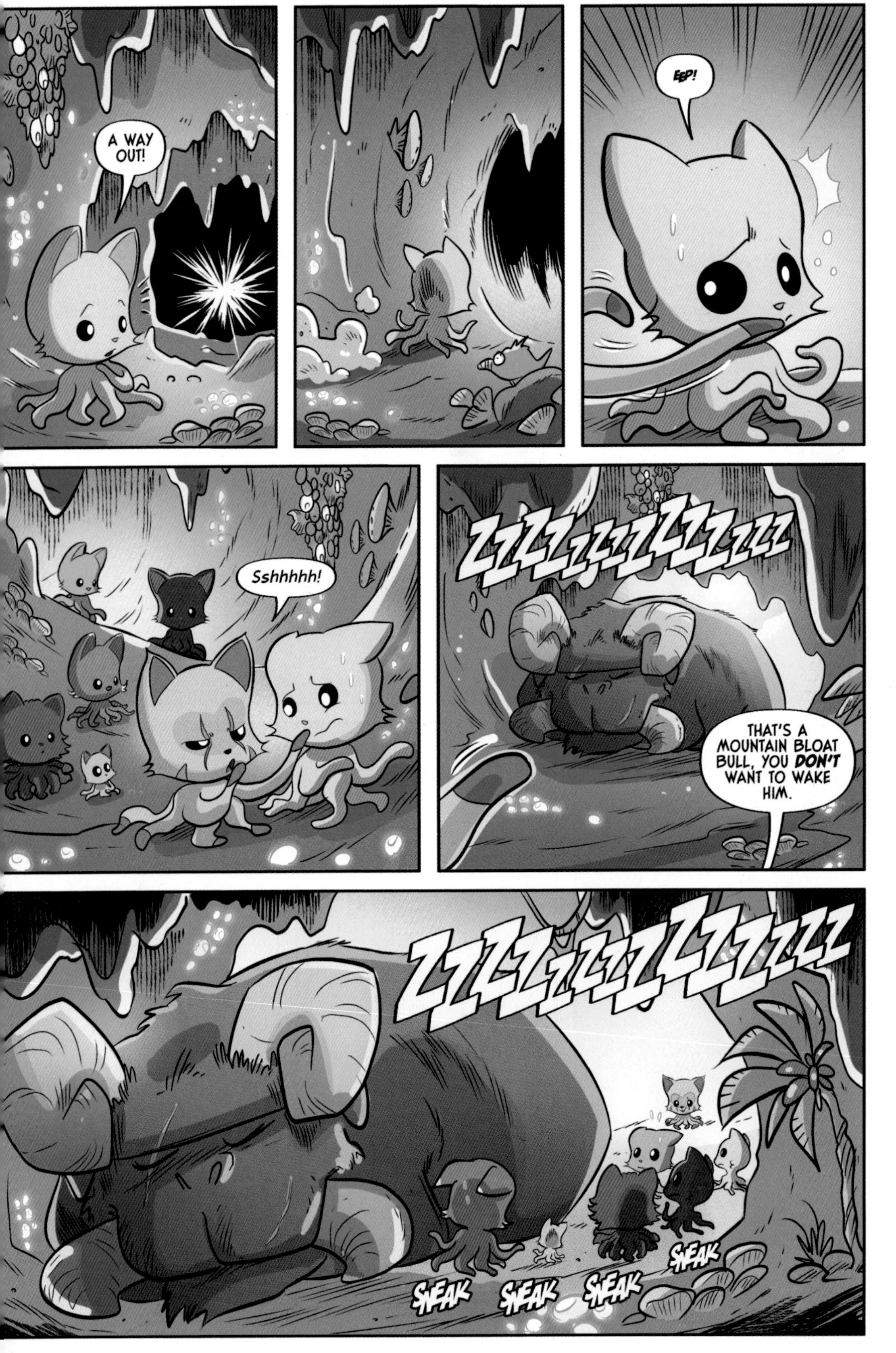
A WAY OUT!
EEP!
Sshhhhh!
ZZZzzzzZZZzzz
THAT'S A MOUNTAIN BLOAT BULL, YOU DON'T WANT TO WAKE HIM.
ZZZzzzzZZZzzzz
SNEAK
SNEAK
SNEAK
SNEAK

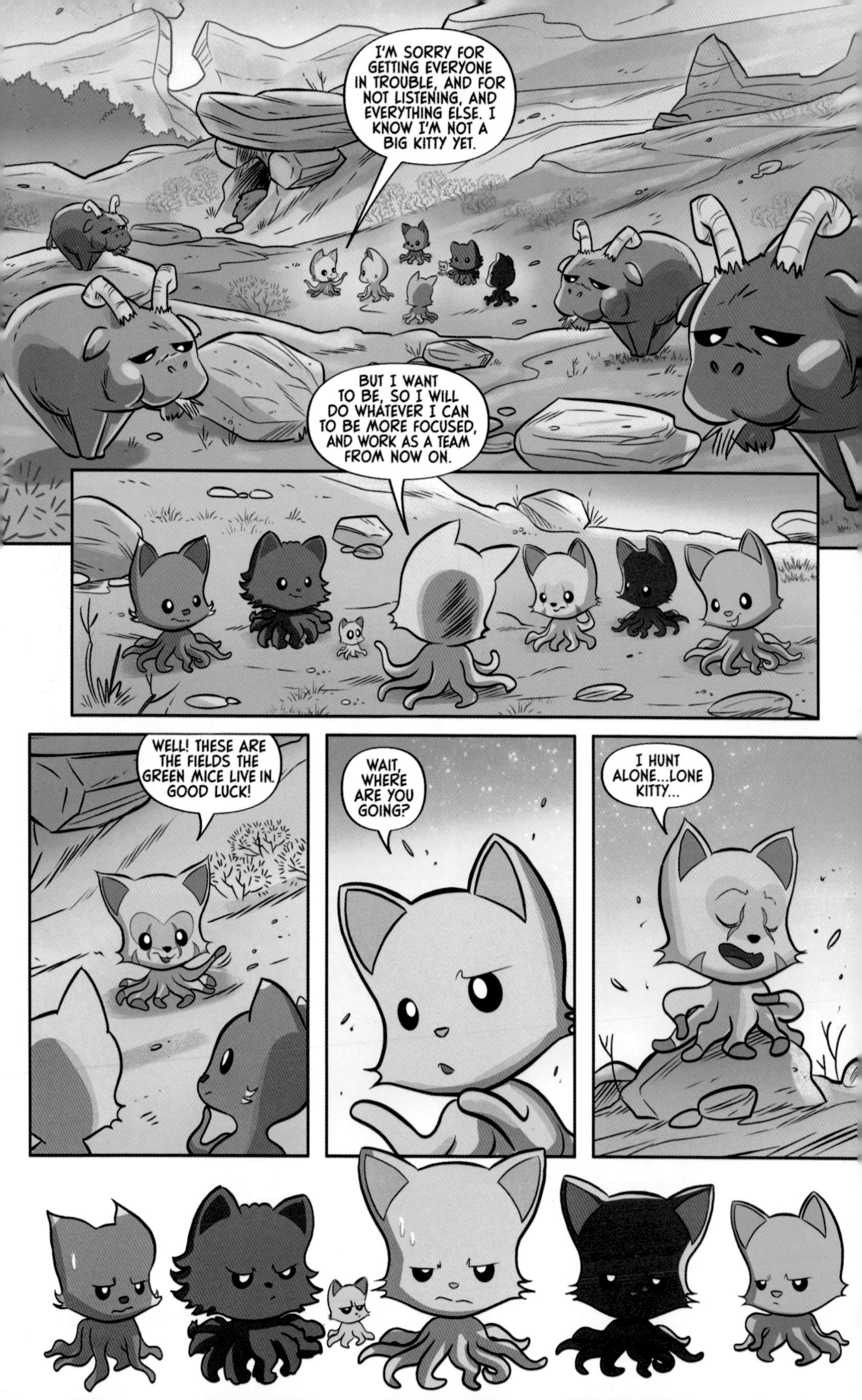
I'M SORRY FOR GETTING EVERYONE IN TROUBLE, AND FOR NOT LISTENING, AND EVERYTHING ELSE. I KNOW I'M NOT A BIG KITTY YET.
BUT I WANT TO BE, SO I WILL DO WHATEVER I CAN TO BE MORE FOCUSED, AND WORK AS A TEAM FROM NOW ON.
WELL! THESE ARE THE FIELDS THE GREEN MICE LIVE IN. GOOD LUCK!
WAIT, WHERE ARE YOU GOING?
I HUNT ALONE...LONE KITTY...

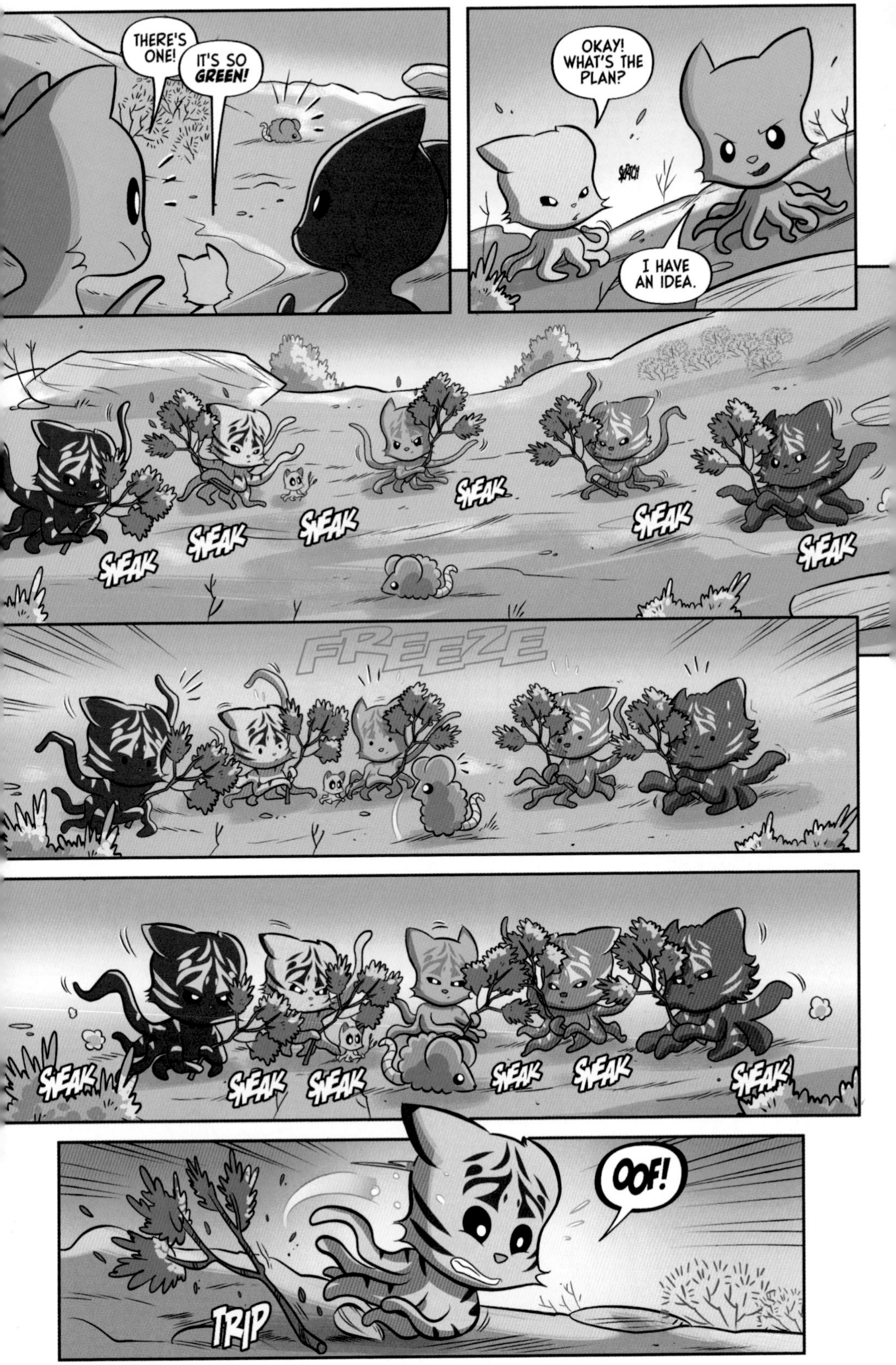
THERE'S ONE!
IT'S SO **GREEN!**
OKAY! WHAT'S THE PLAN?
SKRITCH
I HAVE AN IDEA.
SNEAK
SNEAK
SNEAK
SNEAK
SNEAK
SNEAK
FREEZE
SNEAK
SNEAK
SNEAK
SNEAK
SNEAK
SNEAK
OOF!
TRIP

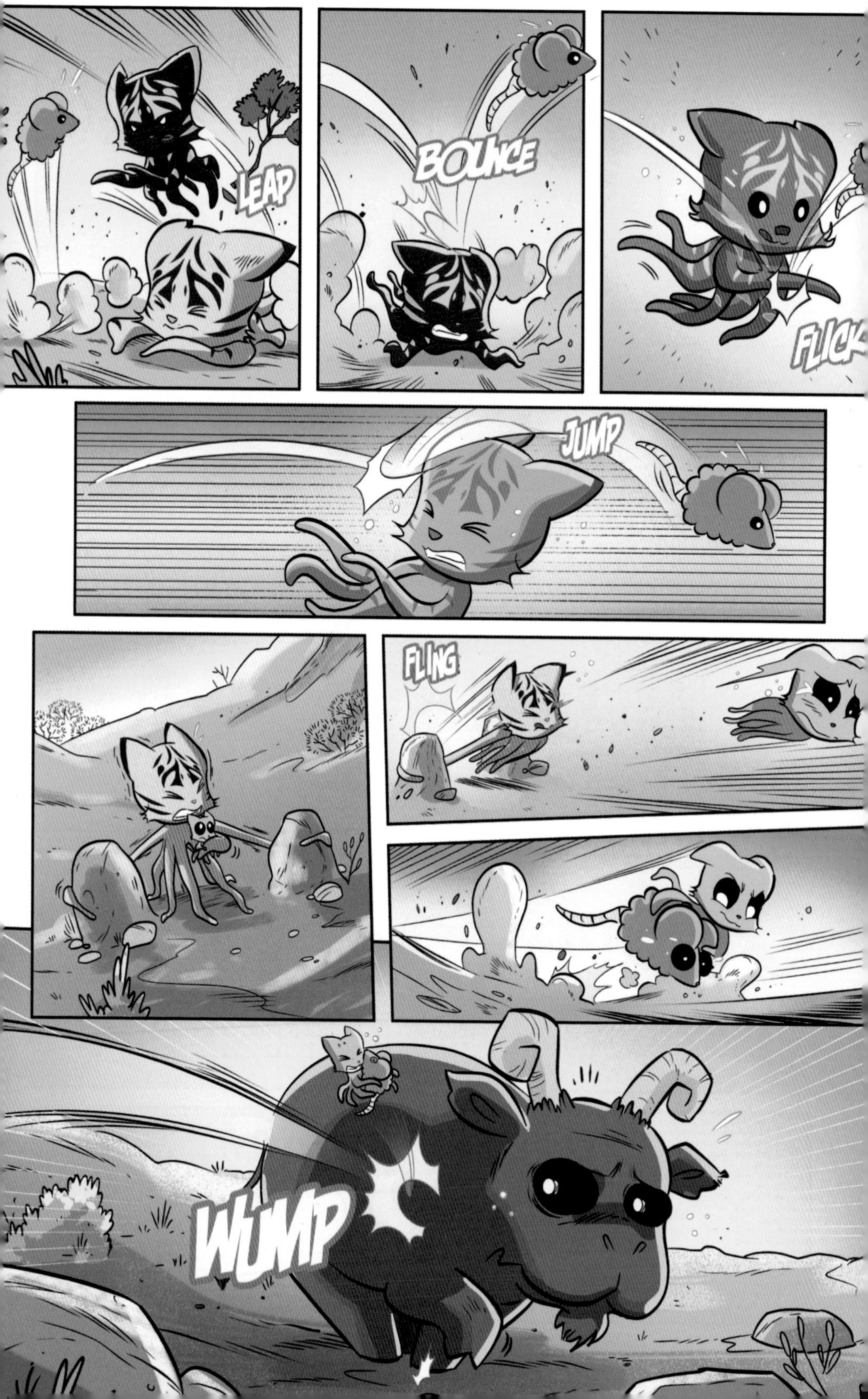
LEAP
BOUNCE
FLICK
JUMP
FLING
WUMP

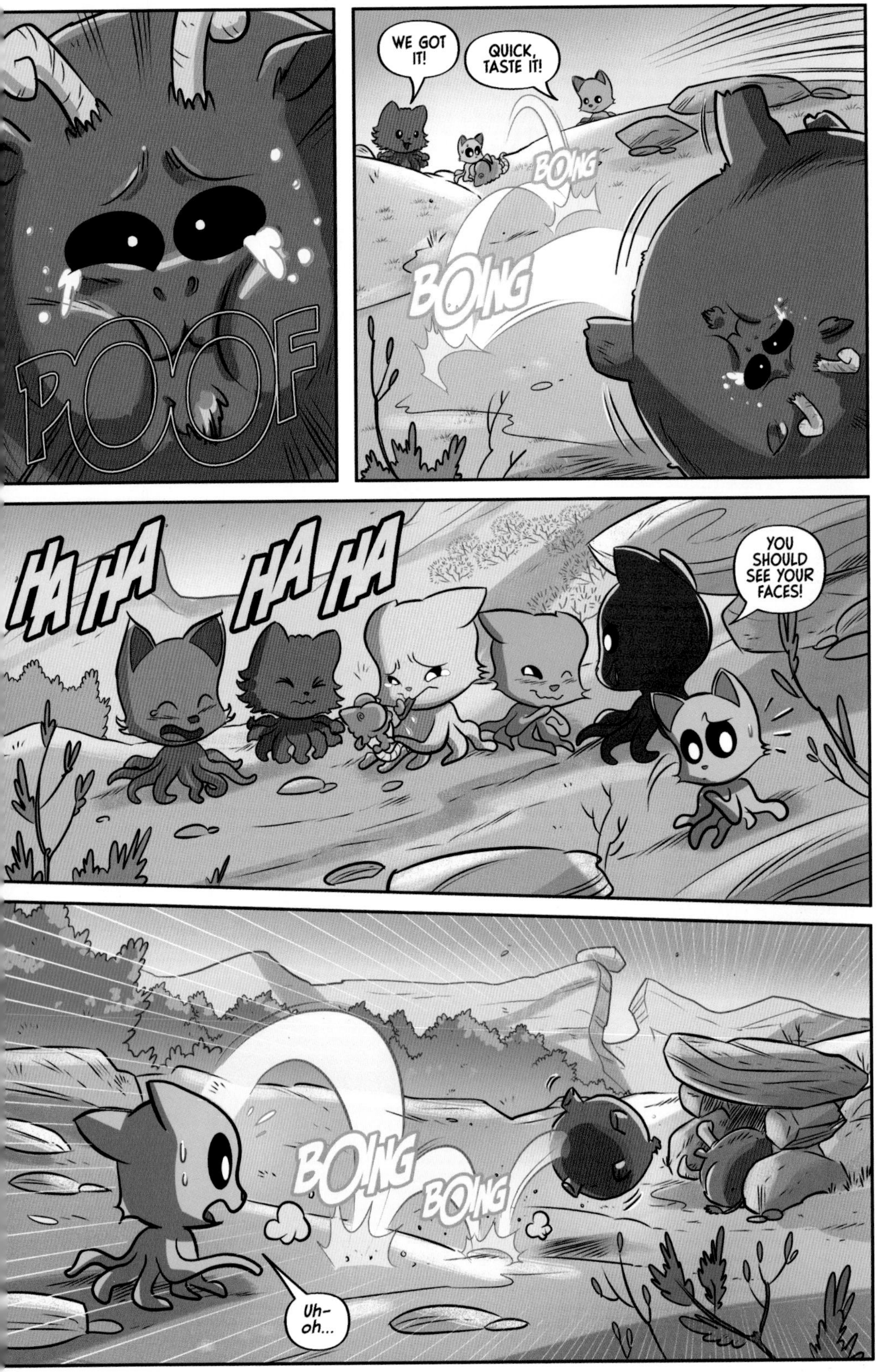
POOF
WE GOT IT!
QUICK, TASTE IT!
BOING
BOING
HA HA
HA HA
YOU SHOULD SEE YOUR FACES!
BOING
BOING
Uh-oh...

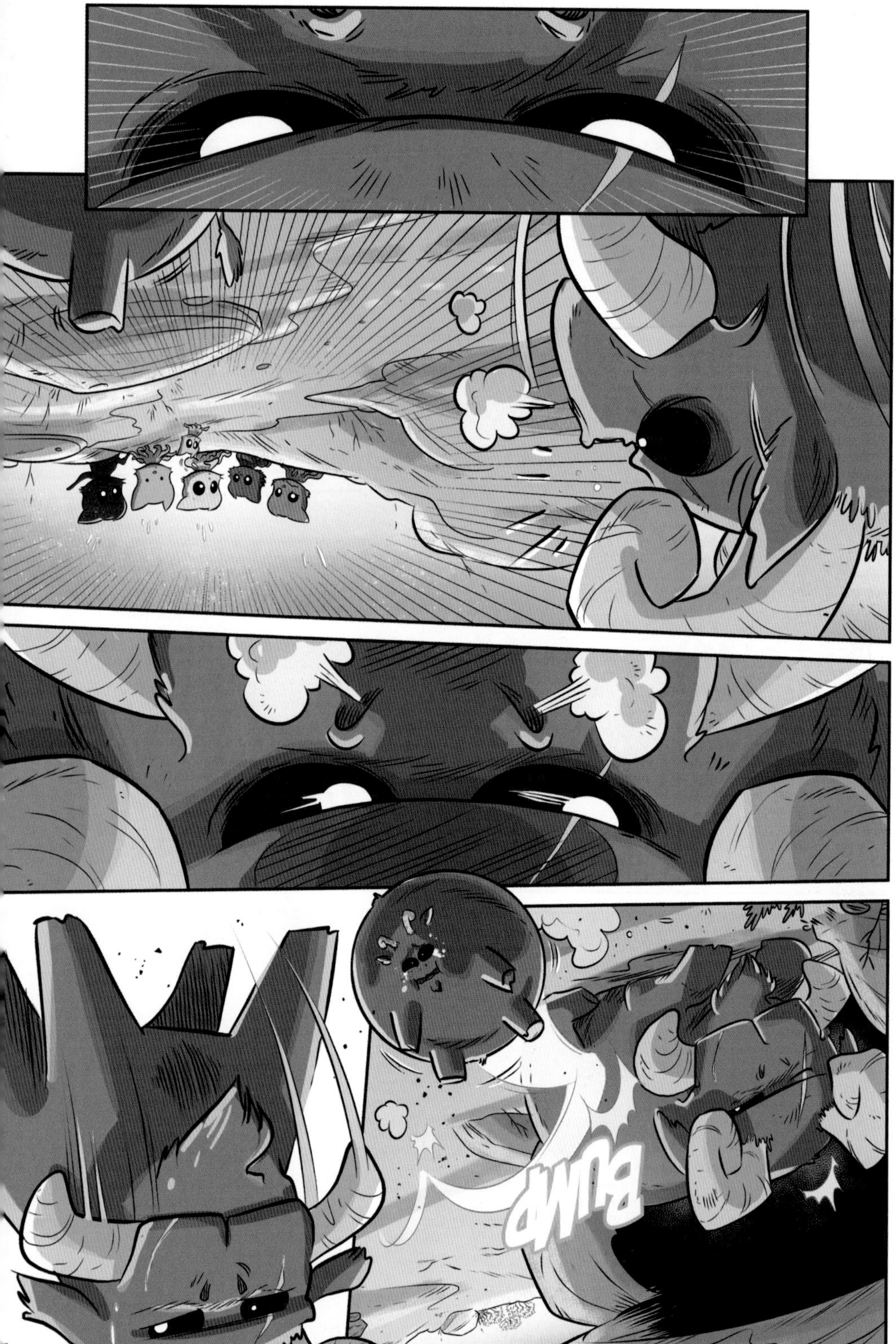
BUMP

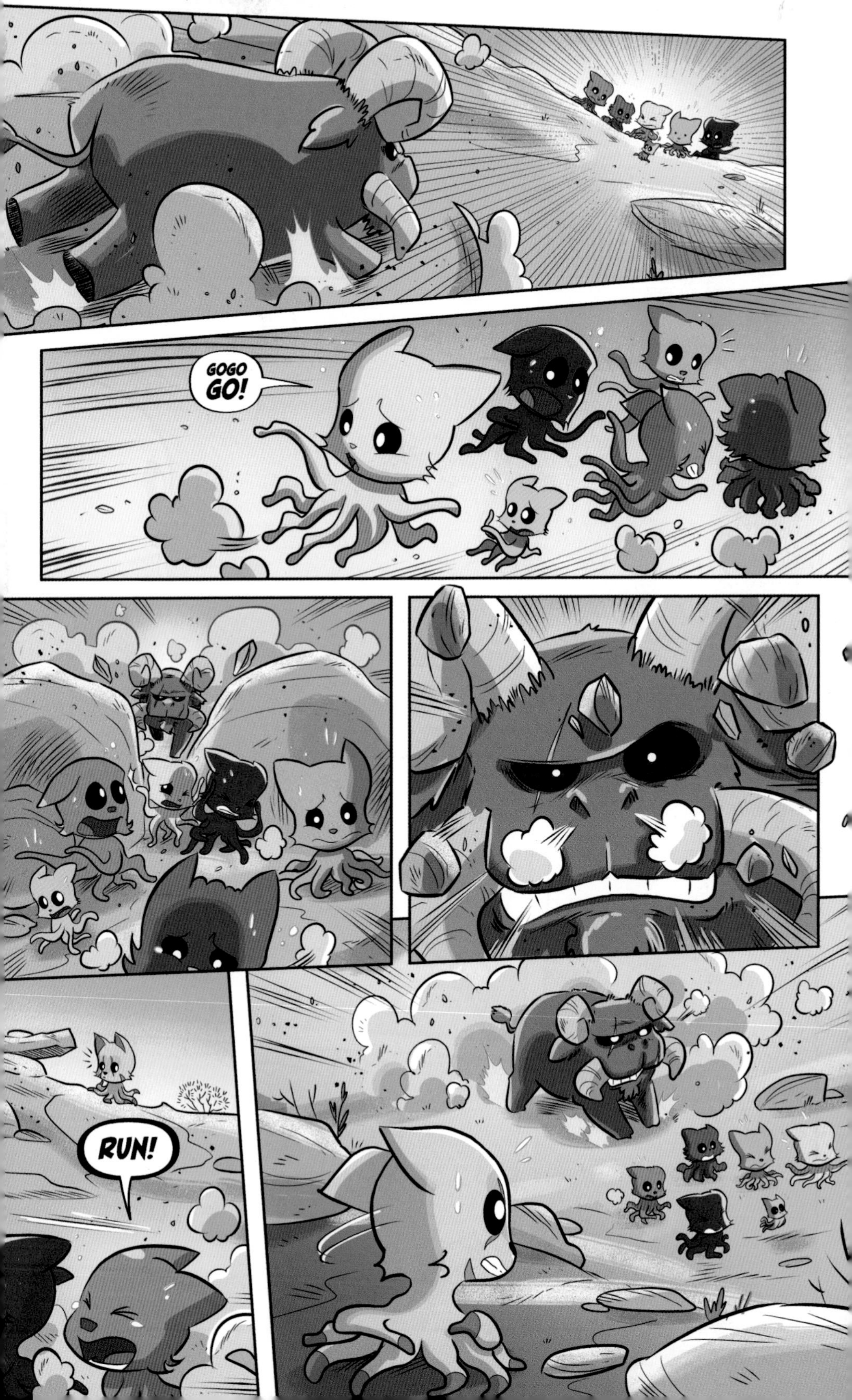
GOGO GO!
RUN!

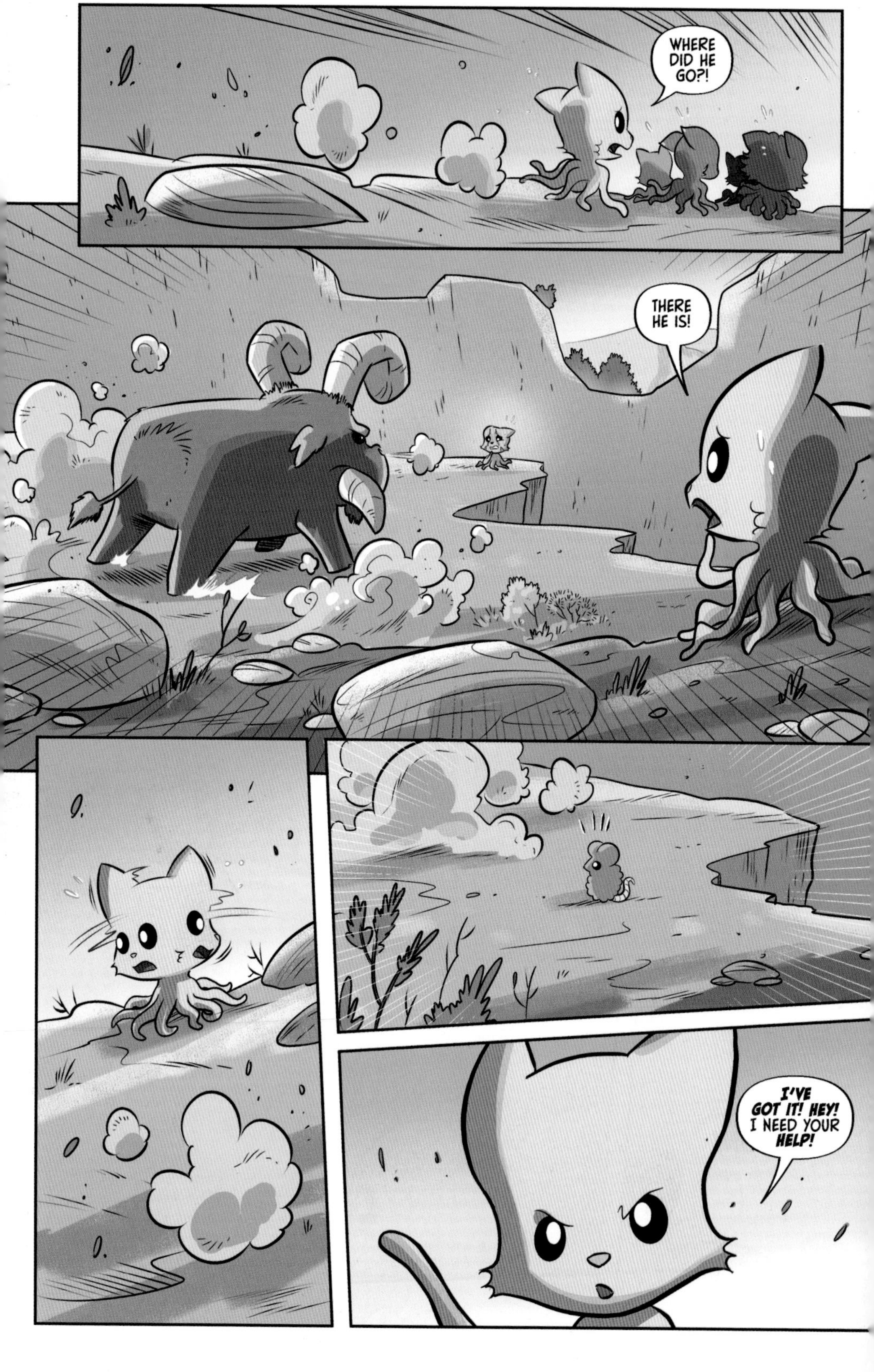
WHERE DID HE GO?!
THERE HE IS!
I'VE GOT IT! HEY! I NEED YOUR HELP!

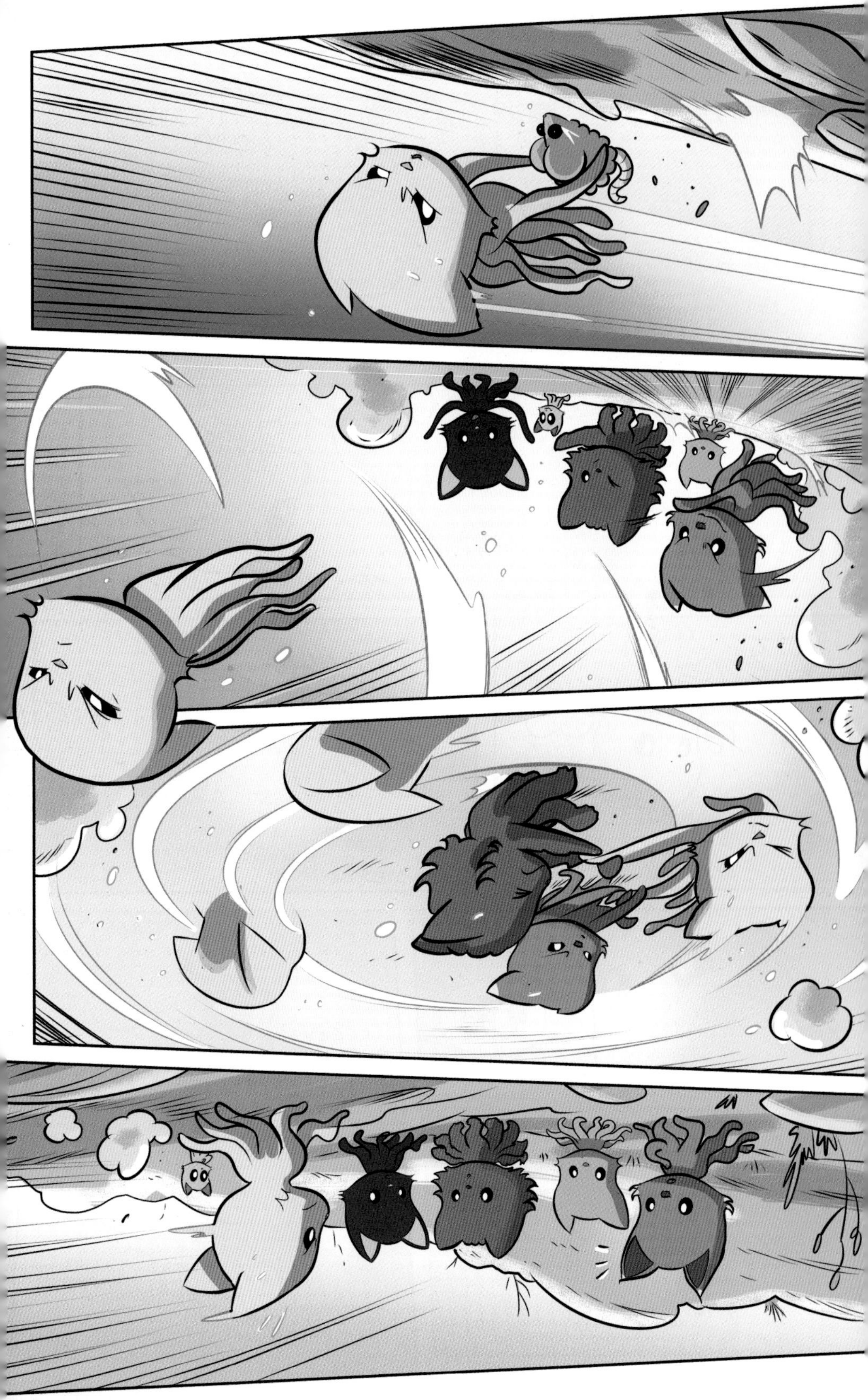

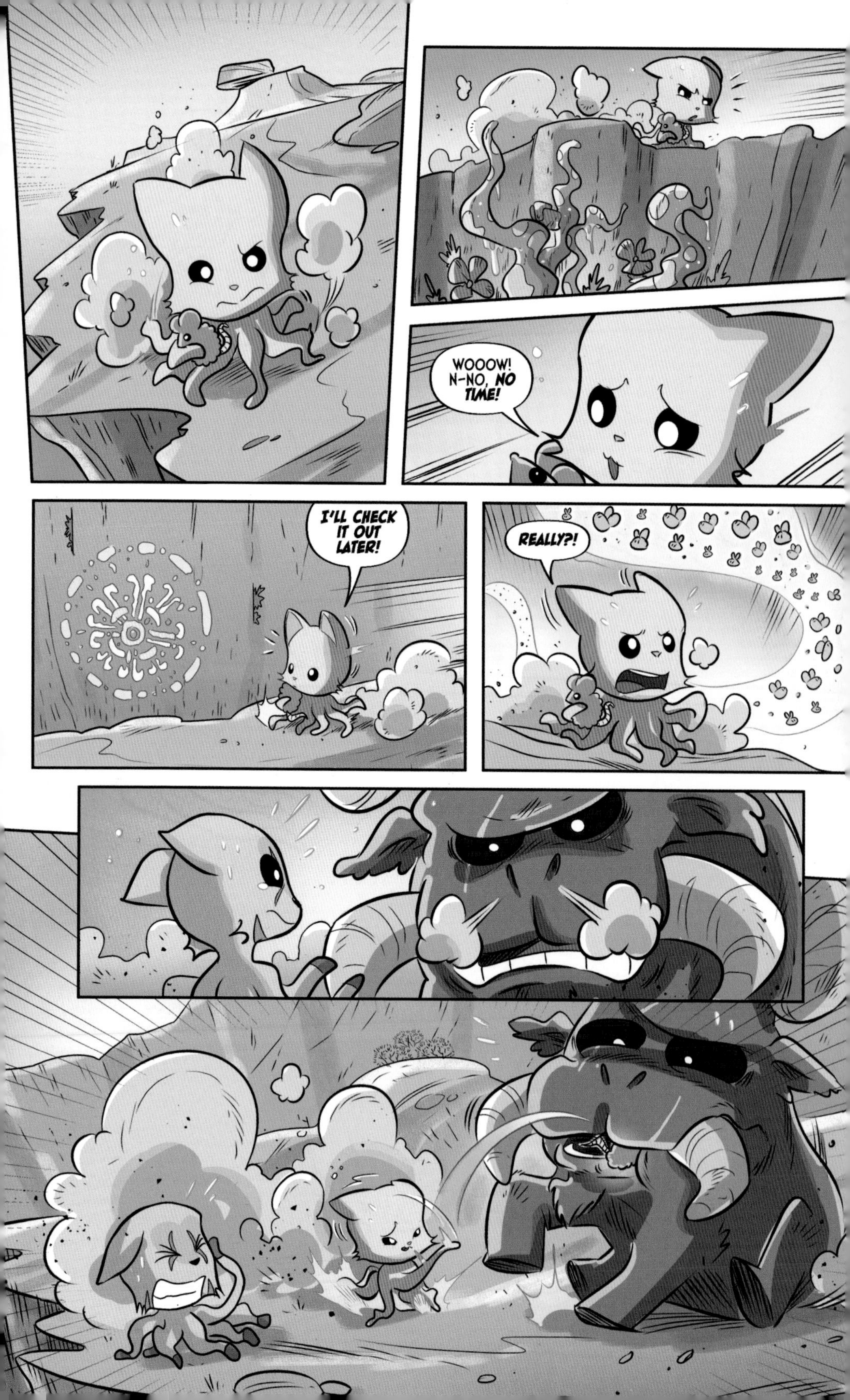
WOOOW! N-NO, NO TIME!
I'LL CHECK IT OUT LATER!
REALLY?!

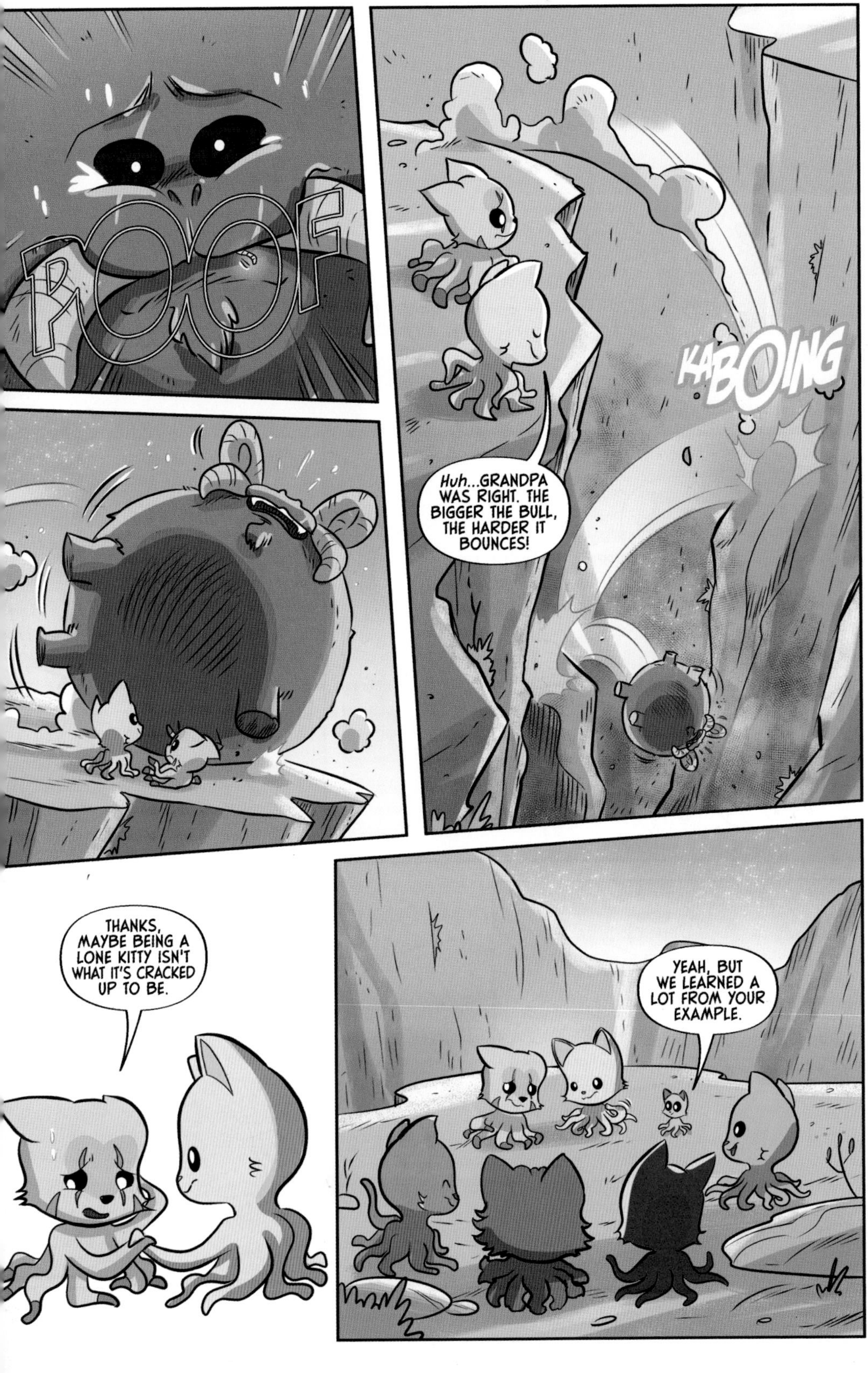
POOF
KABOING
Huh...GRANDPA WAS RIGHT. THE BIGGER THE BULL, THE HARDER IT BOUNCES!
THANKS, MAYBE BEING A LONE KITTY ISN'T WHAT IT'S CRACKED UP TO BE.
YEAH, BUT WE LEARNED A LOT FROM YOUR EXAMPLE.

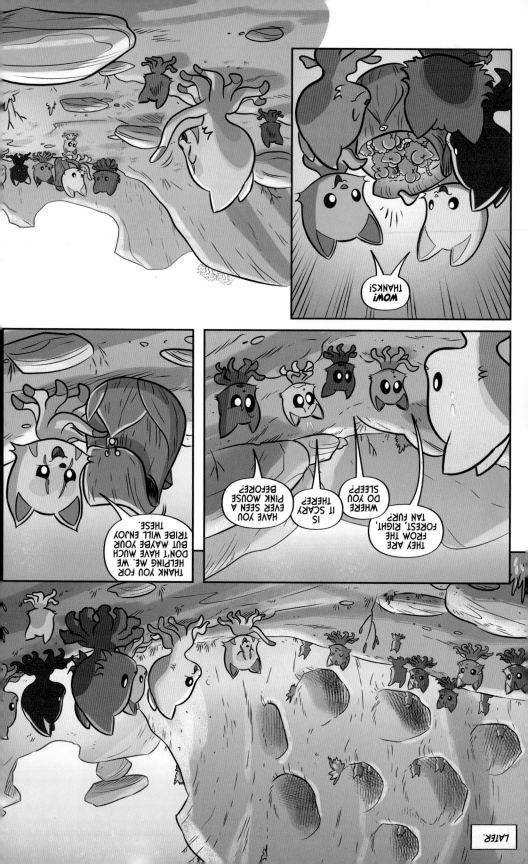

WOW! THANKS!

THANK YOU FOR HELPING ME. WE DON'T HAVE MUCH BUT MAYBE YOUR TRIBE WILL ENJOY THESE.

THEY ARE FROM THE FOREST, RIGHT, TAN FUR?

WHERE DO YOU SLEEP?

IS IT SCARY THERE?

HAVE YOU EVER SEEN A PINK MOUSE BEFORE?

LATER.

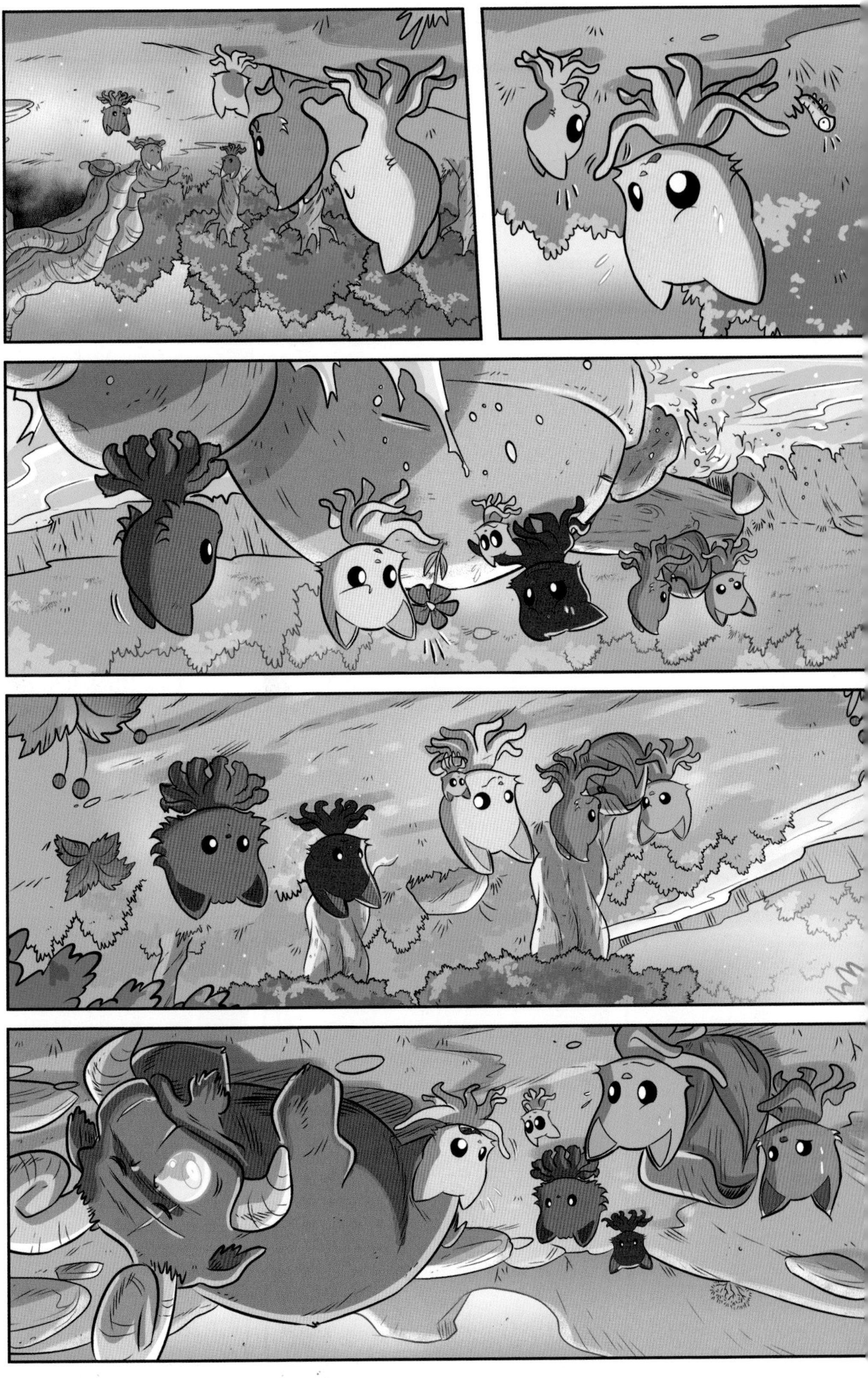

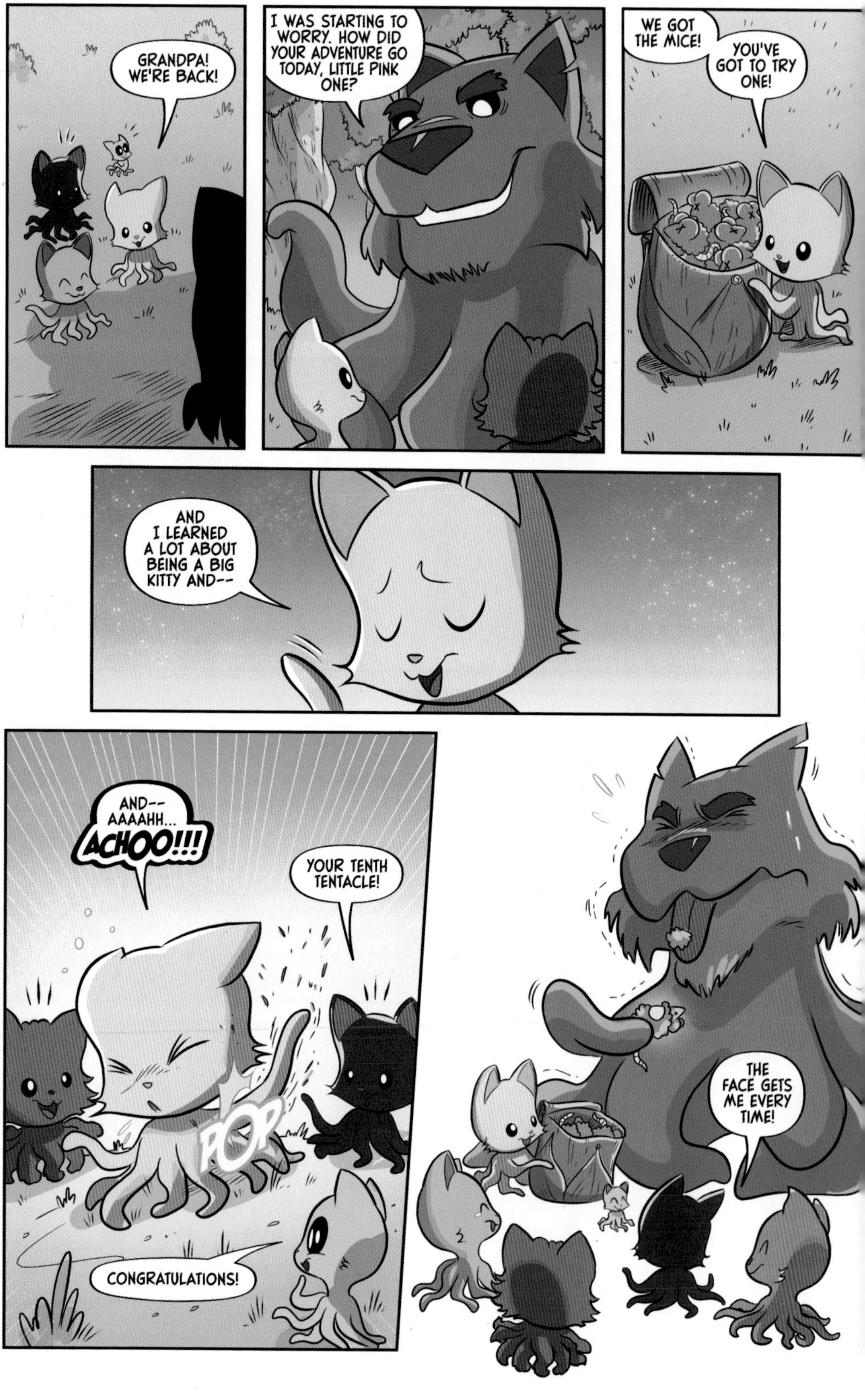
GRANDPA! WE'RE BACK!
I WAS STARTING TO WORRY. HOW DID YOUR ADVENTURE GO TODAY, LITTLE PINK ONE?
WE GOT THE MICE!
YOU'VE GOT TO TRY ONE!
AND I LEARNED A LOT ABOUT BEING A BIG KITTY AND--
AND-- AAAAHH... ACHOO!!!
YOUR TENTH TENTACLE!
POP
CONGRATULATIONS!
THE FACE GETS ME EVERY TIME!

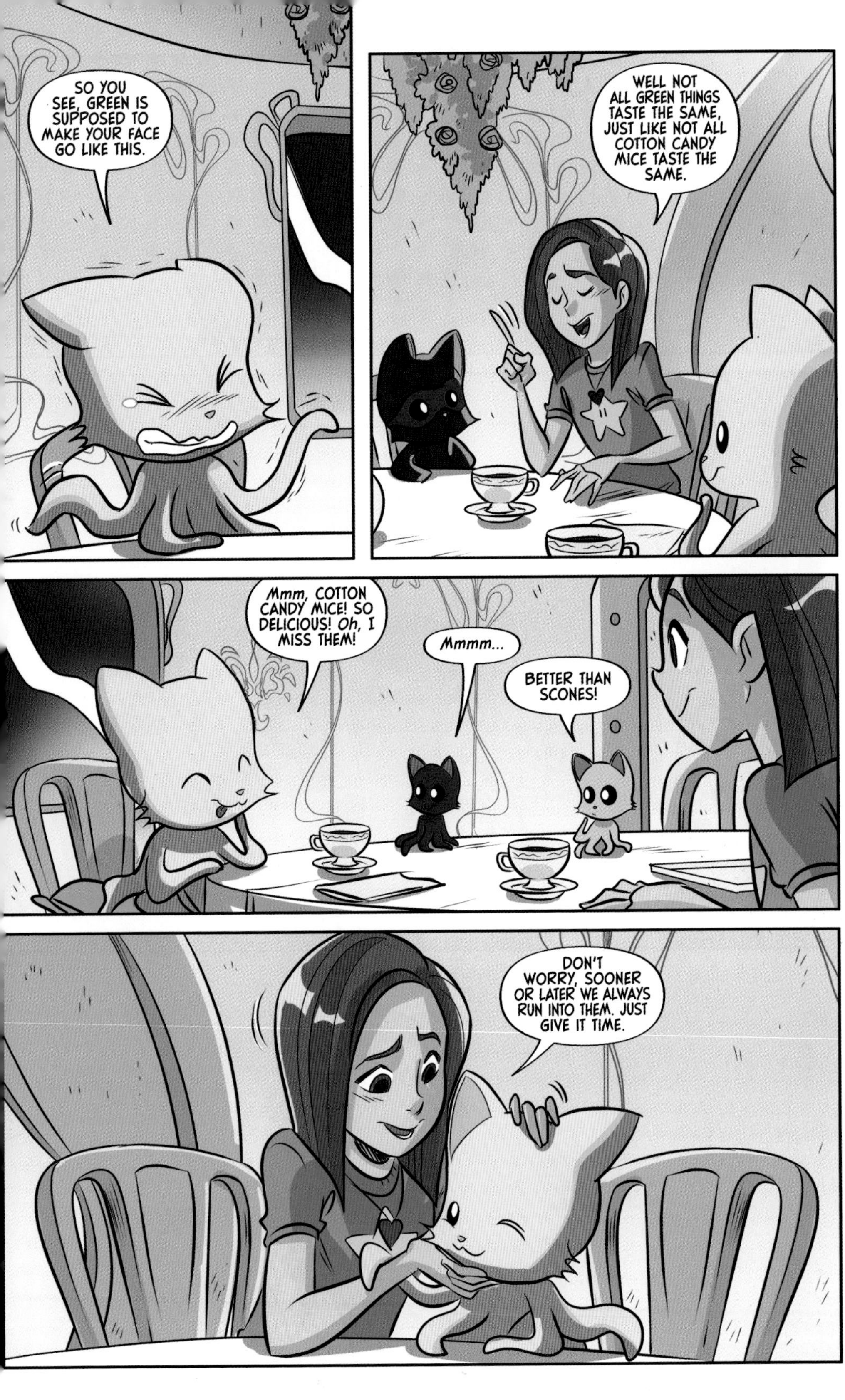
SO YOU SEE, GREEN IS SUPPOSED TO MAKE YOUR FACE GO LIKE THIS.
WELL NOT ALL GREEN THINGS TASTE THE SAME, JUST LIKE NOT ALL COTTON CANDY MICE TASTE THE SAME.
Mmm, COTTON CANDY MICE! SO DELICIOUS! *Oh*, I MISS THEM!
Mmmm...
BETTER THAN SCONES!
DON'T WORRY, SOONER OR LATER WE ALWAYS RUN INTO THEM. JUST GIVE IT TIME.

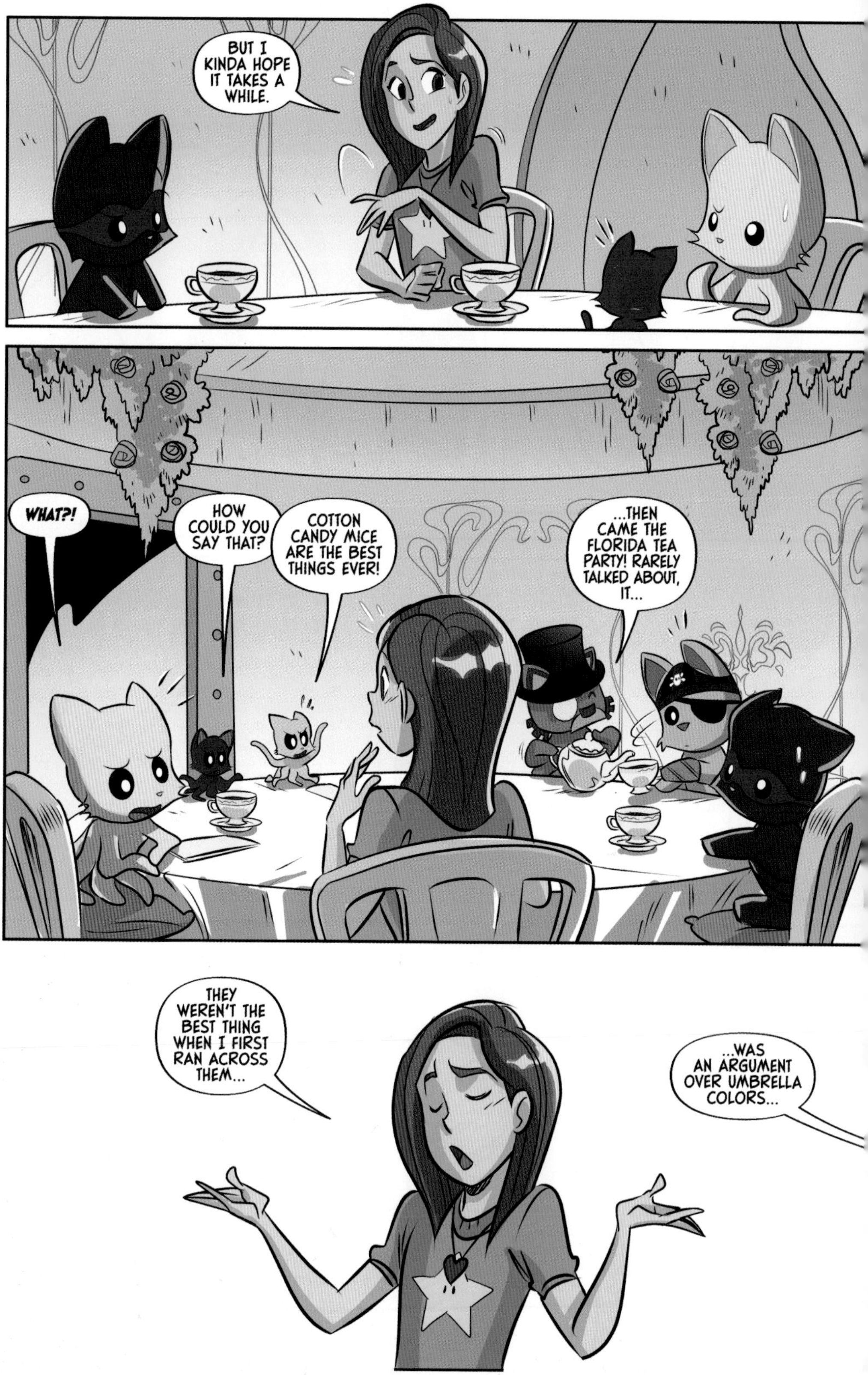
BUT I KINDA HOPE IT TAKES A WHILE.
WHAT?!
HOW COULD YOU SAY THAT?
COTTON CANDY MICE ARE THE BEST THINGS EVER!
...THEN CAME THE FLORIDA TEA PARTY! RARELY TALKED ABOUT, IT...
THEY WEREN'T THE BEST THING WHEN I FIRST RAN ACROSS THEM...
...WAS AN ARGUMENT OVER UMBRELLA COLORS...

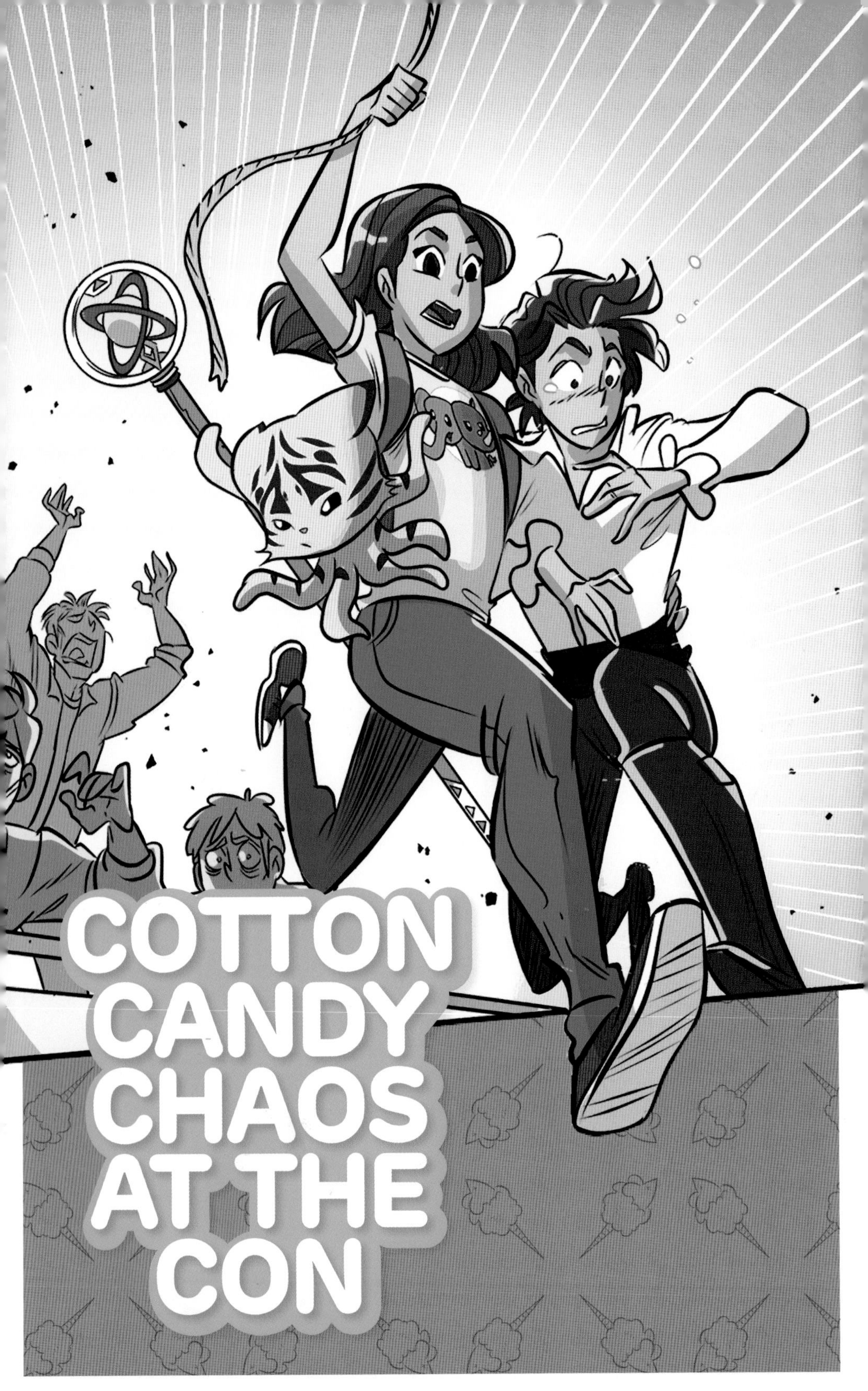
COTTON CANDY CHAOS AT THE CON

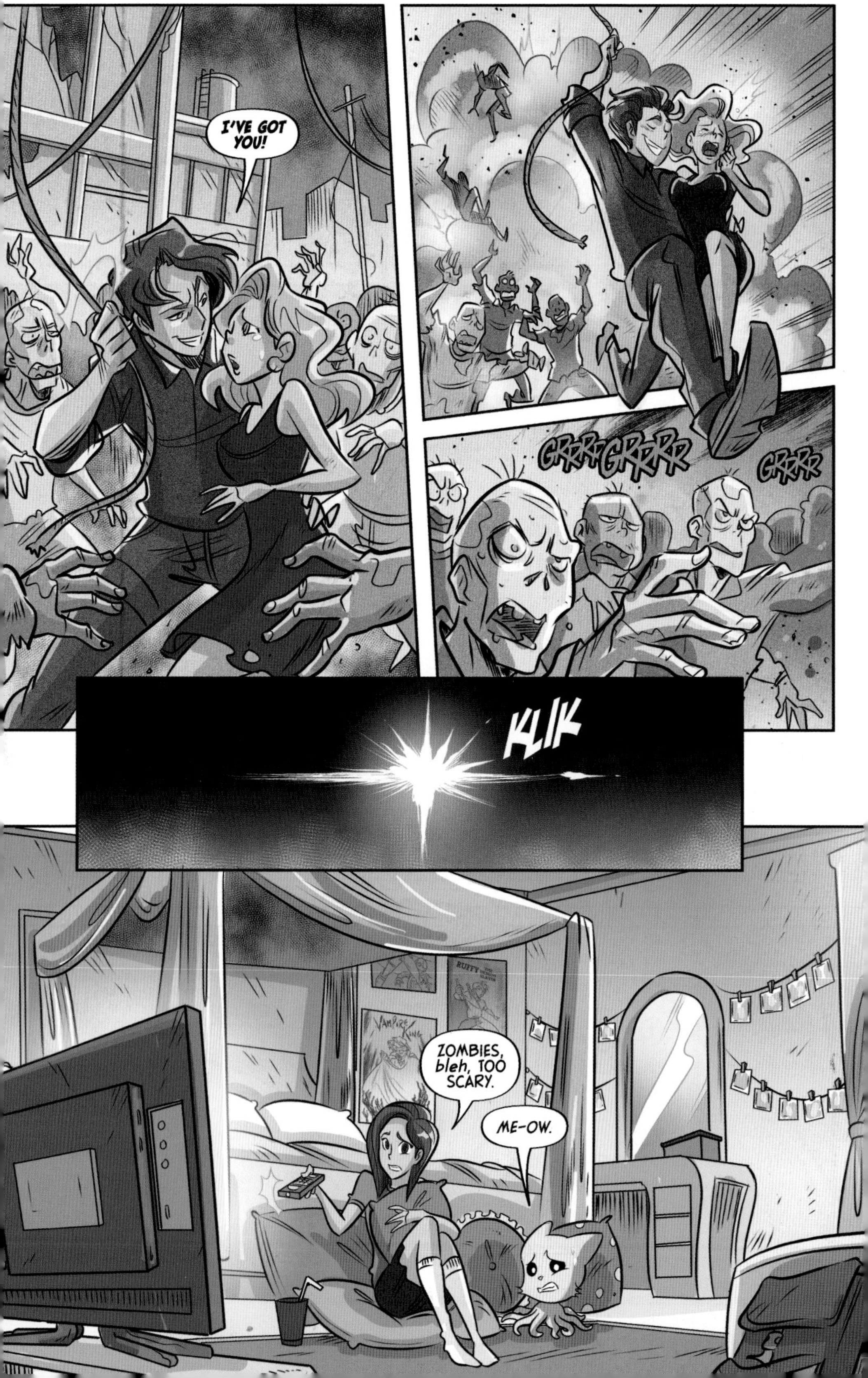
I'VE GOT YOU!
GRRR
GRRRGRRRR
KLIK
ZOMBIES, bleh, TOO SCARY.
ME-OW.

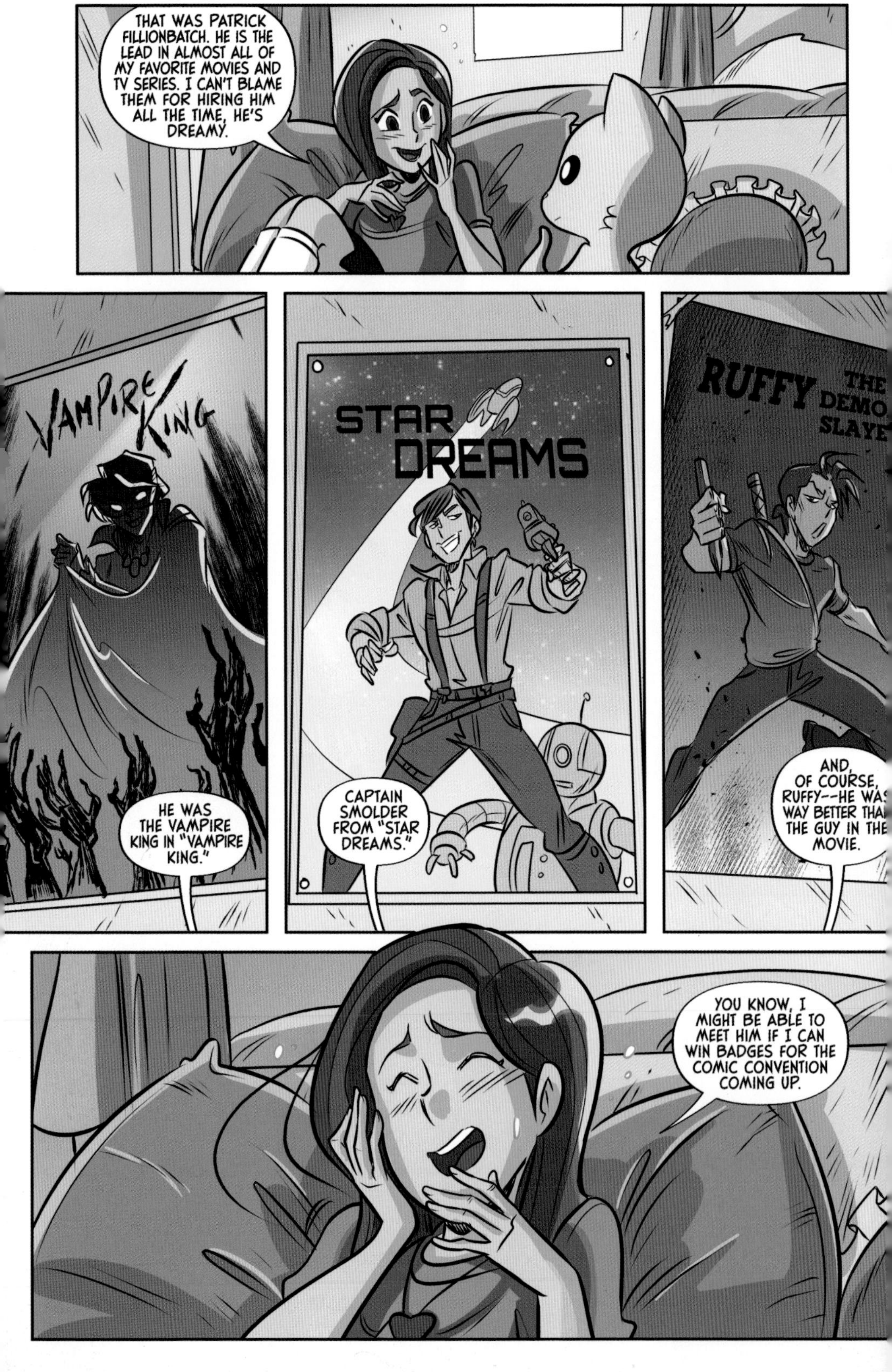
THAT WAS PATRICK FILLIONBATCH. HE IS THE LEAD IN ALMOST ALL OF MY FAVORITE MOVIES AND TV SERIES. I CAN'T BLAME THEM FOR HIRING HIM ALL THE TIME, HE'S DREAMY.
VAMPIRE KING
HE WAS THE VAMPIRE KING IN "VAMPIRE KING."
STAR DREAMS
CAPTAIN SMOLDER FROM "STAR DREAMS."
RUFFY
AND, OF COURSE, RUFFY--HE WAS WAY BETTER THAN THE GUY IN THE MOVIE.
YOU KNOW, I MIGHT BE ABLE TO MEET HIM IF I CAN WIN BADGES FOR THE COMIC CONVENTION COMING UP.

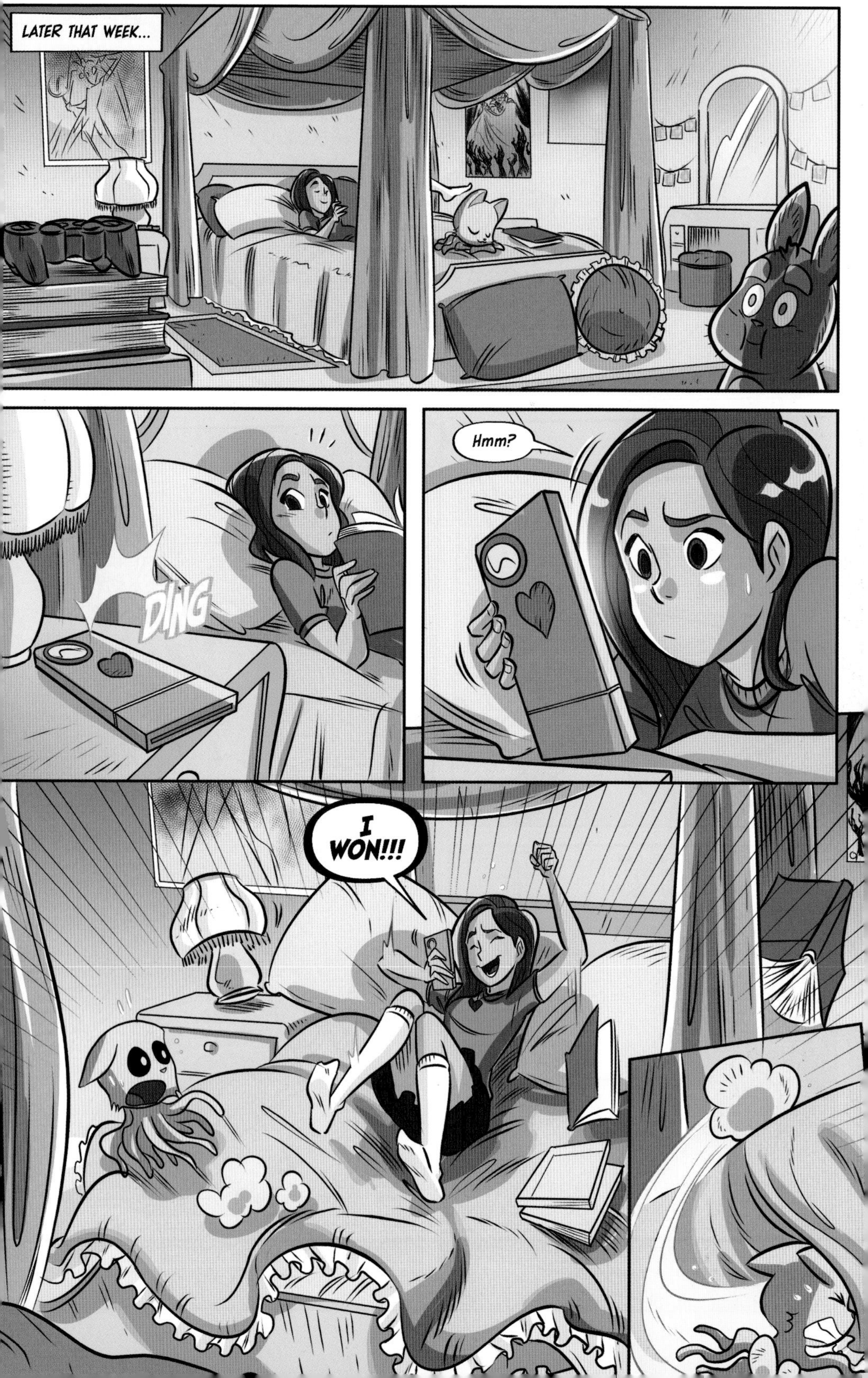
LATER THAT WEEK...
DING
Hmm?
I WON!!!

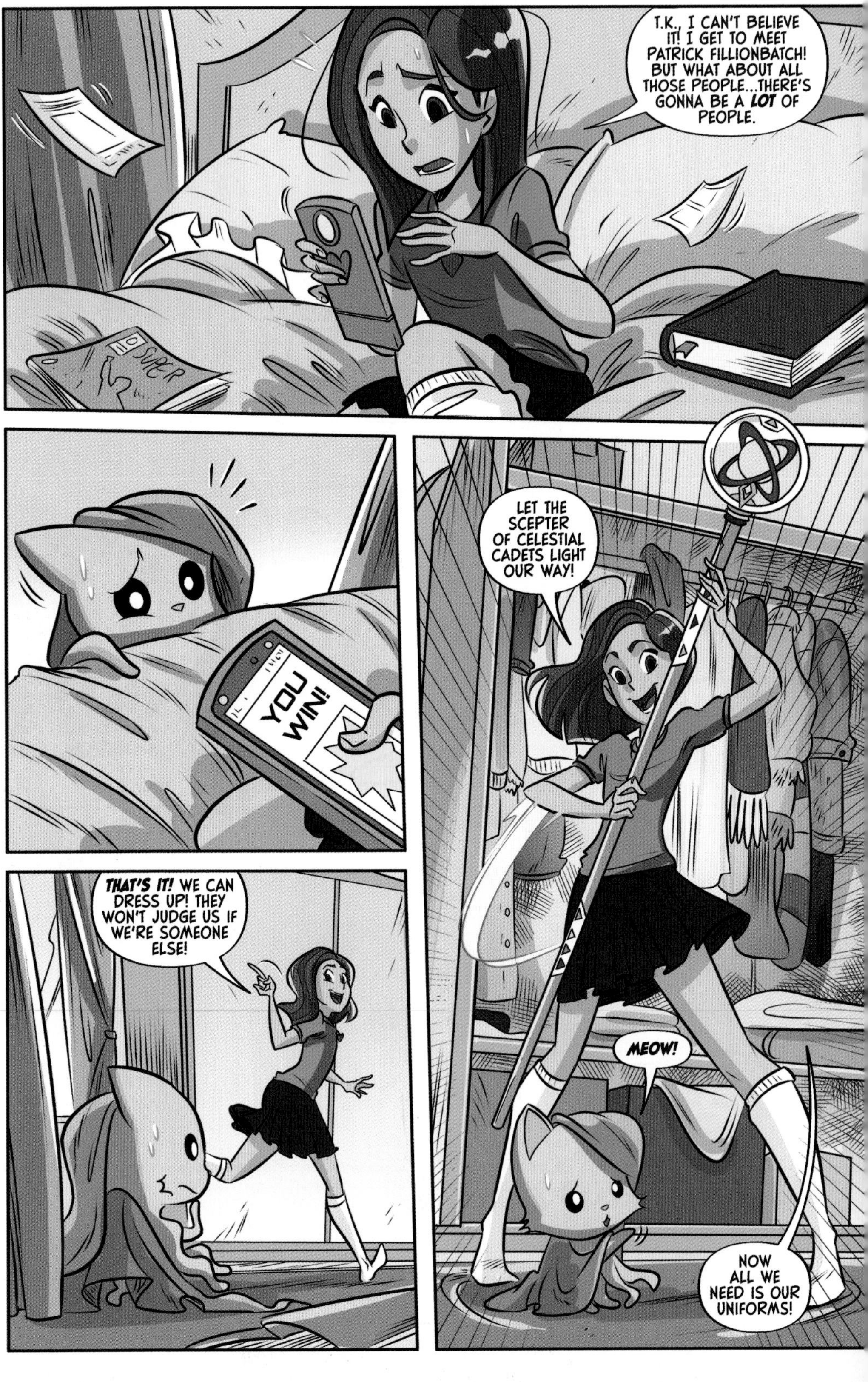
T.K., I CAN'T BELIEVE IT! I GET TO MEET PATRICK FILLIONBATCH! BUT WHAT ABOUT ALL THOSE PEOPLE...THERE'S GONNA BE A ***LOT*** OF PEOPLE.
SUPER
YOU WIN!
THAT'S IT! WE CAN DRESS UP! THEY WON'T JUDGE US IF WE'RE SOMEONE ELSE!
LET THE SCEPTER OF CELESTIAL CADETS LIGHT OUR WAY!
MEOW!
NOW ALL WE NEED IS OUR UNIFORMS!

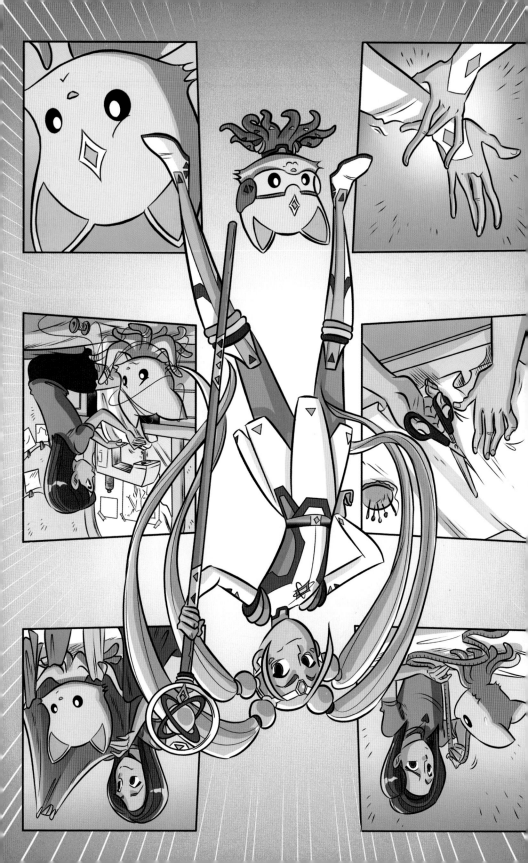

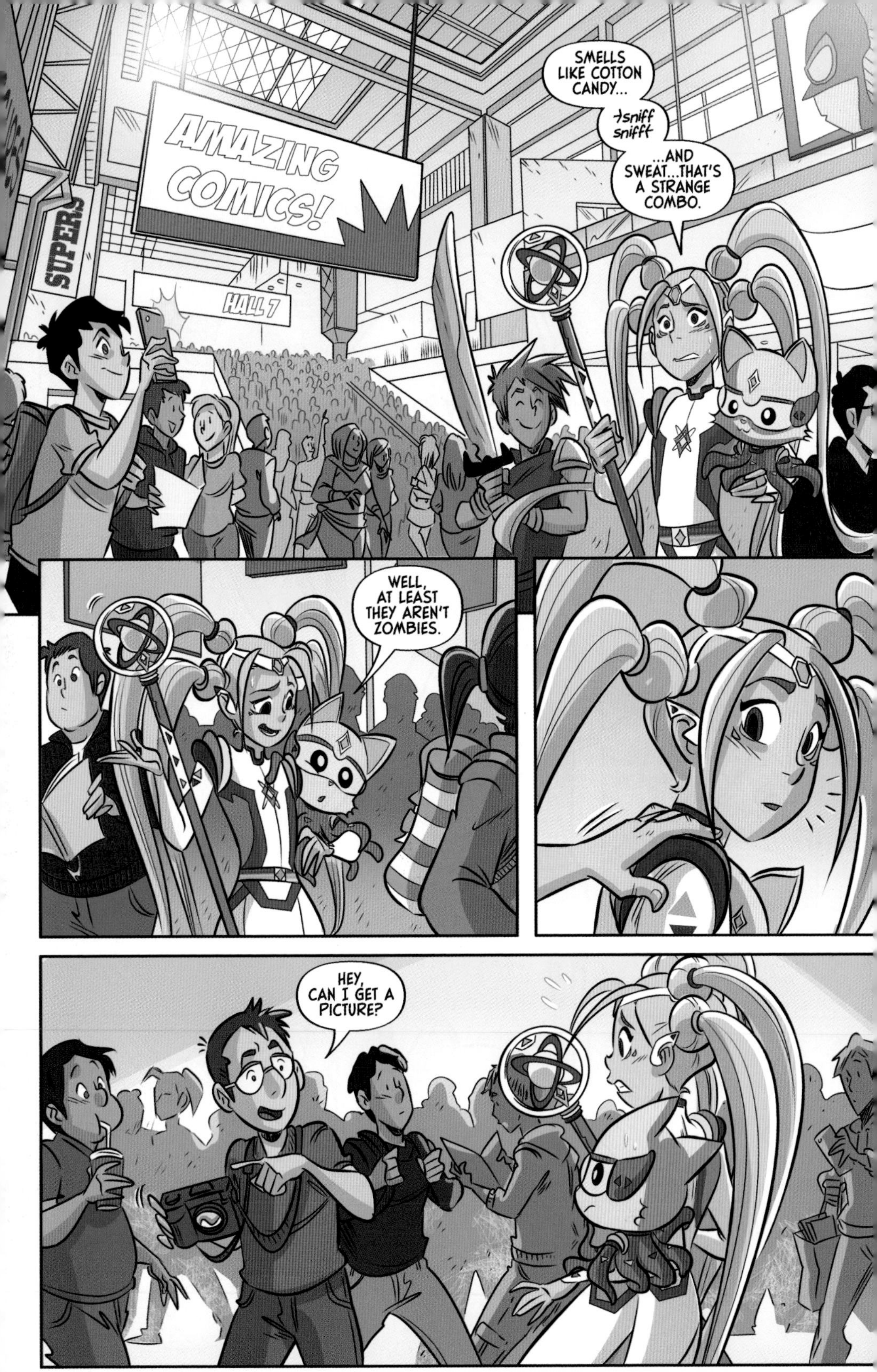
AMAZING COMICS!
SUPERS
HALL 7
SMELLS LIKE COTTON CANDY...
sniff sniff
...AND SWEAT...THAT'S A STRANGE COMBO.
WELL, AT LEAST THEY AREN'T ZOMBIES.
HEY, CAN I GET A PICTURE?

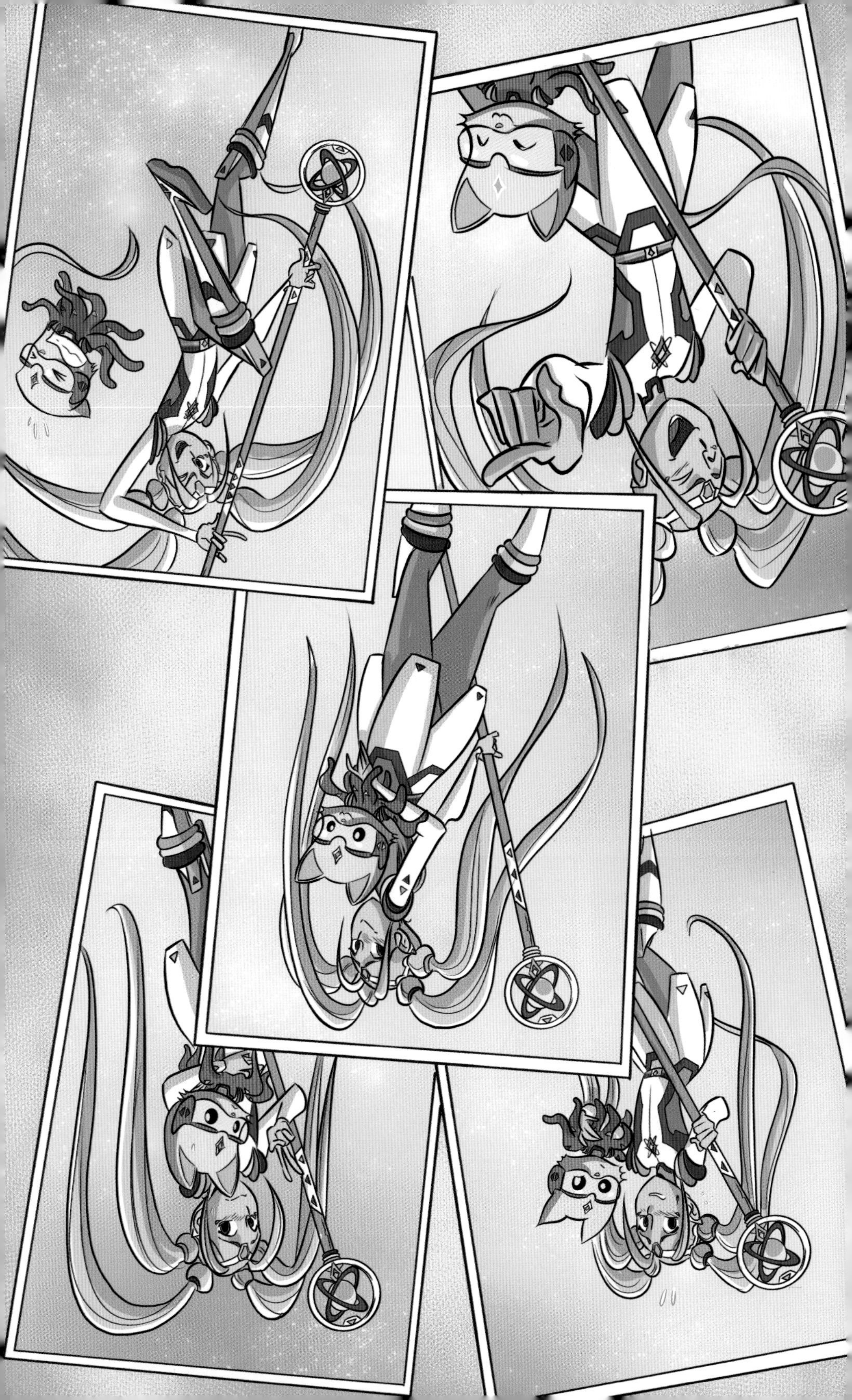

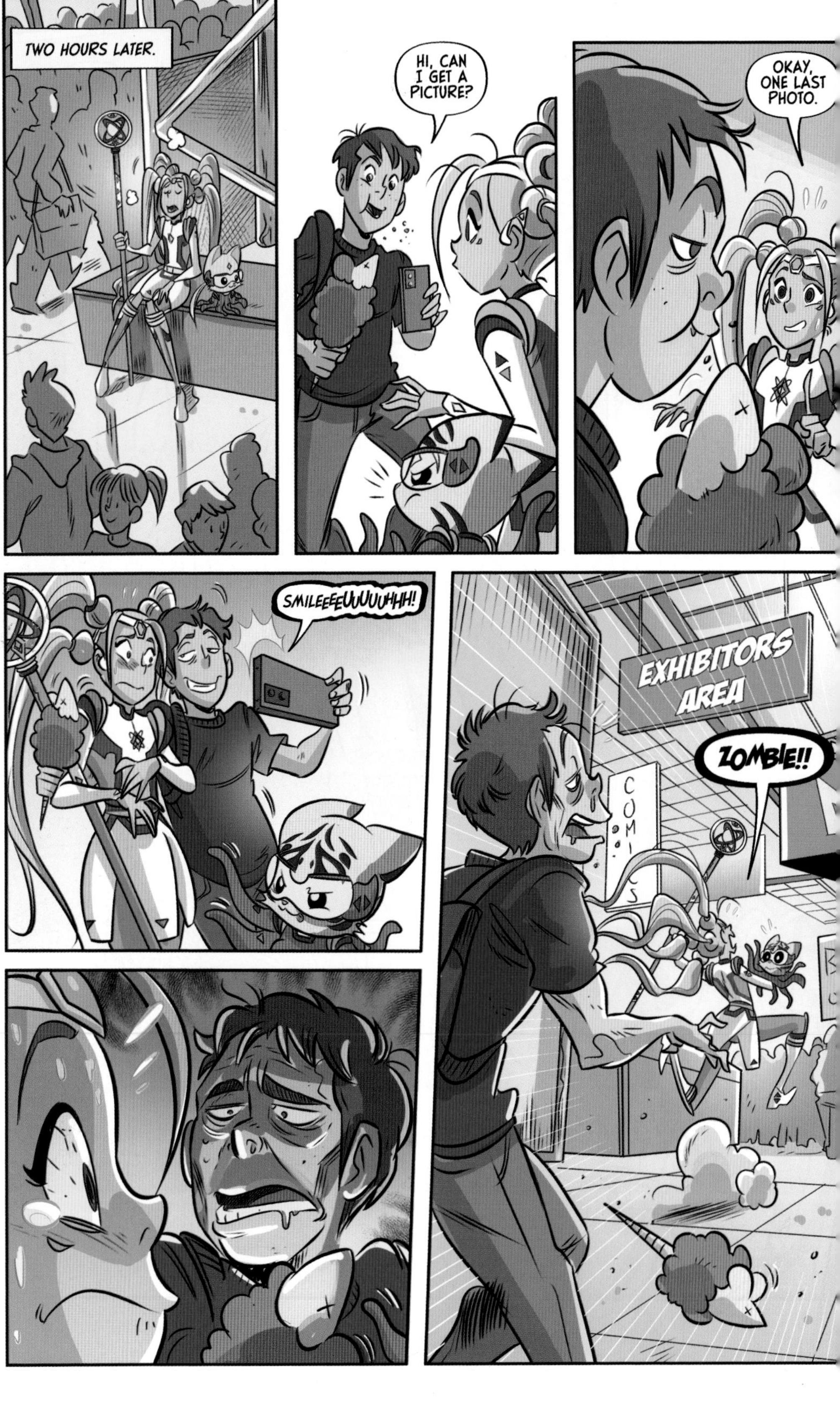
TWO HOURS LATER.
HI, CAN I GET A PICTURE?
OKAY, ONE LAST PHOTO.
SMILEEEEUUUUUHHH!
EXHIBITORS AREA
COMI
ZOMBIE!!

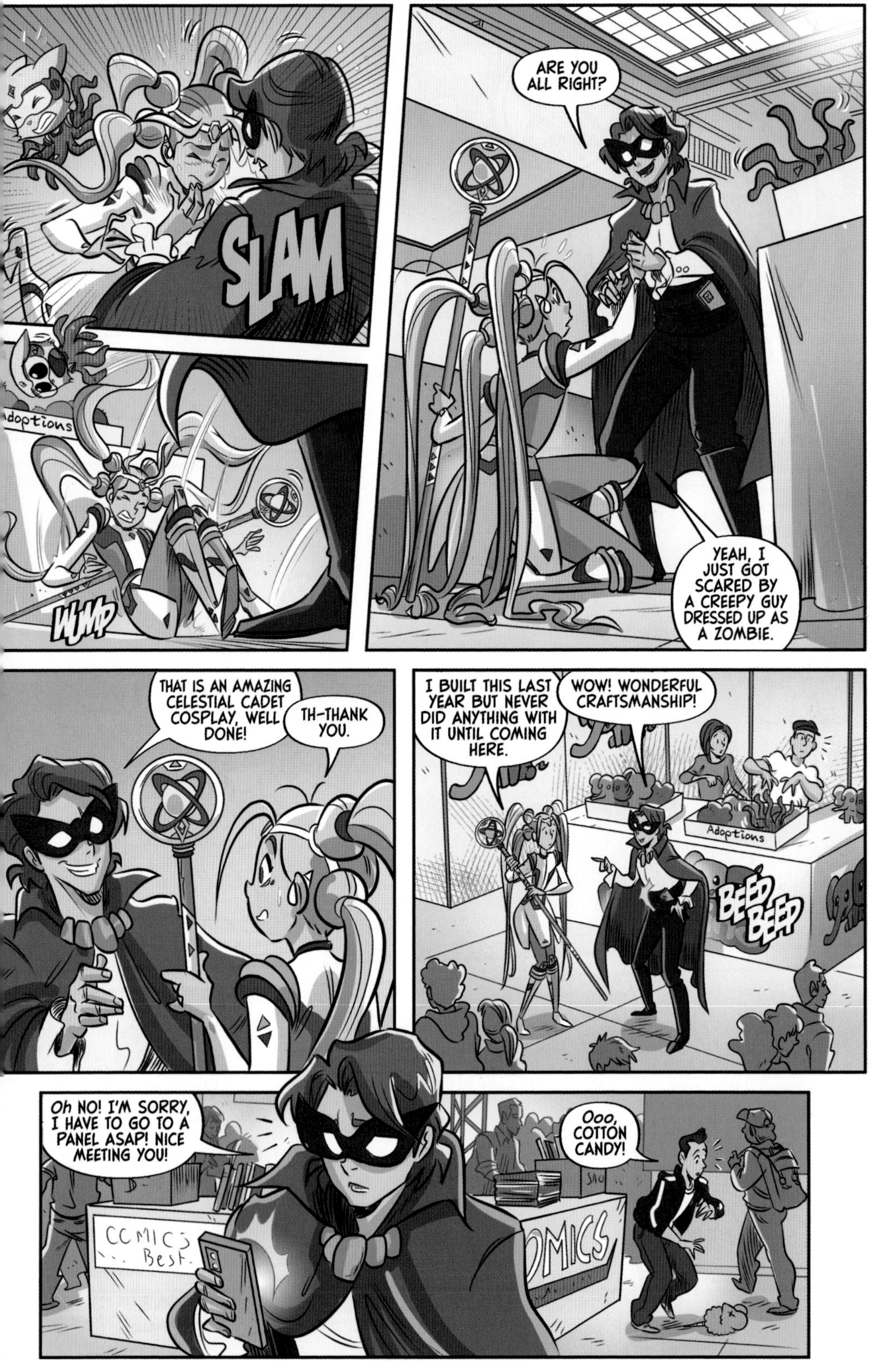
SLAM
Adoptions
WUMP
ARE YOU ALL RIGHT?
YEAH, I JUST GOT SCARED BY A CREEPY GUY DRESSED UP AS A ZOMBIE.
THAT IS AN AMAZING CELESTIAL CADET COSPLAY, WELL DONE!
TH-THANK YOU.
I BUILT THIS LAST YEAR BUT NEVER DID ANYTHING WITH IT UNTIL COMING HERE.
WOW! WONDERFUL CRAFTSMANSHIP!
Adoptions
BEEP BEEP
Oh NO! I'M SORRY, I HAVE TO GO TO A PANEL ASAP! NICE MEETING YOU!
Ooo, COTTON CANDY!
COMICS Best.
OMICS

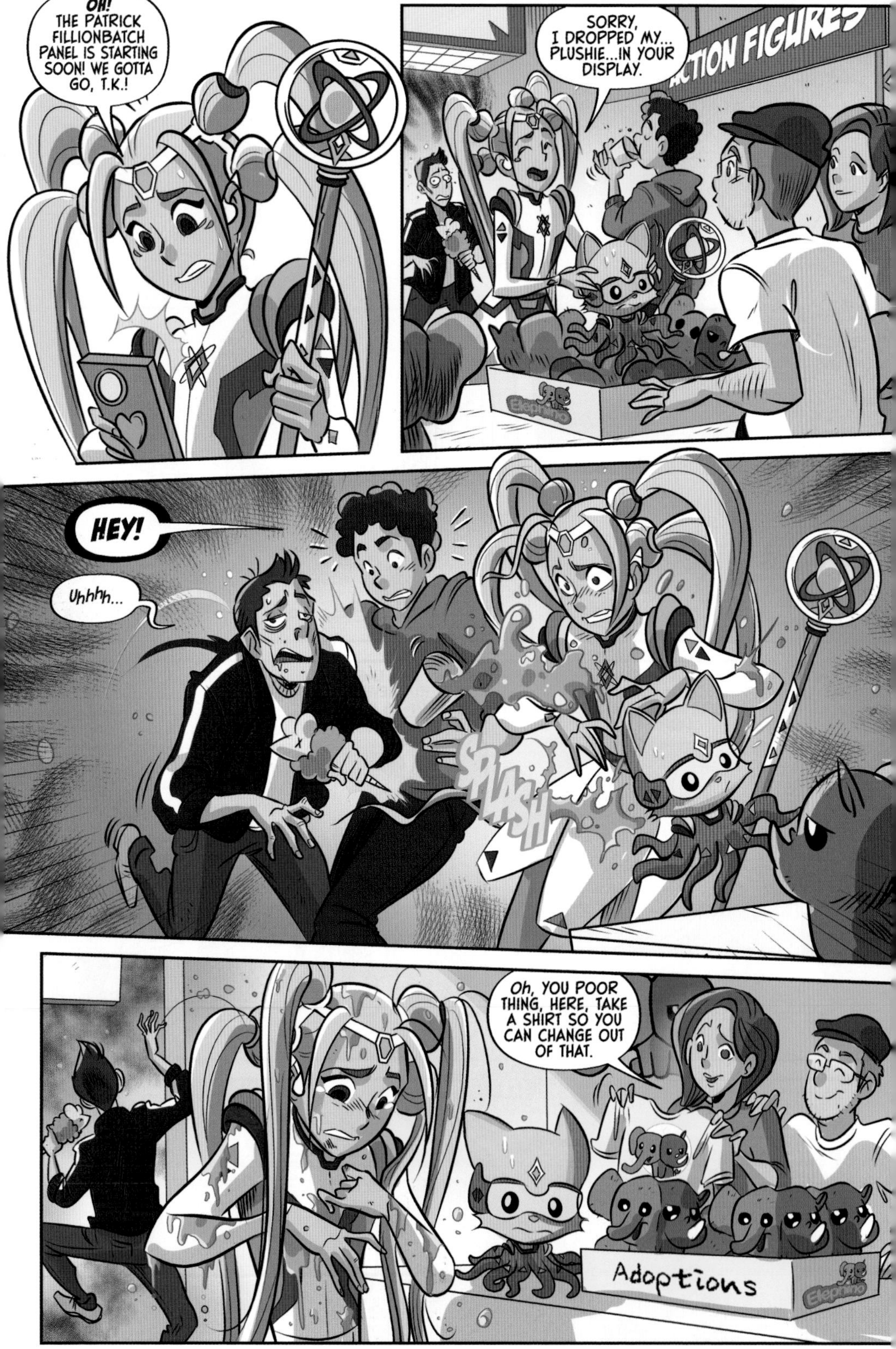
OH!
THE PATRICK FILLIONBATCH PANEL IS STARTING SOON! WE GOTTA GO, T.K.!
SORRY, I DROPPED MY... PLUSHIE...IN YOUR DISPLAY.
ACTION FIGURES
HEY!
Uhhhh...
SPLASH
Oh, YOU POOR THING, HERE, TAKE A SHIRT SO YOU CAN CHANGE OUT OF THAT.
Adoptions

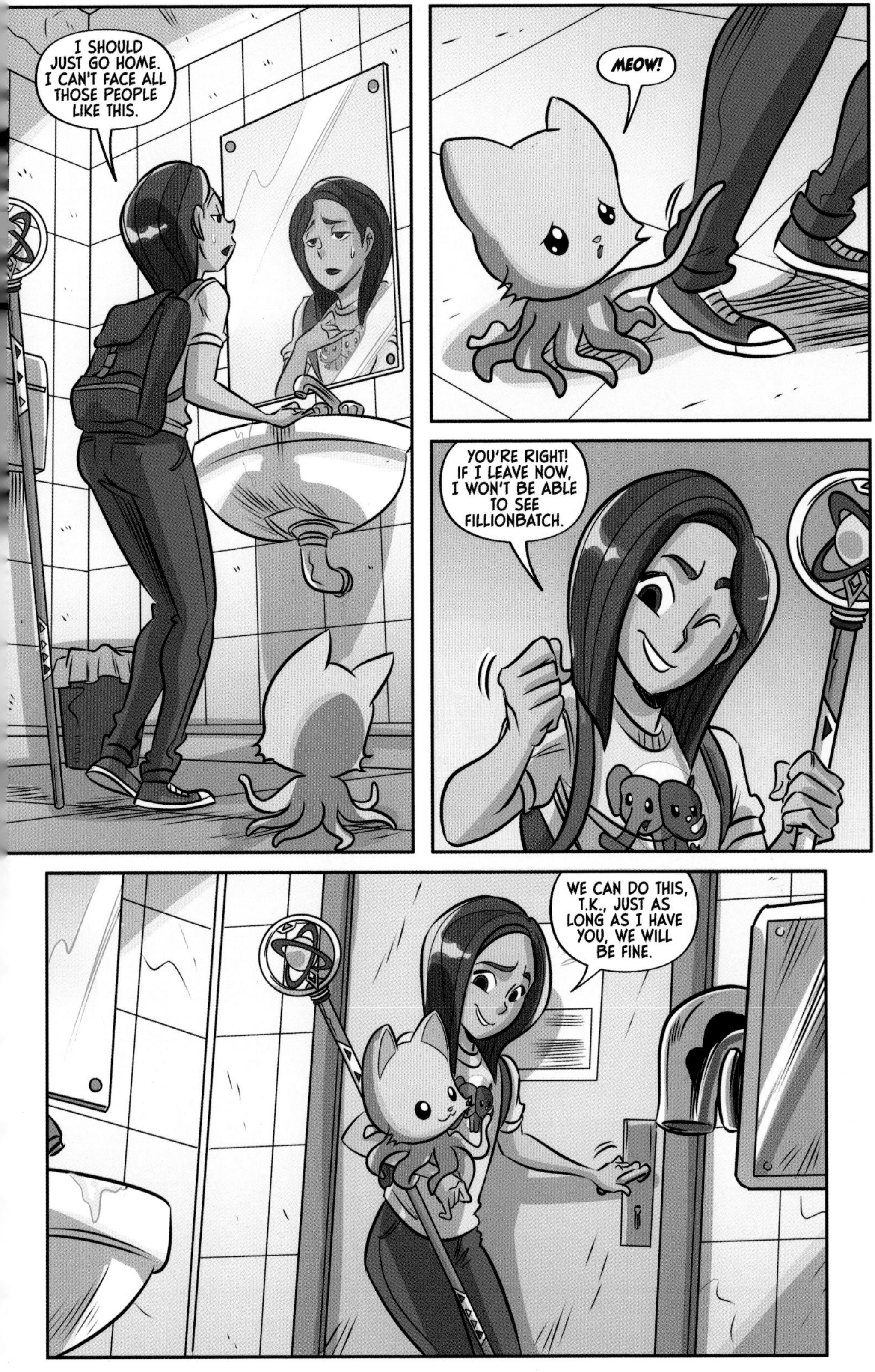
I SHOULD JUST GO HOME. I CAN'T FACE ALL THOSE PEOPLE LIKE THIS.
MEOW!
YOU'RE RIGHT! IF I LEAVE NOW, I WON'T BE ABLE TO SEE FILLIONBATCH.
WE CAN DO THIS, T.K., JUST AS LONG AS I HAVE YOU, WE WILL BE FINE.

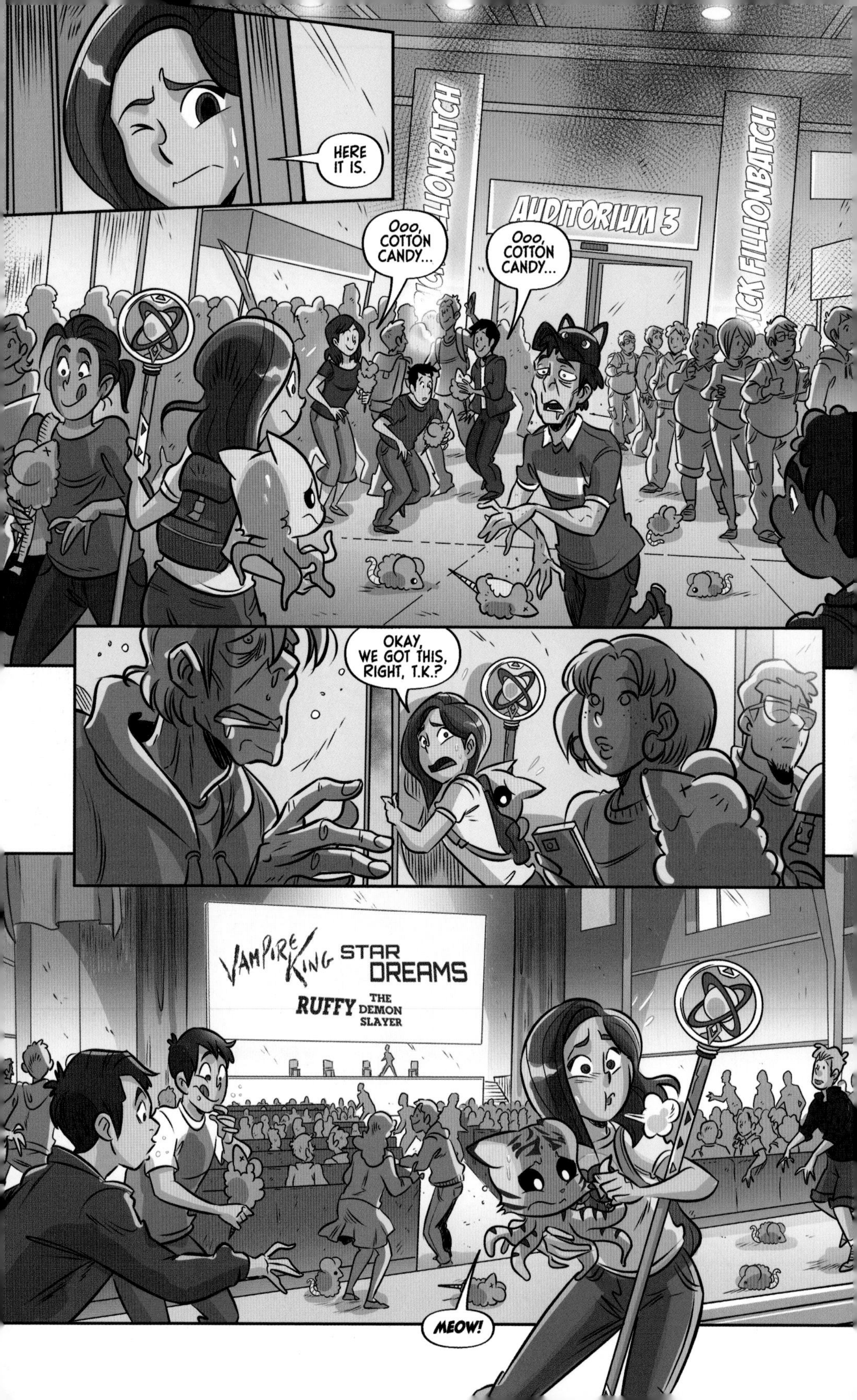
HERE IT IS.
AUDITORIUM 3
FILLIONBATCH
ICK FILLIONBATCH
Ooo, COTTON CANDY...
Ooo, COTTON CANDY...
OKAY, WE GOT THIS, RIGHT, T.K.?
VAMPIRE KING
STAR DREAMS
RUFFY THE DEMON SLAYER
MEOW!

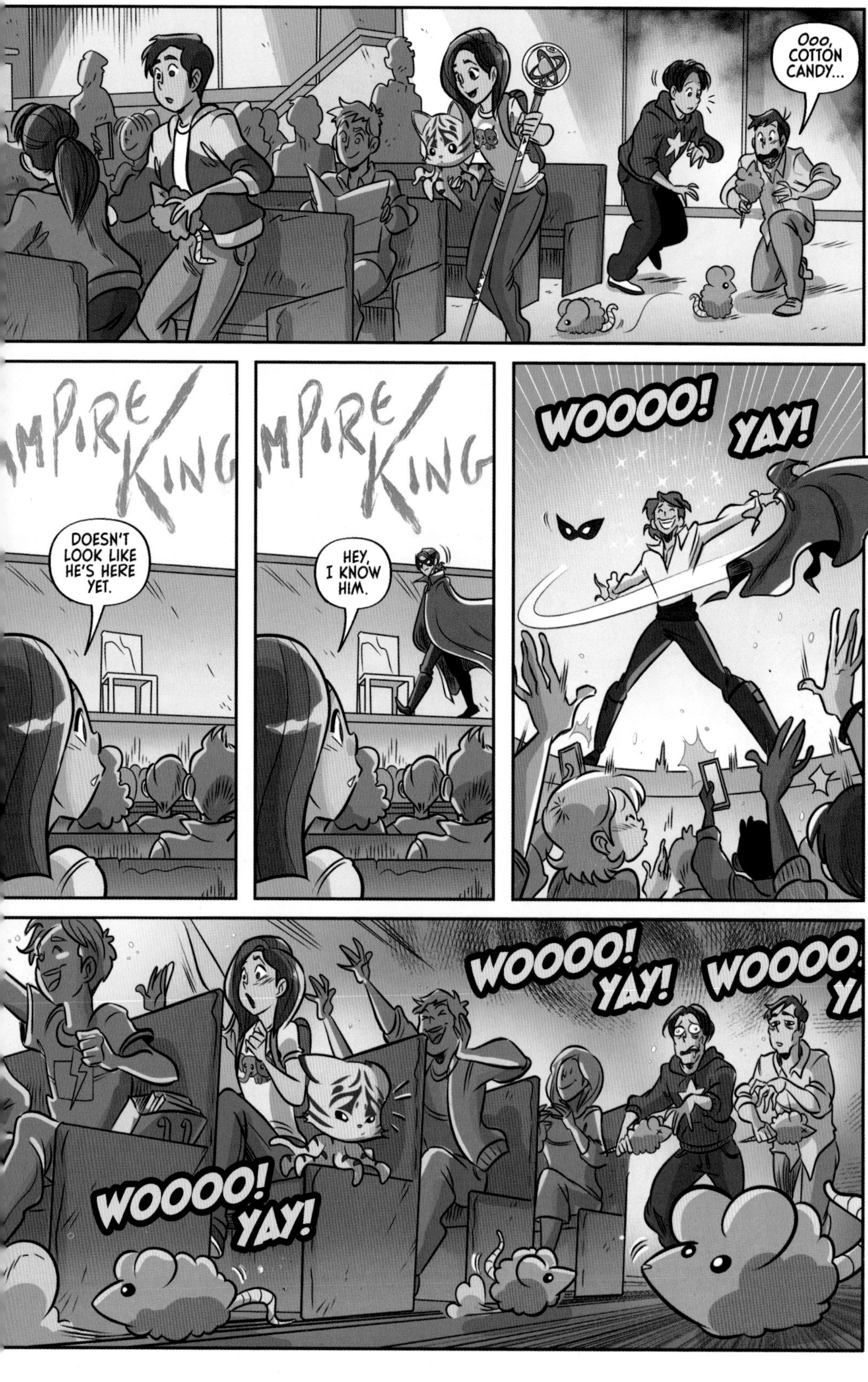
Ooo, COTTON CANDY...
MPIRE KING
DOESN'T LOOK LIKE HE'S HERE YET.
MPIRE KING
HEY, I KNOW HIM.
WOOOO! YAY!
WOOOO! YAY!
WOOOO!
WOOOO! YAY!

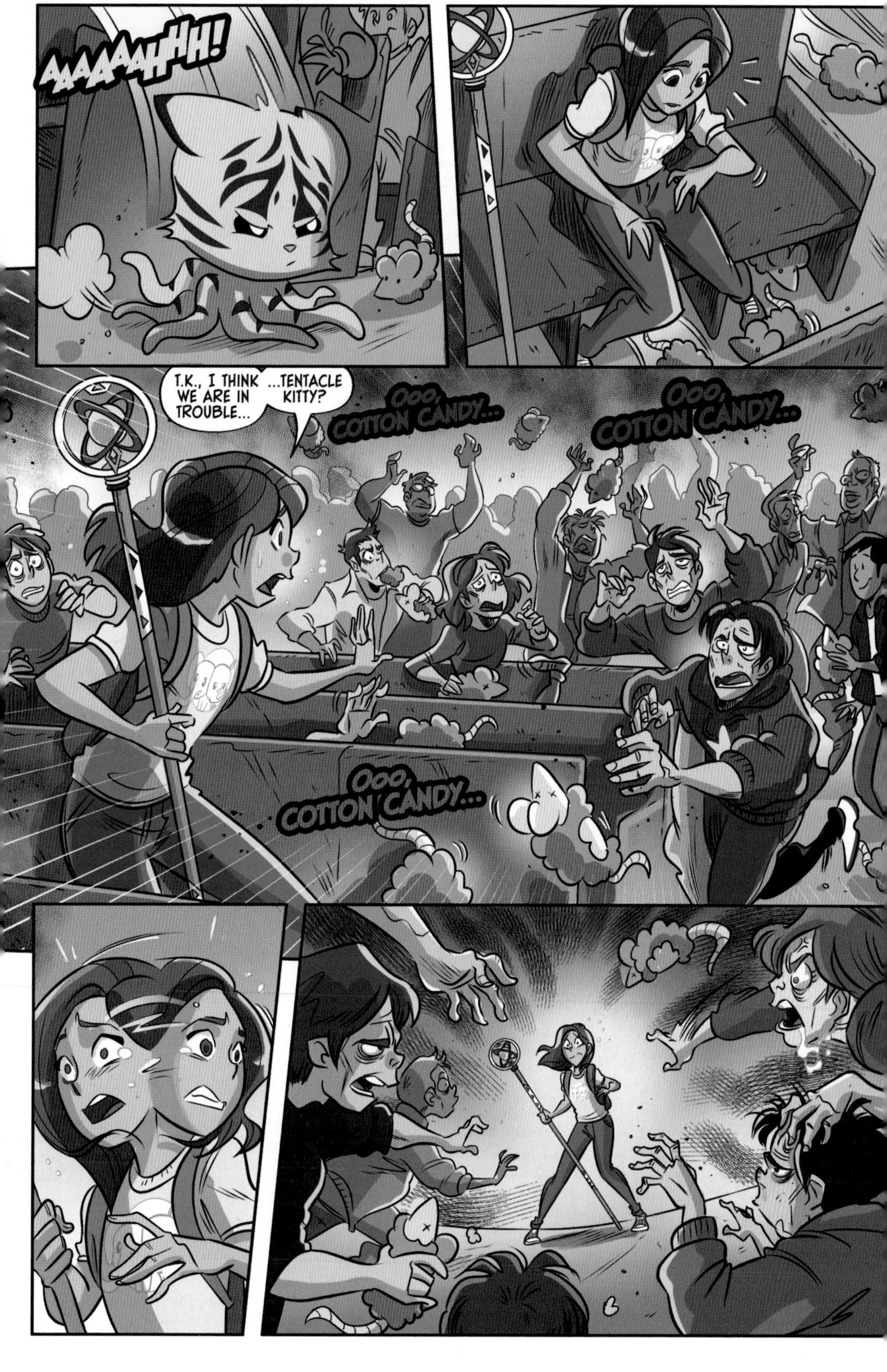
AAAAAAHHH!
T.K., I THINK WE ARE IN TROUBLE...
...TENTACLE KITTY?
Ooo, COTTON CANDY...
Ooo, COTTON CANDY...
Ooo, COTTON CANDY...

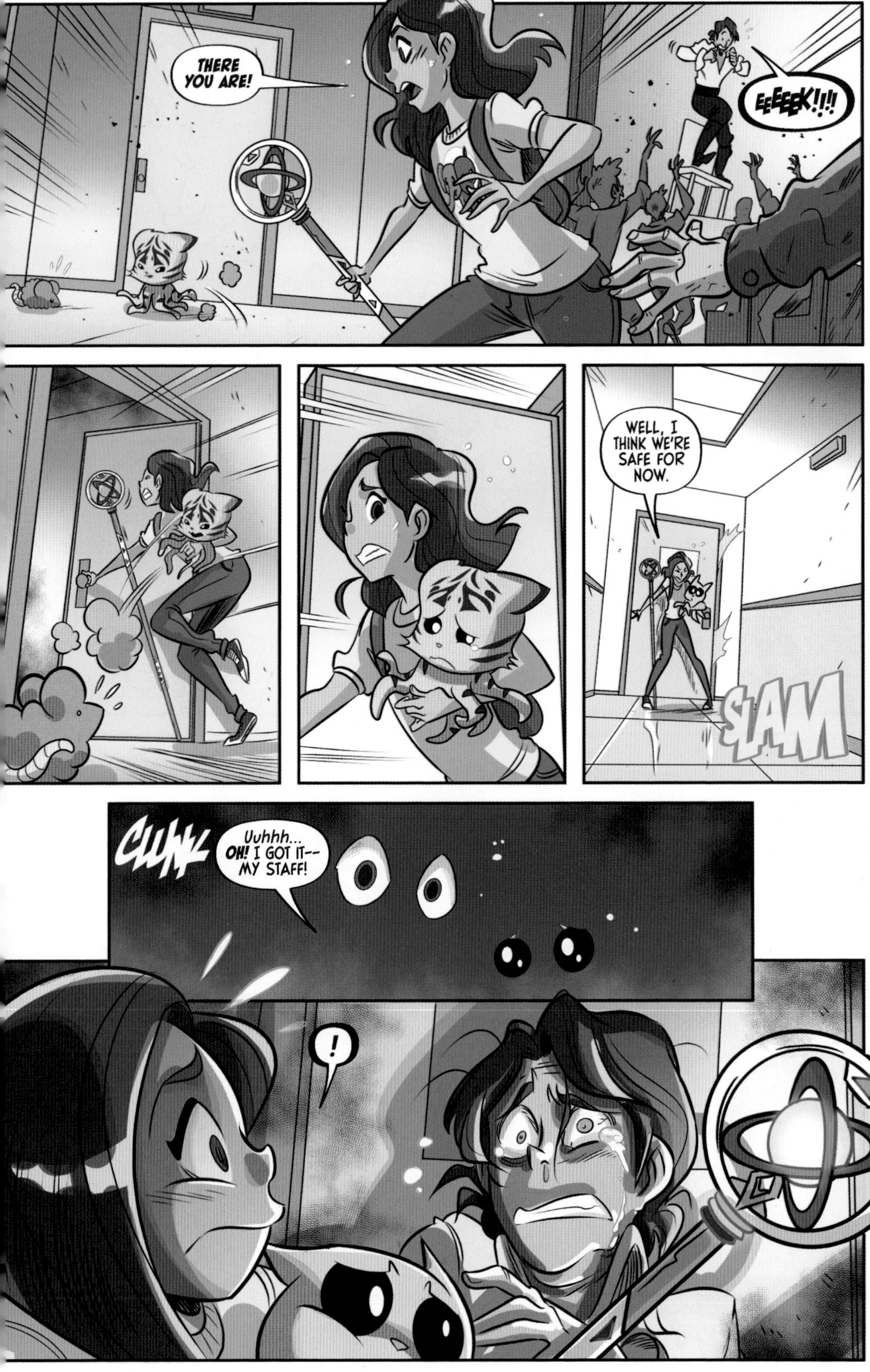
THERE YOU ARE!
EEEEEK!!!!
WELL, I THINK WE'RE SAFE FOR NOW.
SLAM
CLUNK
Uuhhh... OH! I GOT IT-- MY STAFF!
!

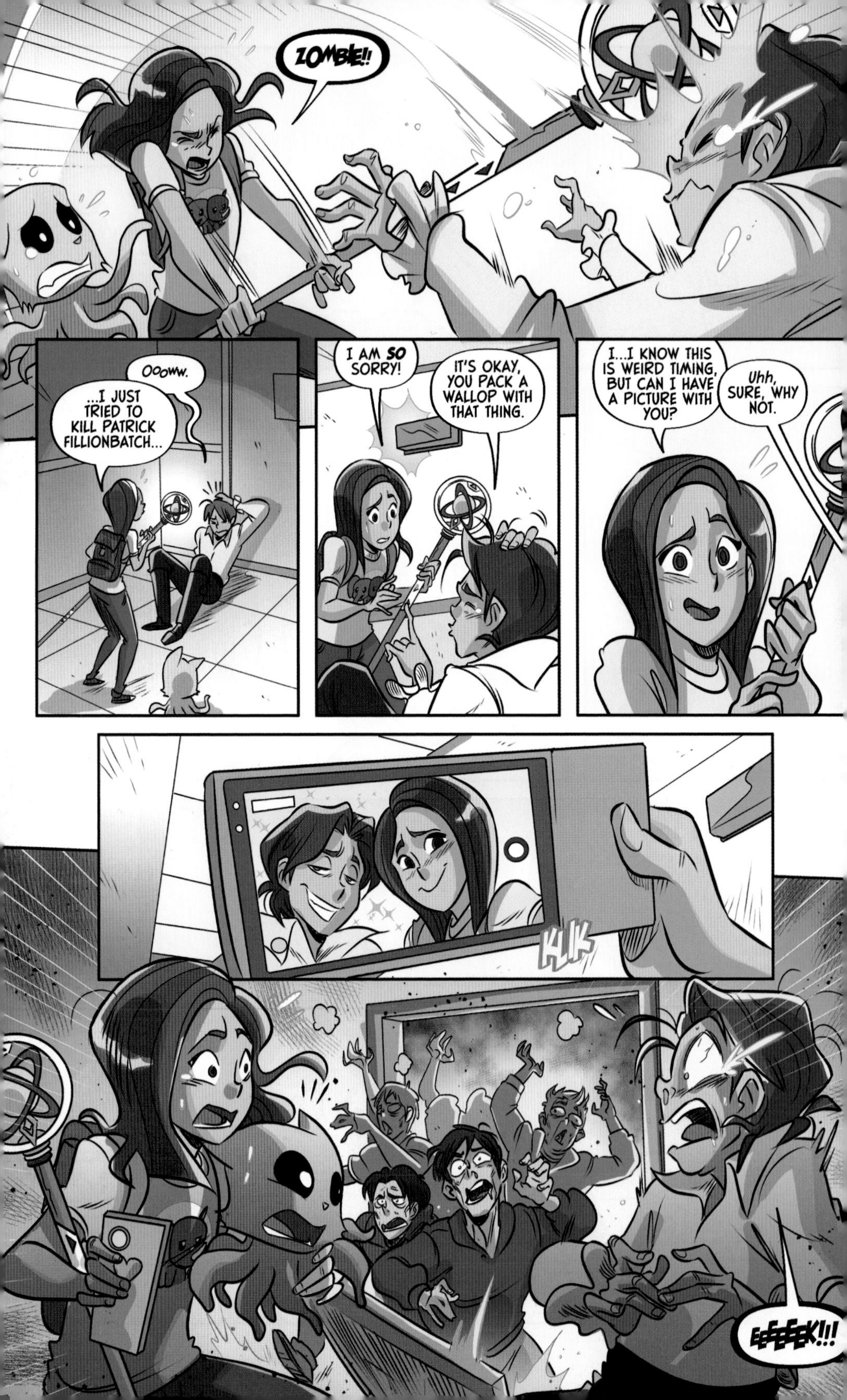
ZOMBIE!!
OOOWW.
...I JUST TRIED TO KILL PATRICK FILLIONBATCH...
I AM SO SORRY!
IT'S OKAY, YOU PACK A WALLOP WITH THAT THING.
I...I KNOW THIS IS WEIRD TIMING, BUT CAN I HAVE A PICTURE WITH YOU?
Uhh, SURE, WHY NOT.
KLIK
EEEEEEK!!!

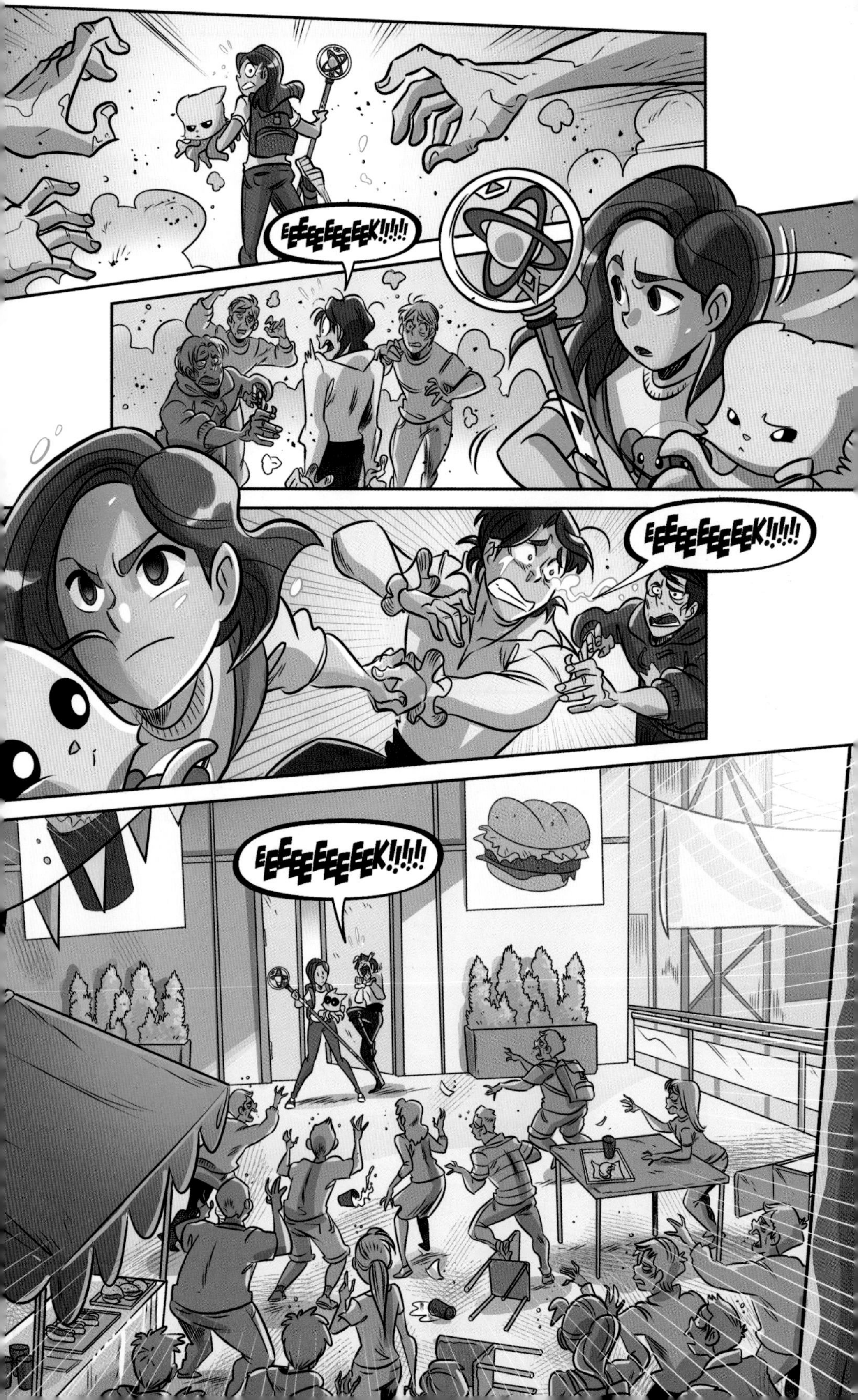
EEEEEEEEEK!!!!!
EEEEEEEEEK!!!!!
EEEEEEEEEK!!!!!

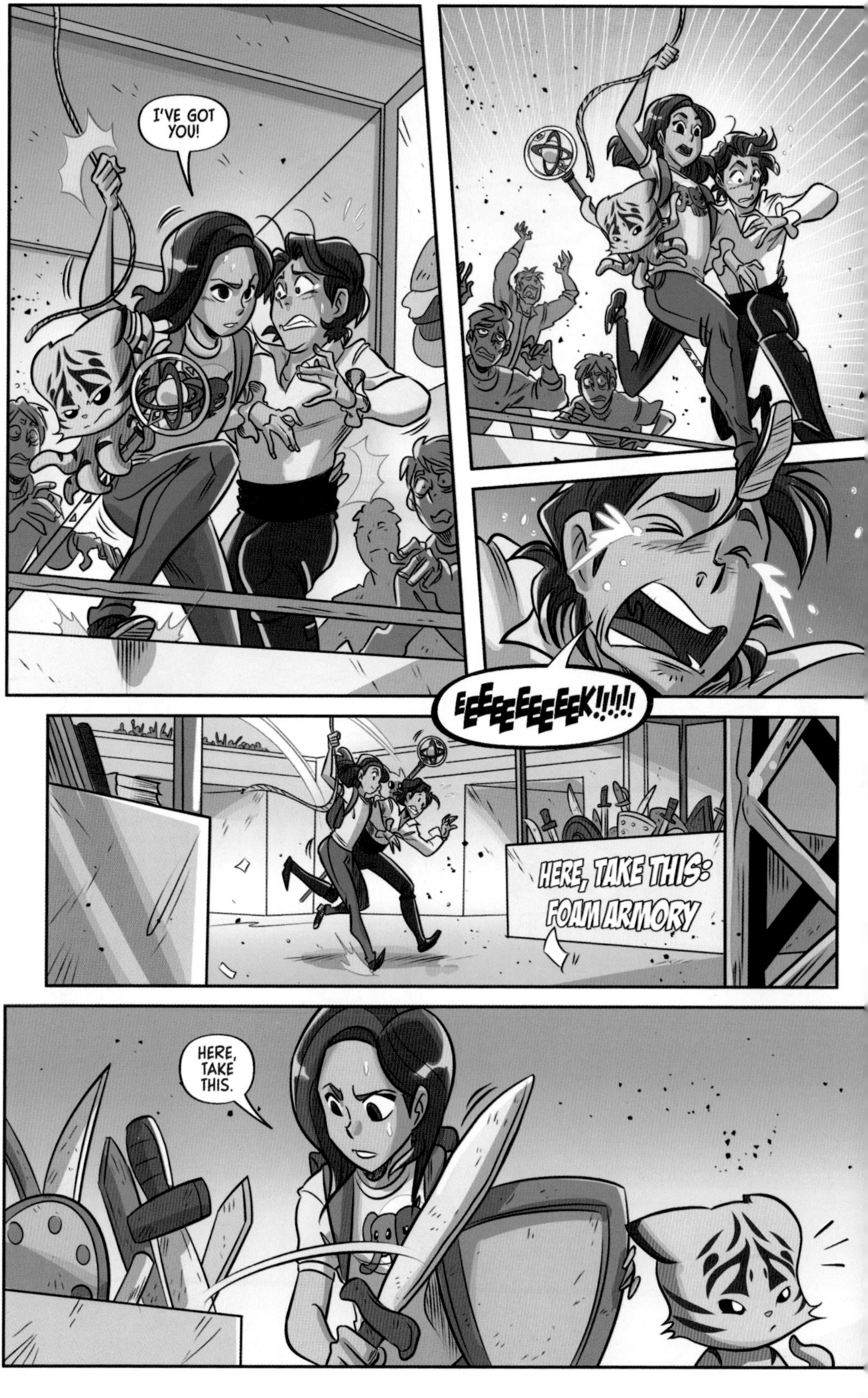
I'VE GOT YOU!
EEEEEEEEEEK!!!!!!
HERE, TAKE THIS:
FOAM ARMORY
HERE, TAKE THIS.

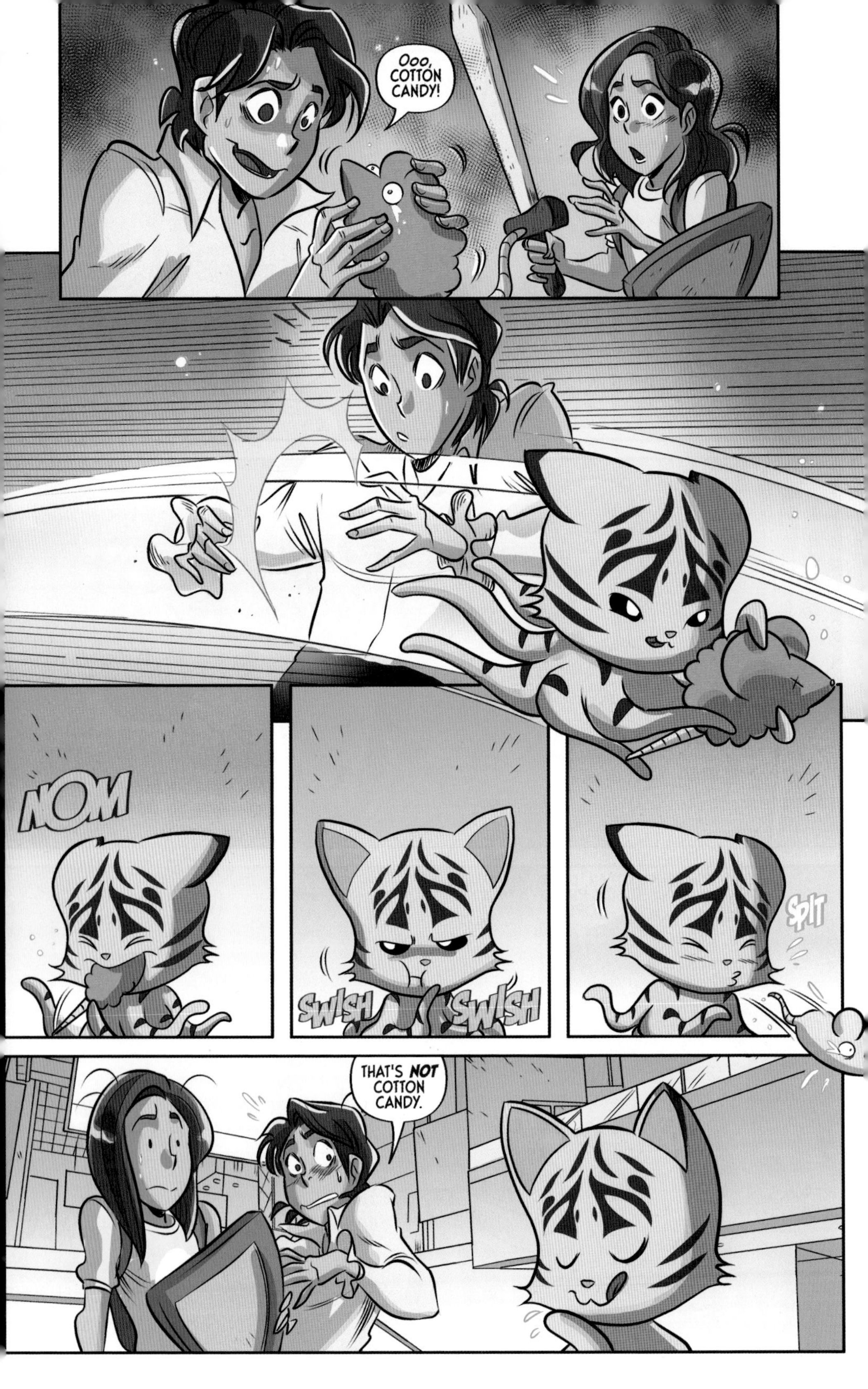
Ooo, COTTON CANDY!
NOM
SWISH
SWISH
SPIT
THAT'S **NOT** COTTON CANDY.

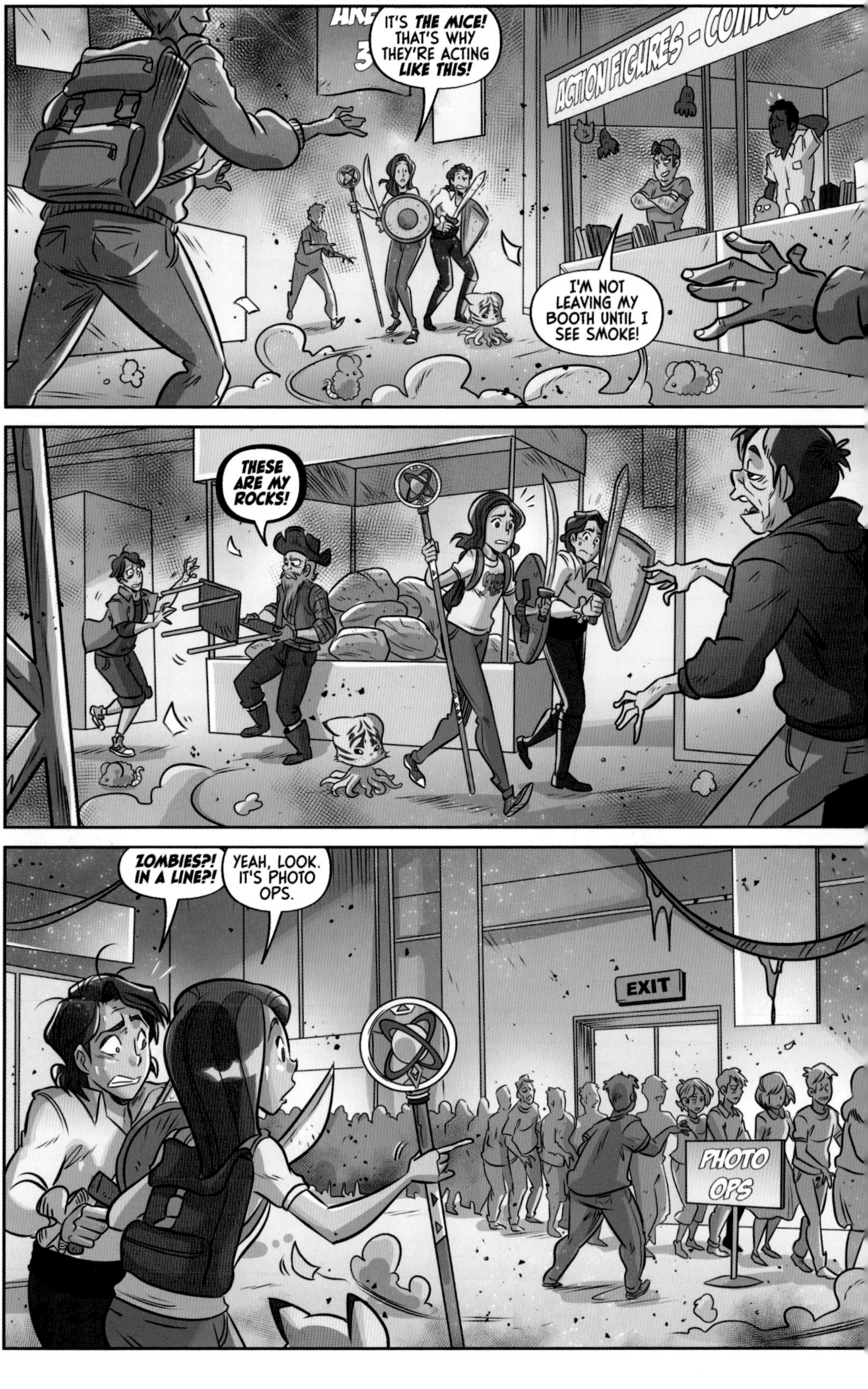
IT'S THE MICE! THAT'S WHY THEY'RE ACTING LIKE THIS!
ACTION FIGURES - COMICS
I'M NOT LEAVING MY BOOTH UNTIL I SEE SMOKE!
THESE ARE MY ROCKS!
ZOMBIES?! IN A LINE?!
YEAH, LOOK. IT'S PHOTO OPS.
EXIT
PHOTO OPS

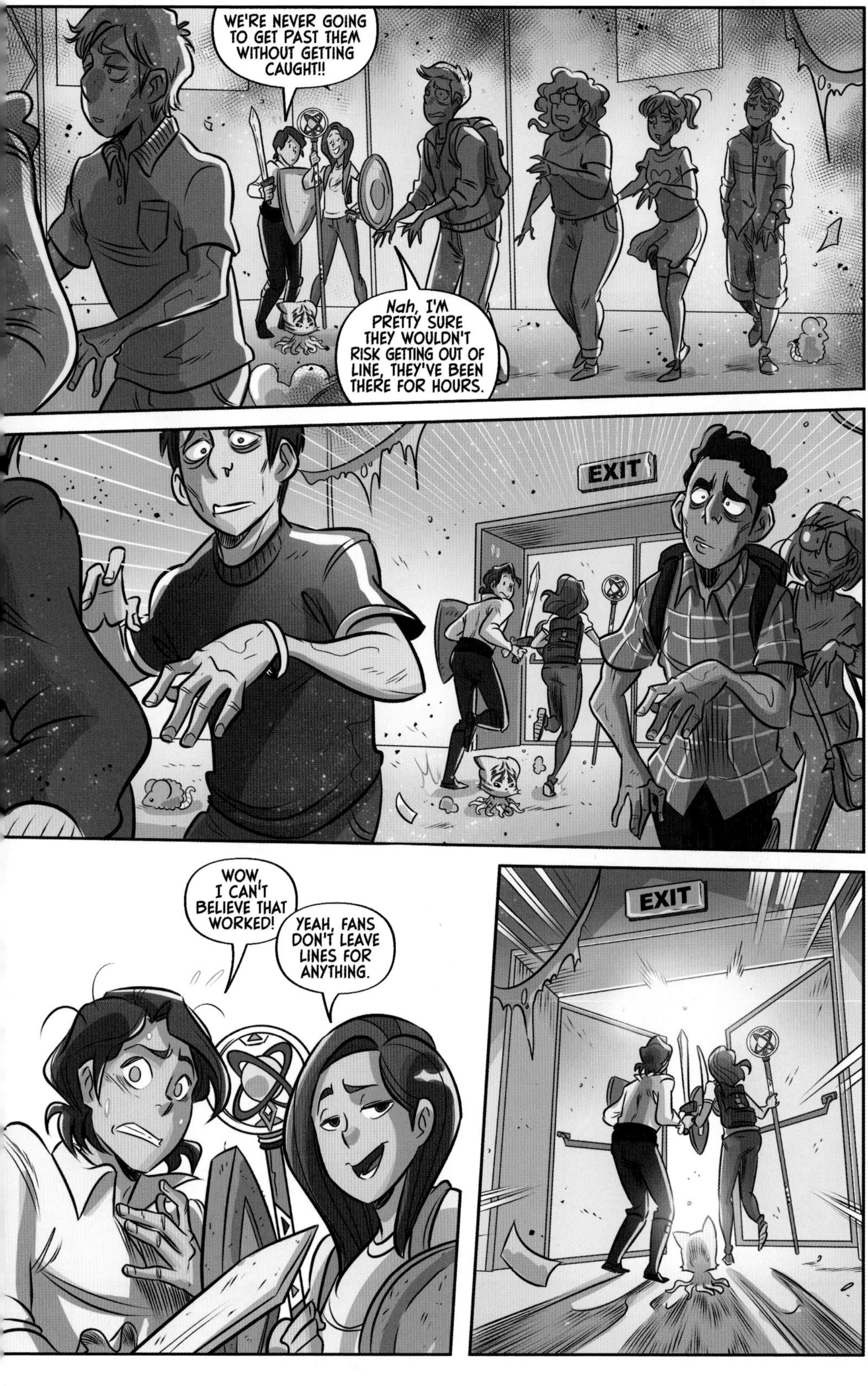
WE'RE NEVER GOING TO GET PAST THEM WITHOUT GETTING CAUGHT!!
Nah, I'M PRETTY SURE THEY WOULDN'T RISK GETTING OUT OF LINE, THEY'VE BEEN THERE FOR HOURS.
EXIT
WOW, I CAN'T BELIEVE THAT WORKED!
YEAH, FANS DON'T LEAVE LINES FOR ANYTHING.
EXIT

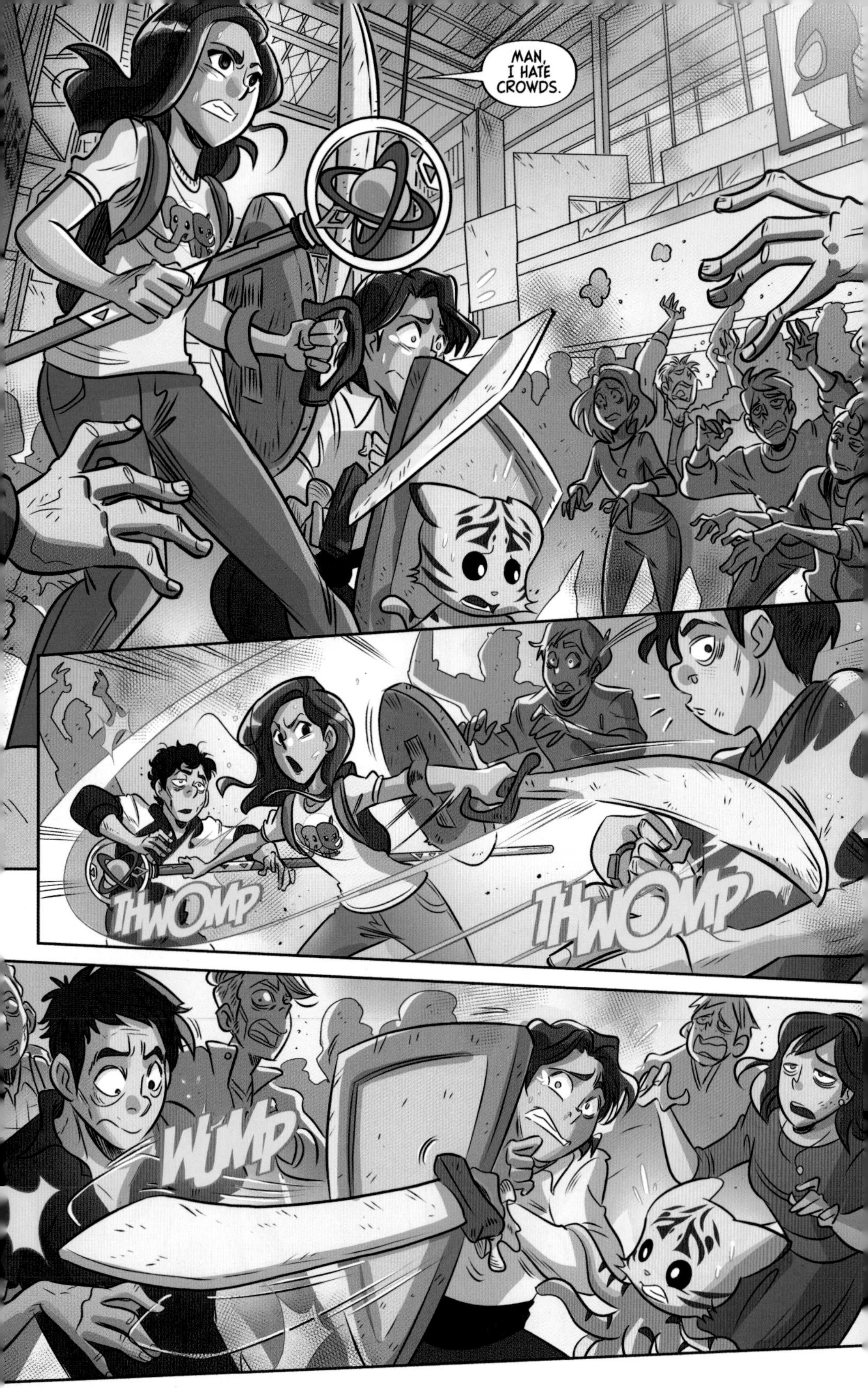
MAN, I HATE CROWDS.
THWOMP
THWOMP
WUMP

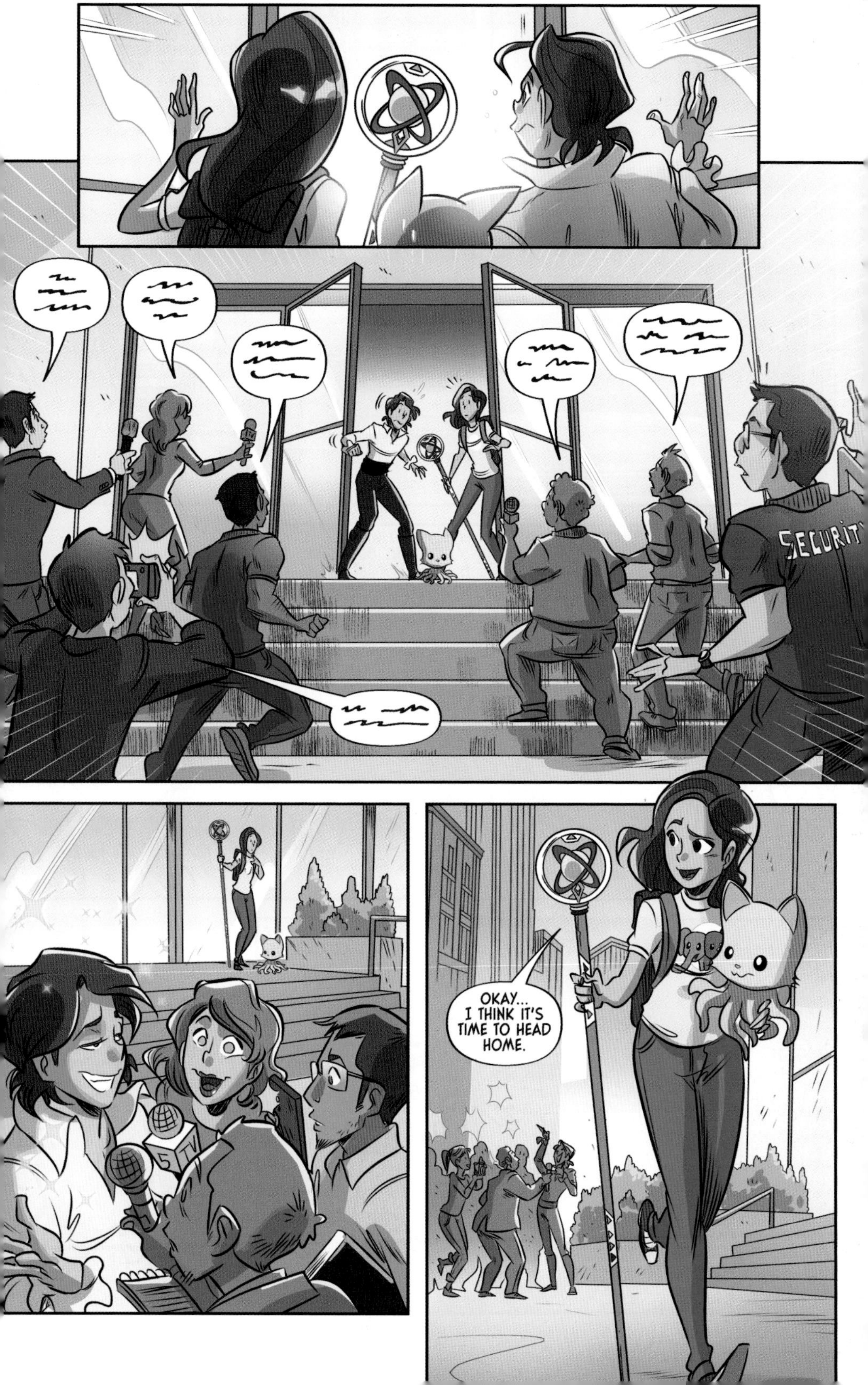
SECURITY
OKAY... I THINK IT'S TIME TO HEAD HOME.

AND TO MY FAVORITE CADET OUT THERE--

--THANKS, YOU'VE GOT AN AMAZING FUTURE AHEAD OF YOU.

YES, IT WAS ALL VERY CHAOTIC, BUT THANKS TO MY EXPERIENCE IN ACTION FILMS I WAS ABLE TO FIGHT OFF THE HORDE WHILE RESCUING A HELPLESS YOUNG GIRL.

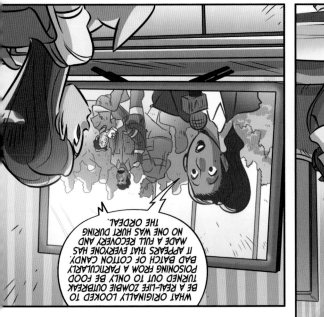

WHAT ORIGINALLY LOOKED TO BE A REAL-LIFE ZOMBIE OUTBREAK TURNED OUT TO ONLY BE FOOD POISONING FROM A PARTICULARLY BAD BATCH OF COTTON CANDY. IT APPEARS THAT EVERYONE HAS MADE A FULL RECOVERY AND NO ONE WAS HURT DURING THE ORDEAL.

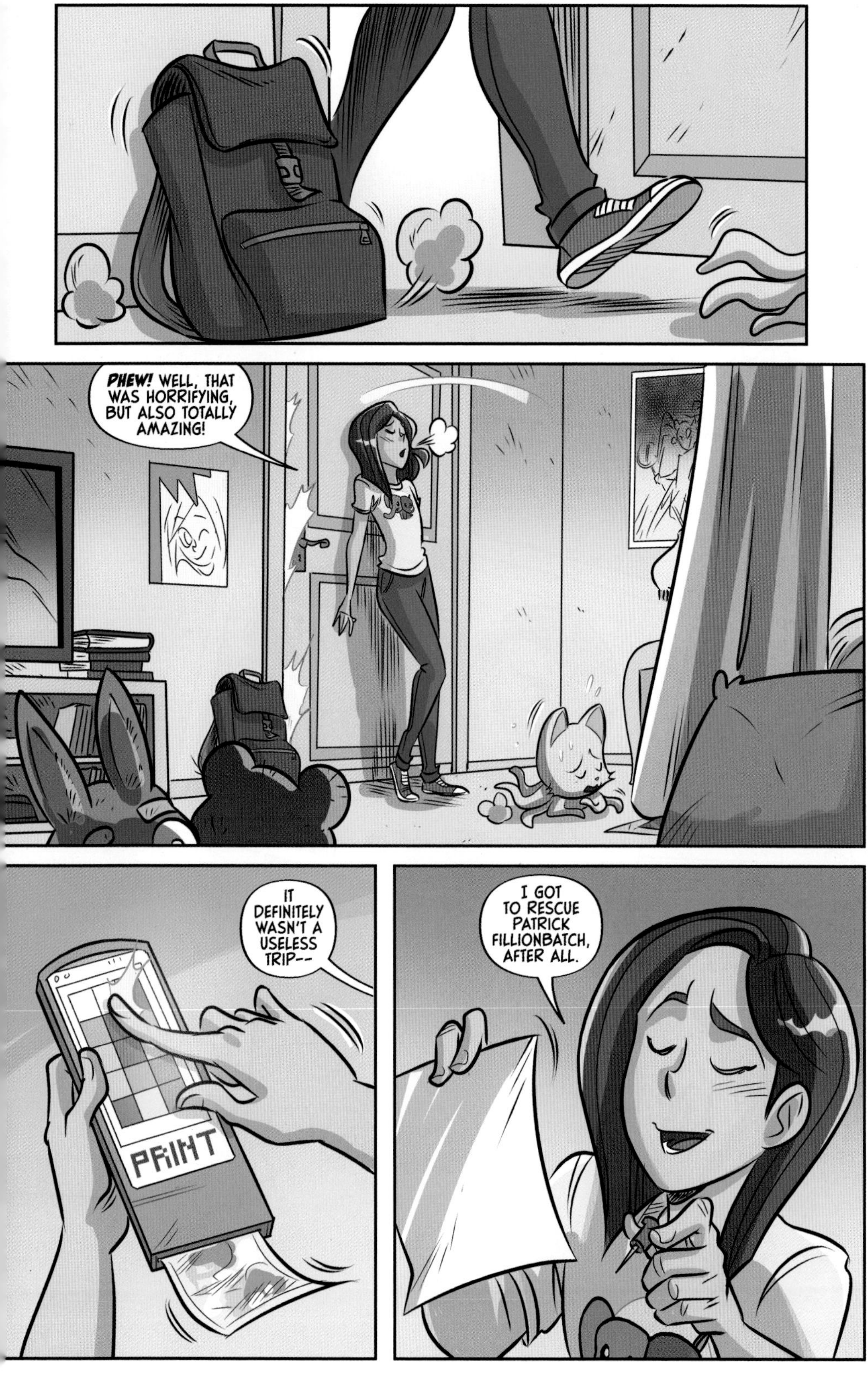
PHEW! WELL, THAT WAS HORRIFYING, BUT ALSO TOTALLY AMAZING!
IT DEFINITELY WASN'T A USELESS TRIP--
PRINT
I GOT TO RESCUE PATRICK FILLIONBATCH, AFTER ALL.

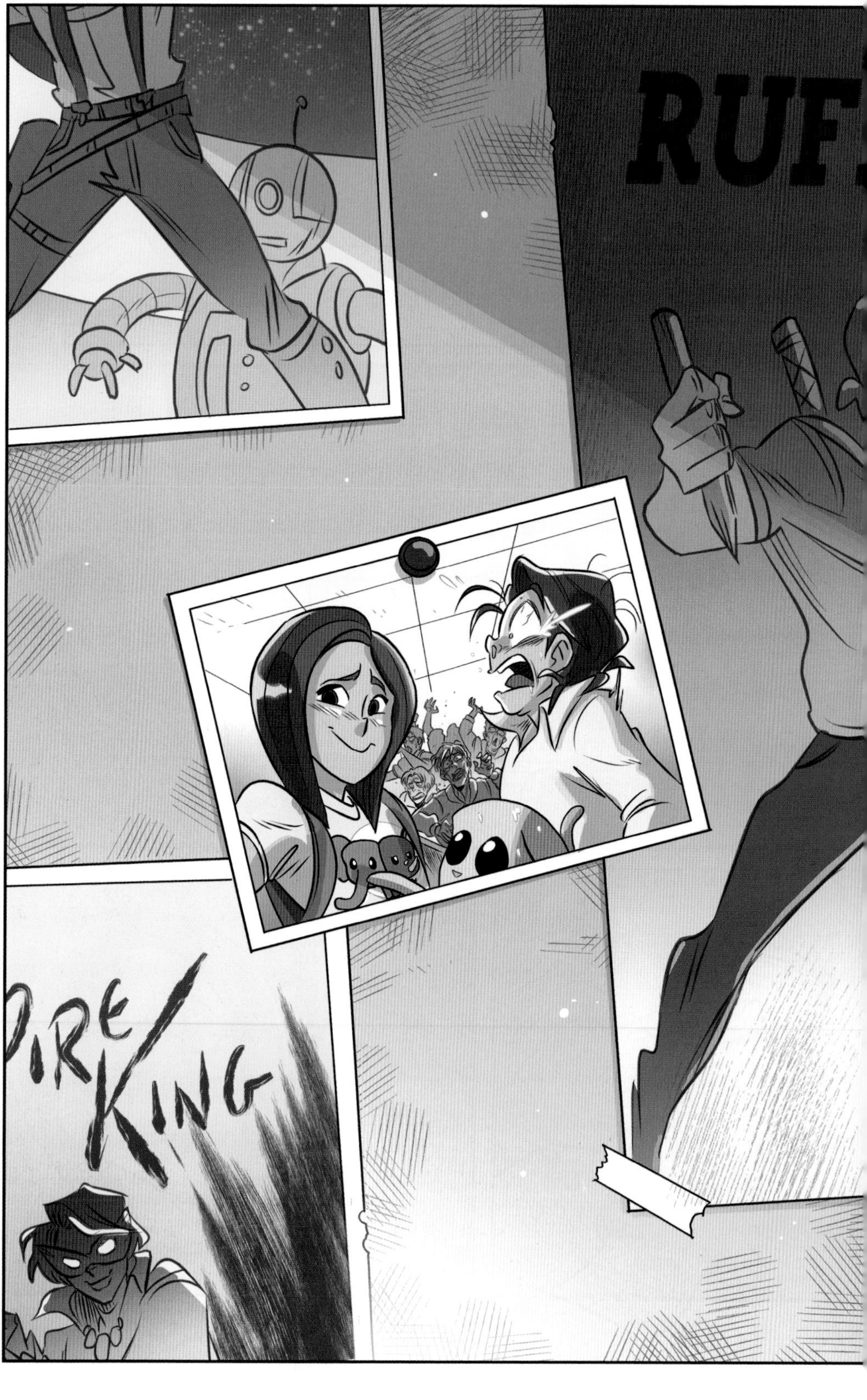
RUF
IRE KING

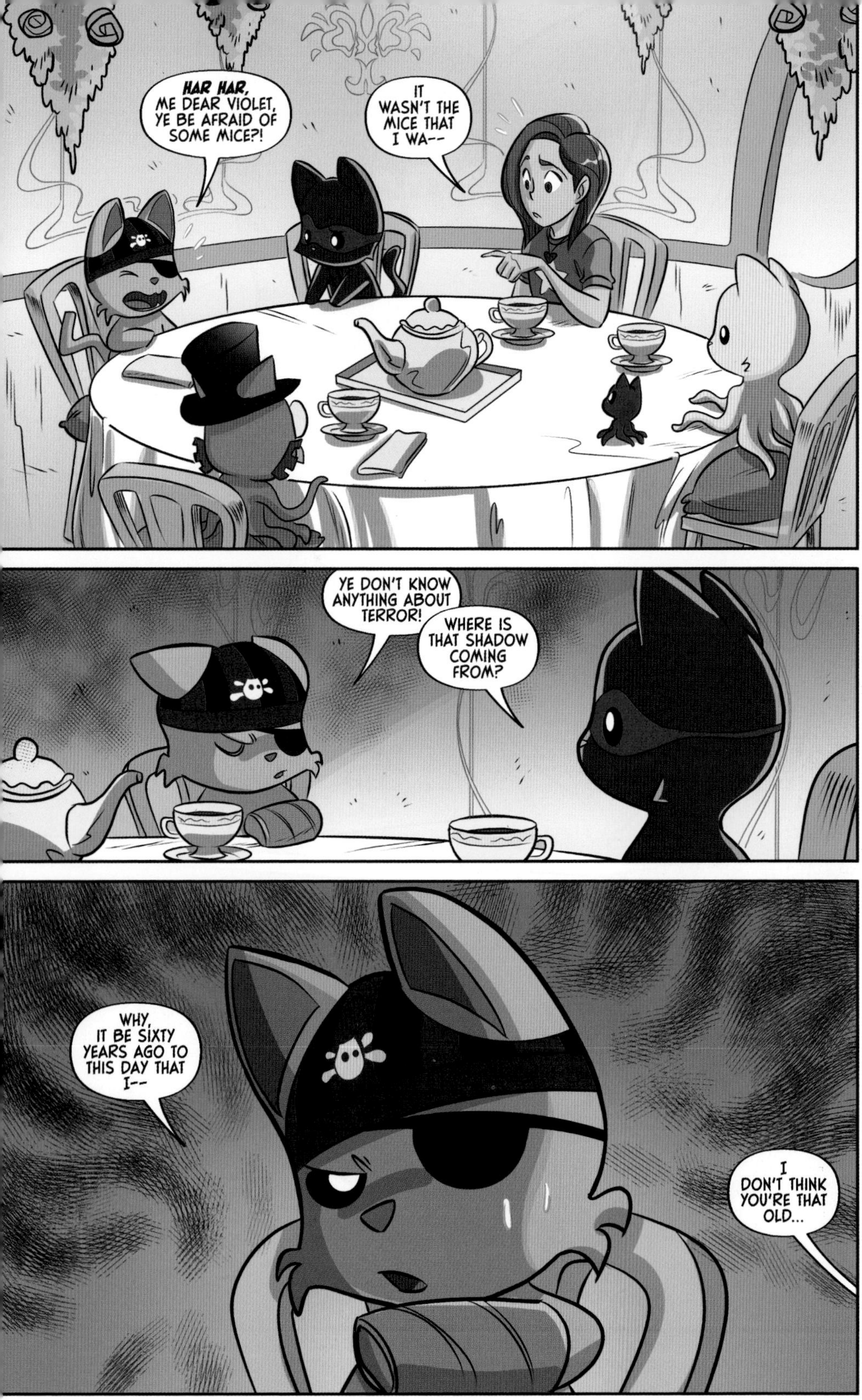
HAR HAR, ME DEAR VIOLET, YE BE AFRAID OF SOME MICE?!
IT WASN'T THE MICE THAT I WA--
YE DON'T KNOW ANYTHING ABOUT TERROR!
WHERE IS THAT SHADOW COMING FROM?
WHY, IT BE SIXTY YEARS AGO TO THIS DAY THAT I--
I DON'T THINK YOU'RE THAT OLD...

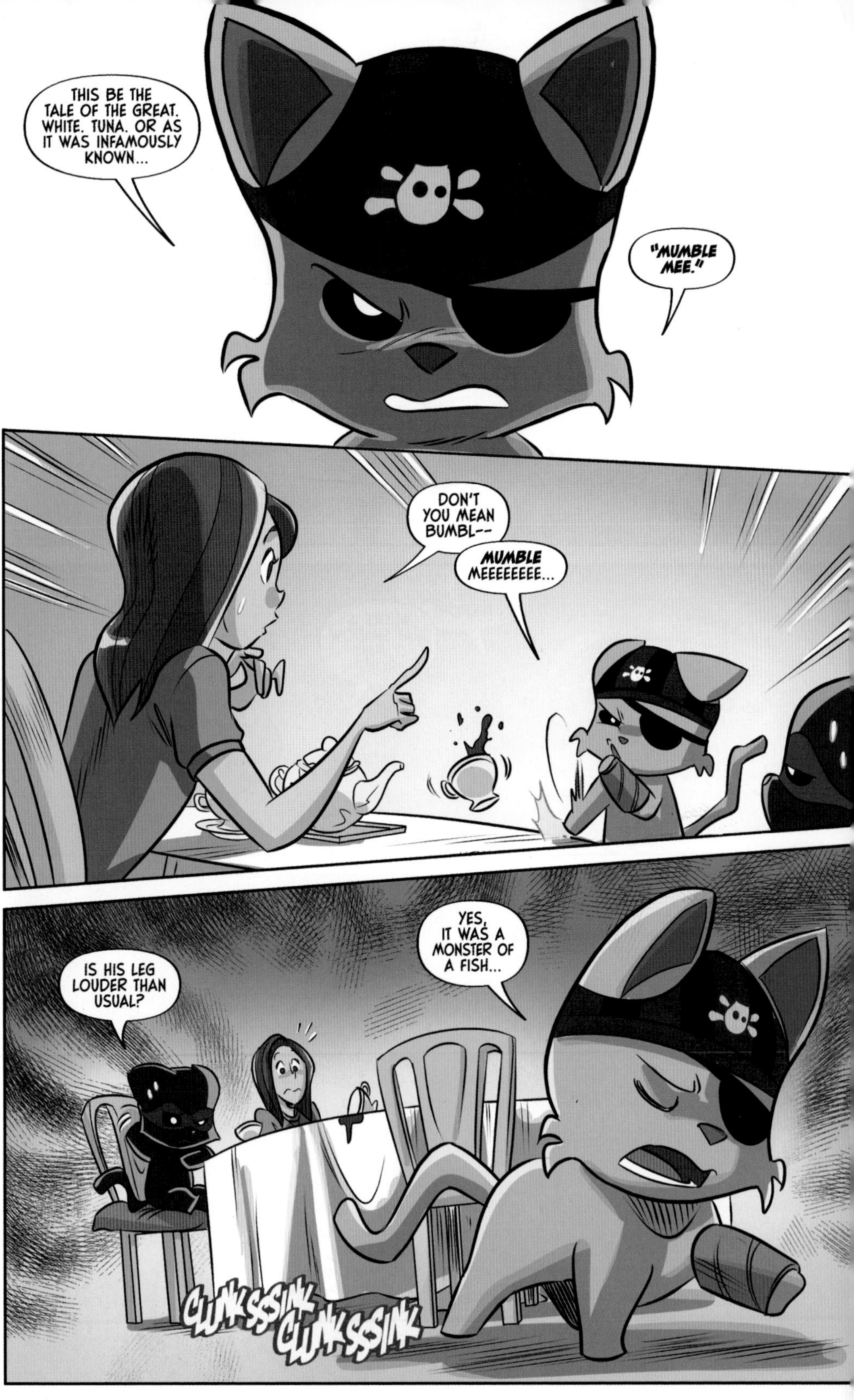
THIS BE THE TALE OF THE GREAT. WHITE. TUNA. OR AS IT WAS INFAMOUSLY KNOWN...
"MUMBLE MEE."
DON'T YOU MEAN BUMBL--
MUMBLE MEEEEEEEE...
IS HIS LEG LOUDER THAN USUAL?
YES, IT WAS A MONSTER OF A FISH...
CLUNK SSSINK CLUNK SSSINK

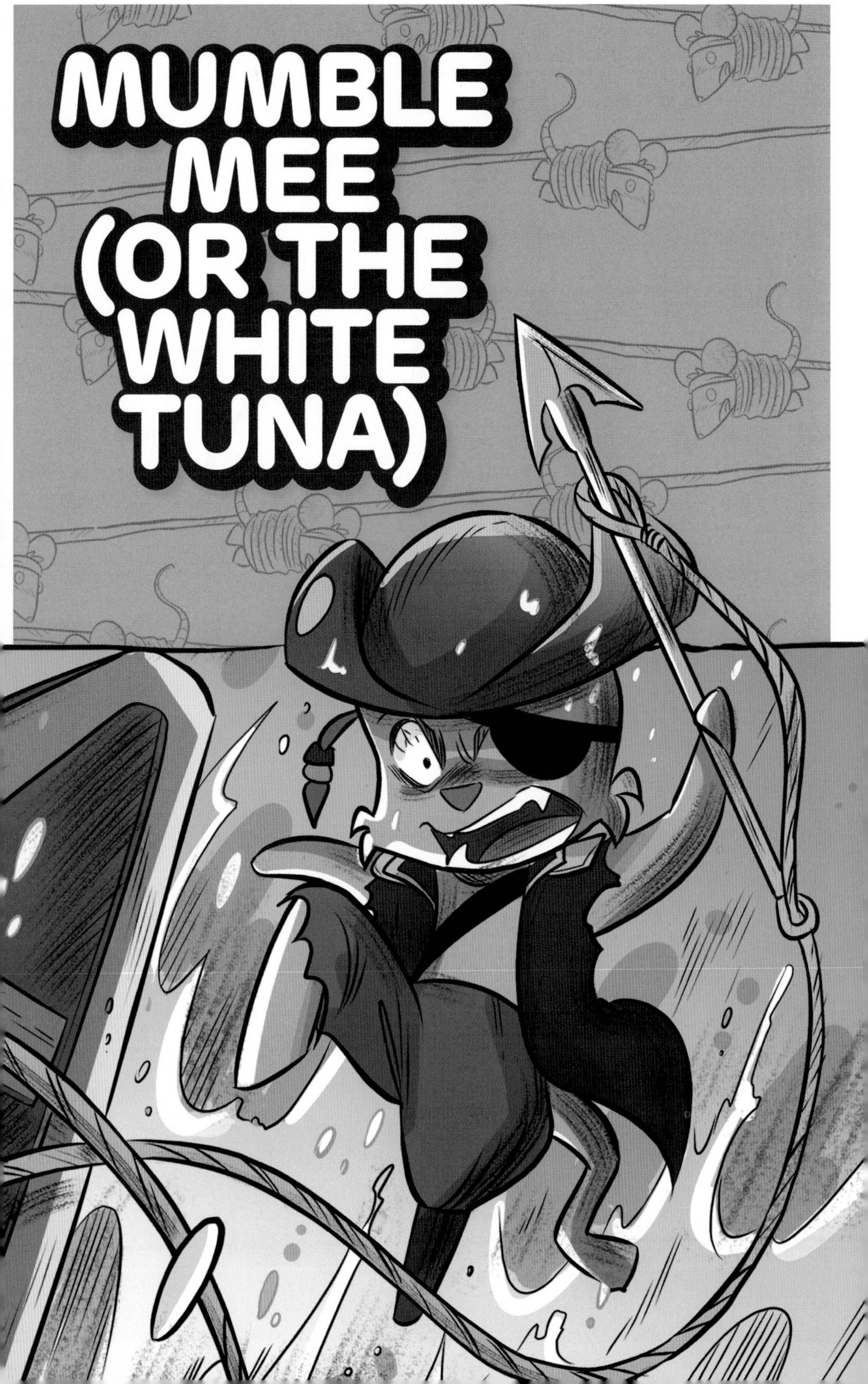
MUMBLE MEE (OR THE WHITE TUNA)

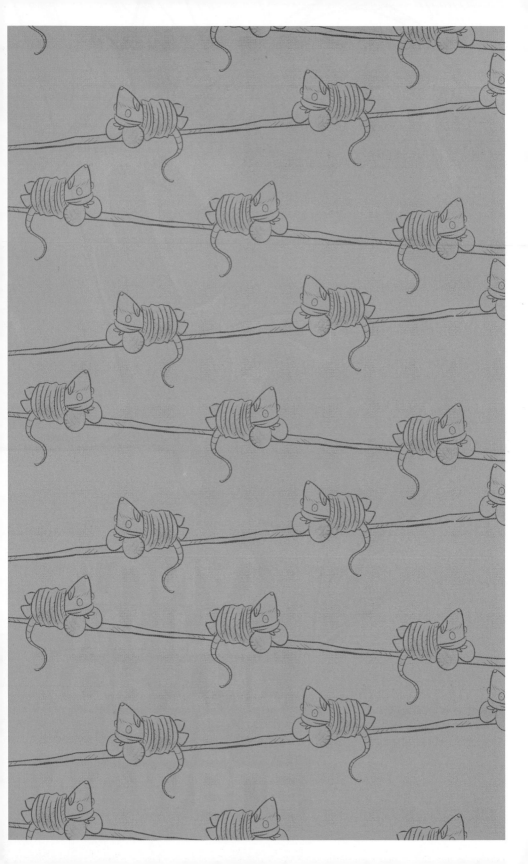

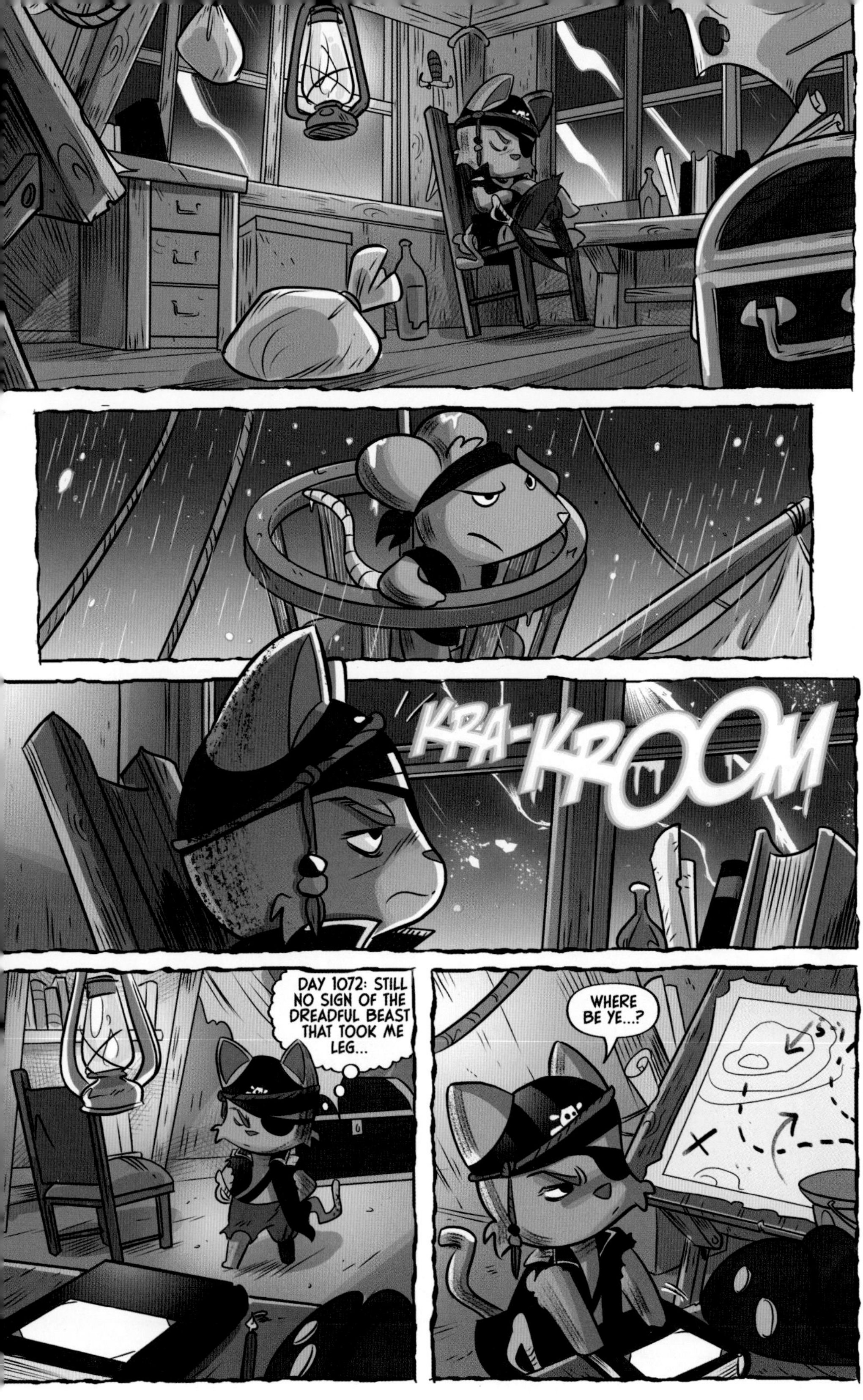
KRA-KROOM
DAY 1072: STILL NO SIGN OF THE DREADFUL BEAST THAT TOOK ME LEG...
WHERE BE YE...?

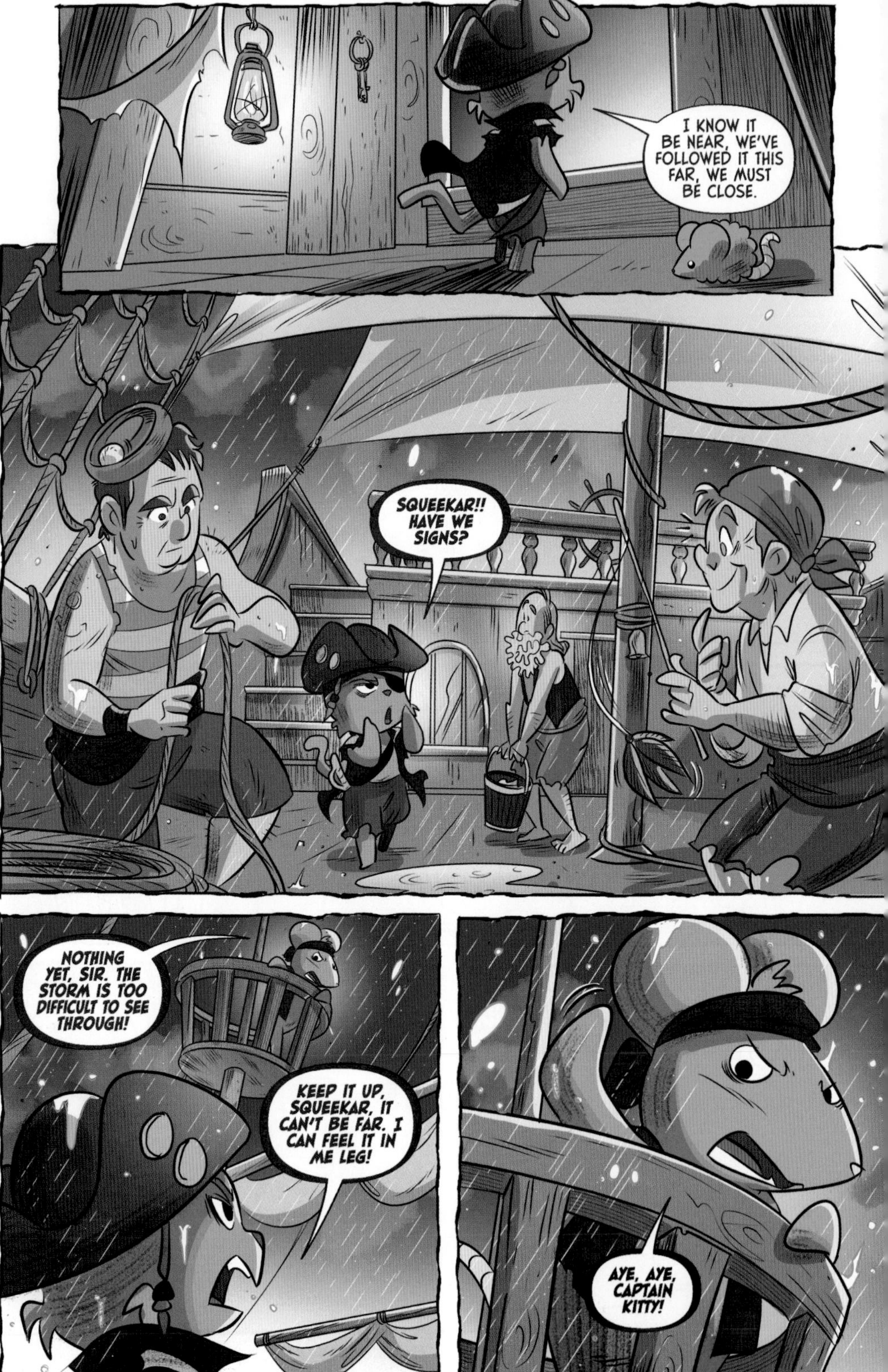
I KNOW IT BE NEAR, WE'VE FOLLOWED IT THIS FAR, WE MUST BE CLOSE.
SQUEEKAR!! HAVE WE SIGNS?
NOTHING YET, SIR. THE STORM IS TOO DIFFICULT TO SEE THROUGH!
KEEP IT UP, SQUEEKAR, IT CAN'T BE FAR. I CAN FEEL IT IN ME LEG!
AYE, AYE, CAPTAIN KITTY!

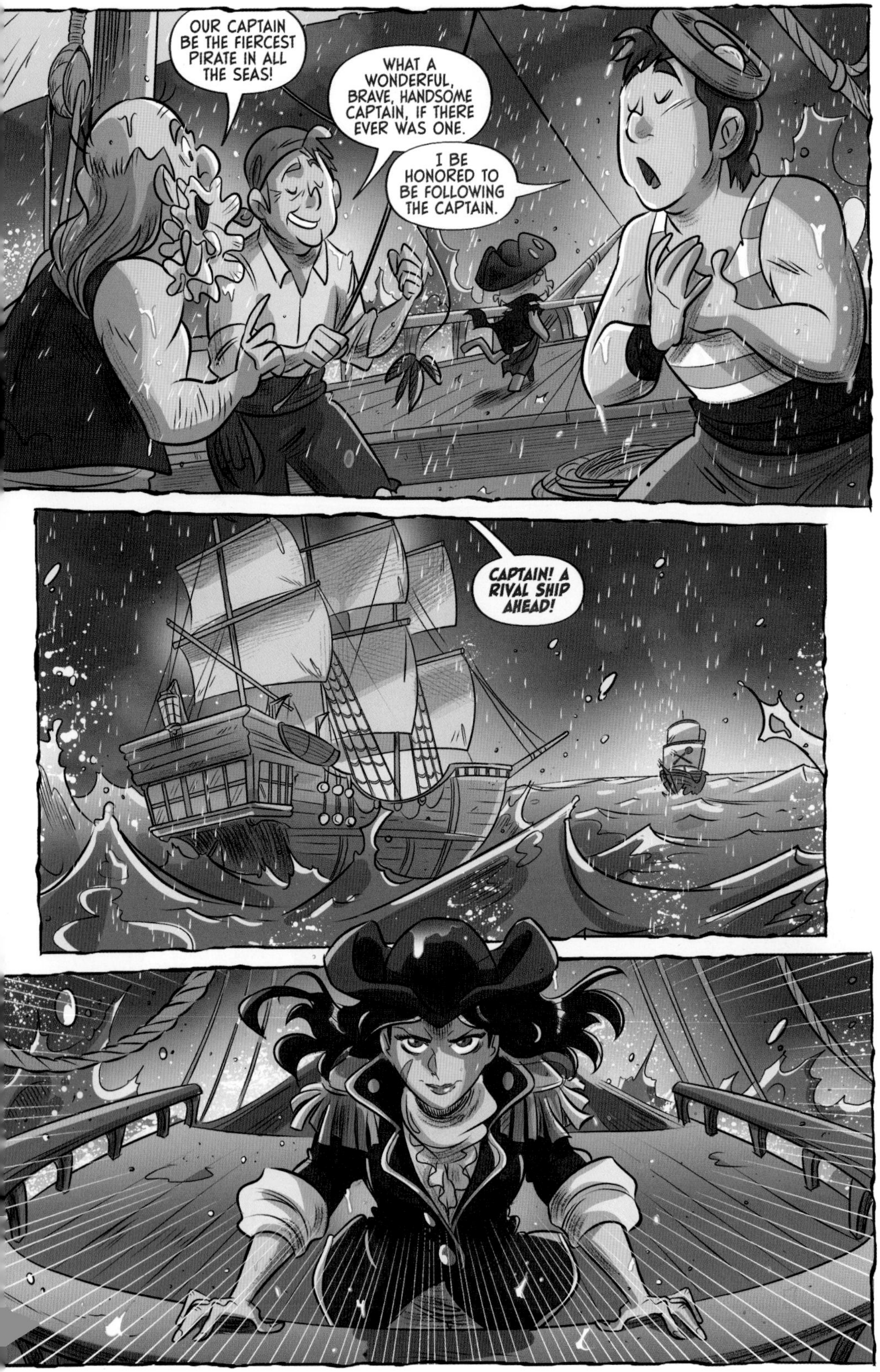
OUR CAPTAIN BE THE FIERCEST PIRATE IN ALL THE SEAS!
WHAT A WONDERFUL, BRAVE, HANDSOME CAPTAIN, IF THERE EVER WAS ONE.
I BE HONORED TO BE FOLLOWING THE CAPTAIN.
CAPTAIN! A RIVAL SHIP AHEAD!

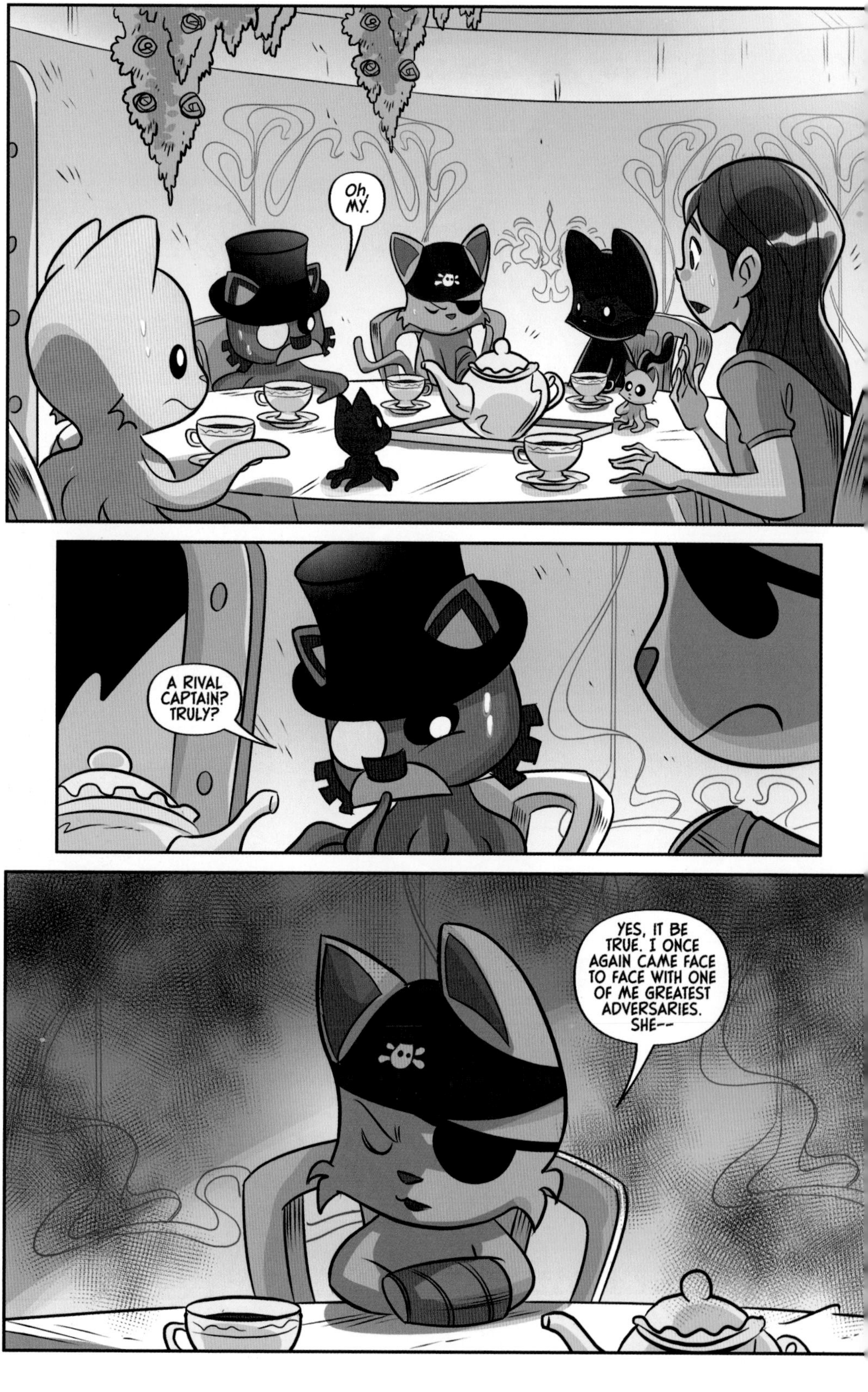
Oh, MY.
A RIVAL CAPTAIN? TRULY?
YES, IT BE TRUE. I ONCE AGAIN CAME FACE TO FACE WITH ONE OF ME GREATEST ADVERSARIES. SHE--

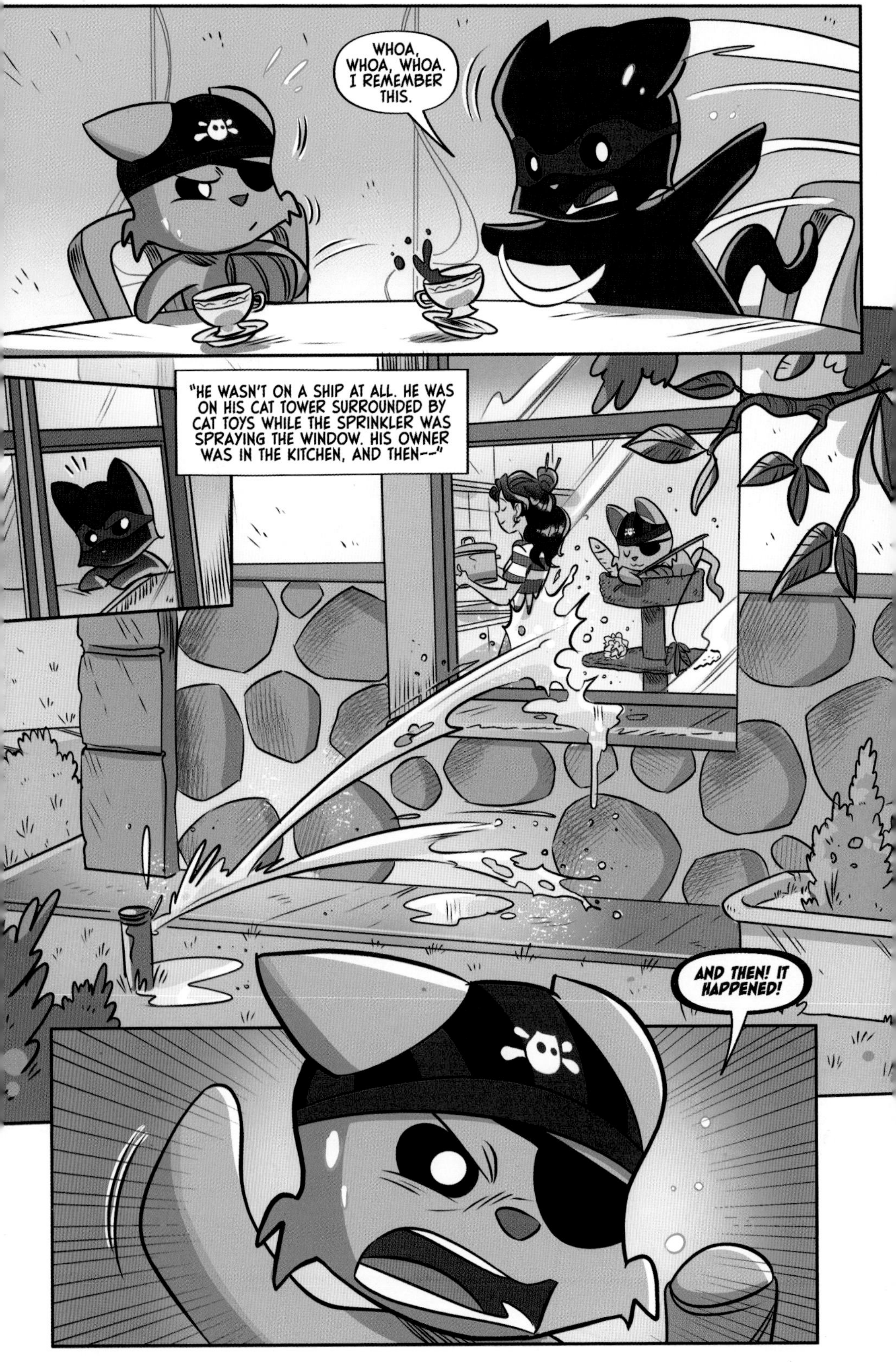
WHOA, WHOA, WHOA. I REMEMBER THIS.
"HE WASN'T ON A SHIP AT ALL. HE WAS ON HIS CAT TOWER SURROUNDED BY CAT TOYS WHILE THE SPRINKLER WAS SPRAYING THE WINDOW. HIS OWNER WAS IN THE KITCHEN, AND THEN--"
AND THEN! IT HAPPENED!

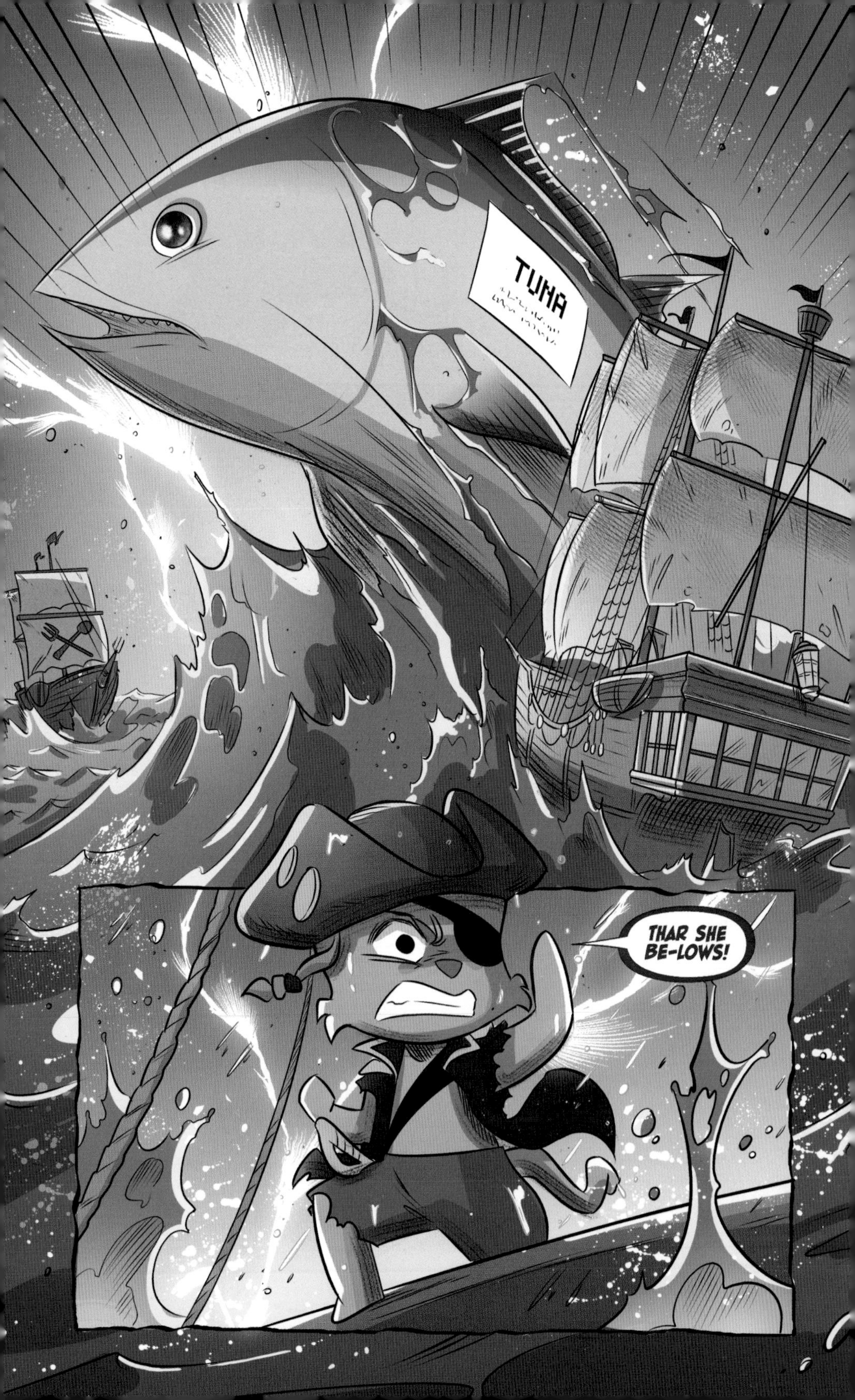
TUNA
THAR SHE BE-LOWS!

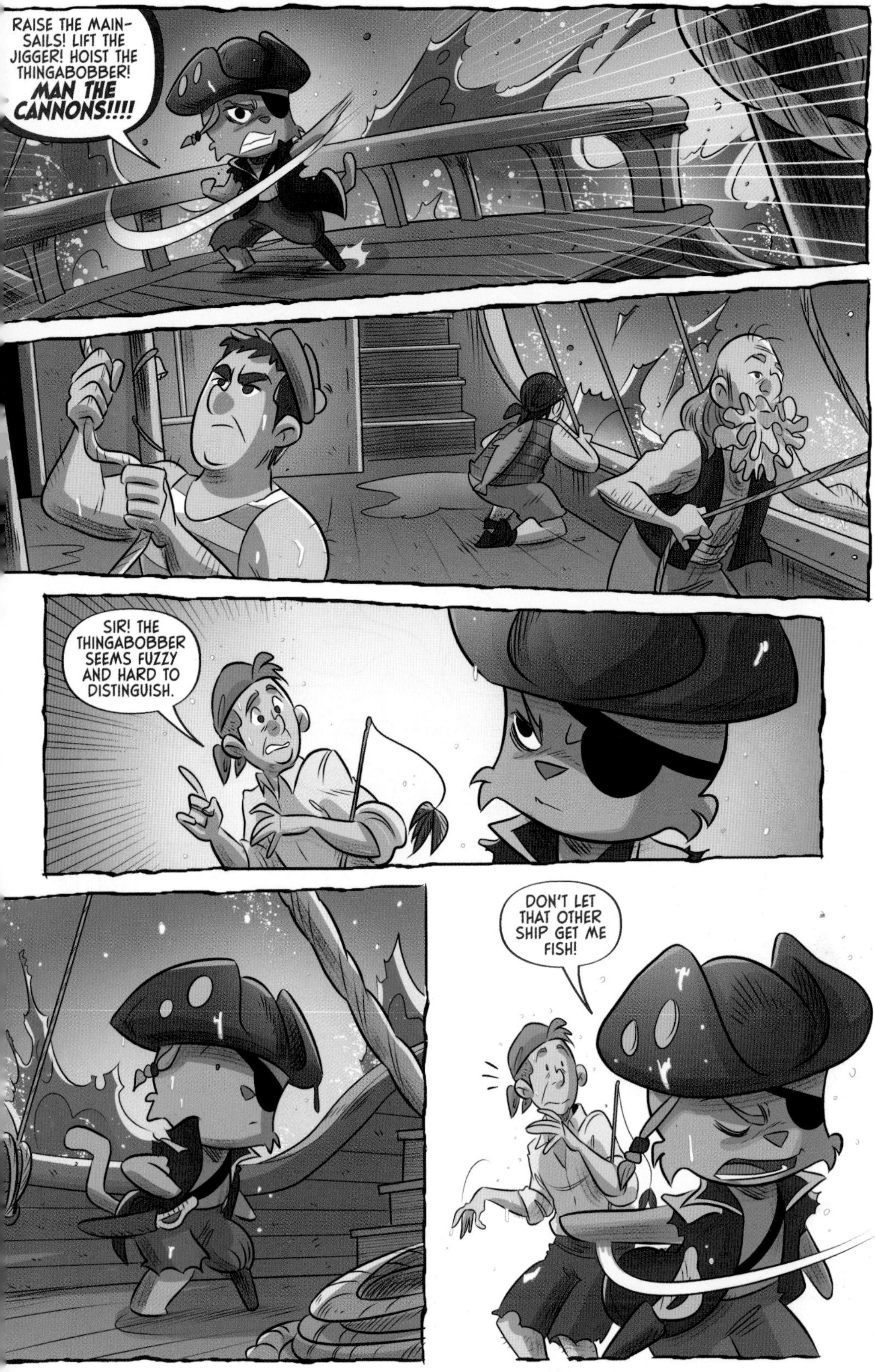
RAISE THE MAIN-SAILS! LIFT THE JIGGER! HOIST THE THINGABOBBER! ***MAN THE CANNONS!!!!***
SIR! THE THINGABOBBER SEEMS FUZZY AND HARD TO DISTINGUISH.
DON'T LET THAT OTHER SHIP GET ME FISH!

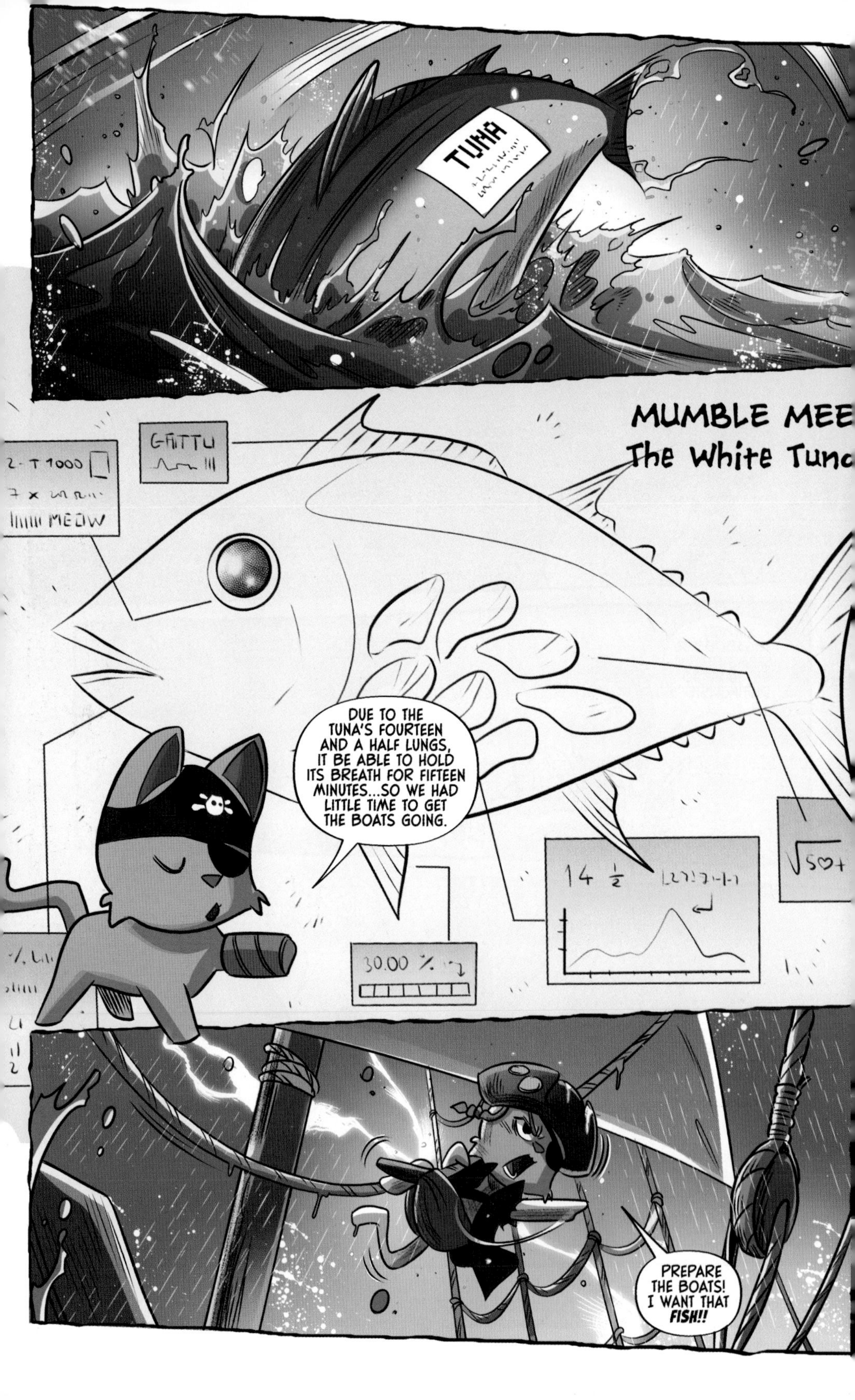
TUNA
MUMBLE MEE
The White Tuna
GATTU
MEOW
DUE TO THE TUNA'S FOURTEEN AND A HALF LUNGS, IT BE ABLE TO HOLD ITS BREATH FOR FIFTEEN MINUTES...SO WE HAD LITTLE TIME TO GET THE BOATS GOING.
14 ½
30.00 %
PREPARE THE BOATS! I WANT THAT *FISH!!*

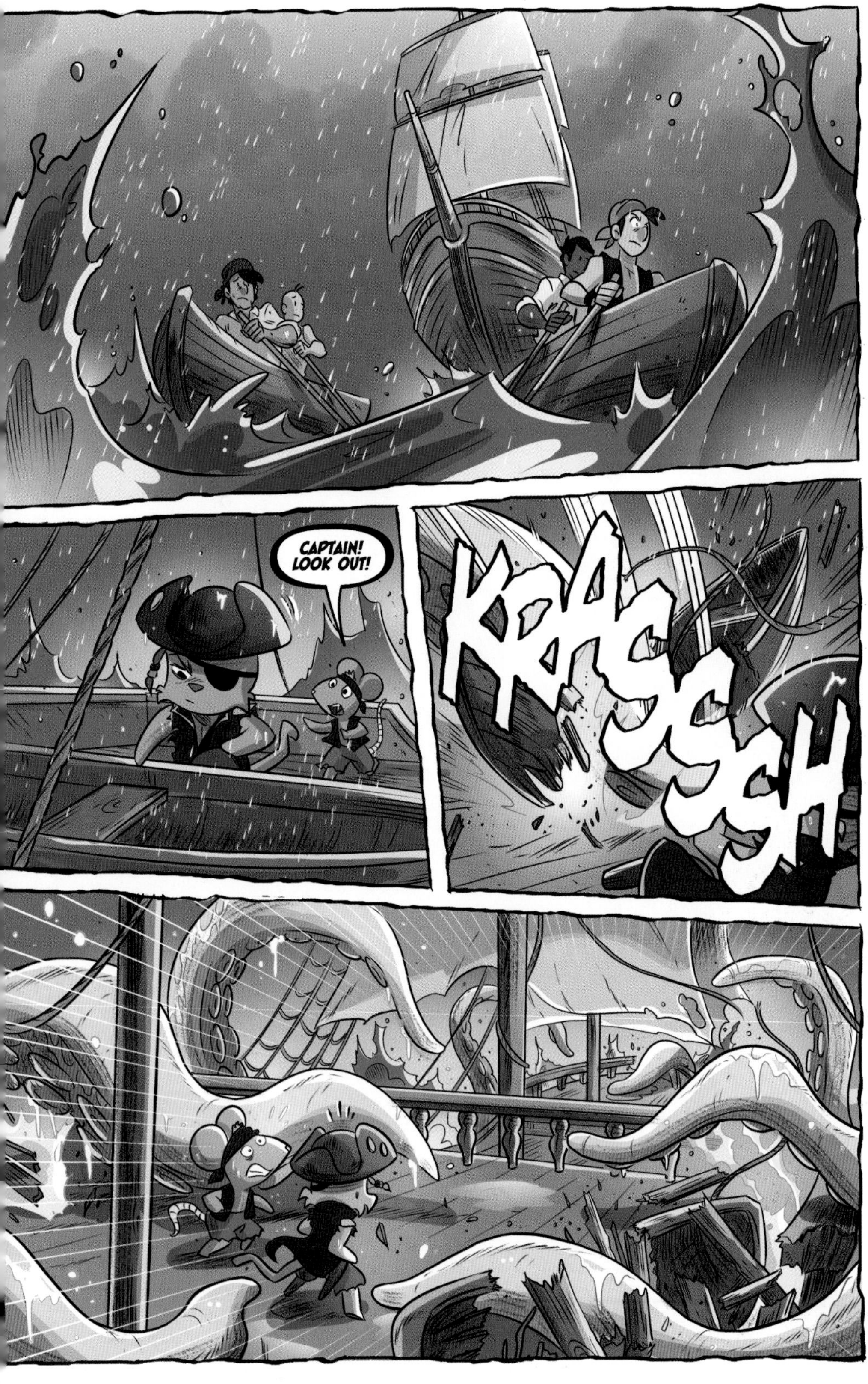
CAPTAIN! LOOK OUT!
KRASSSH

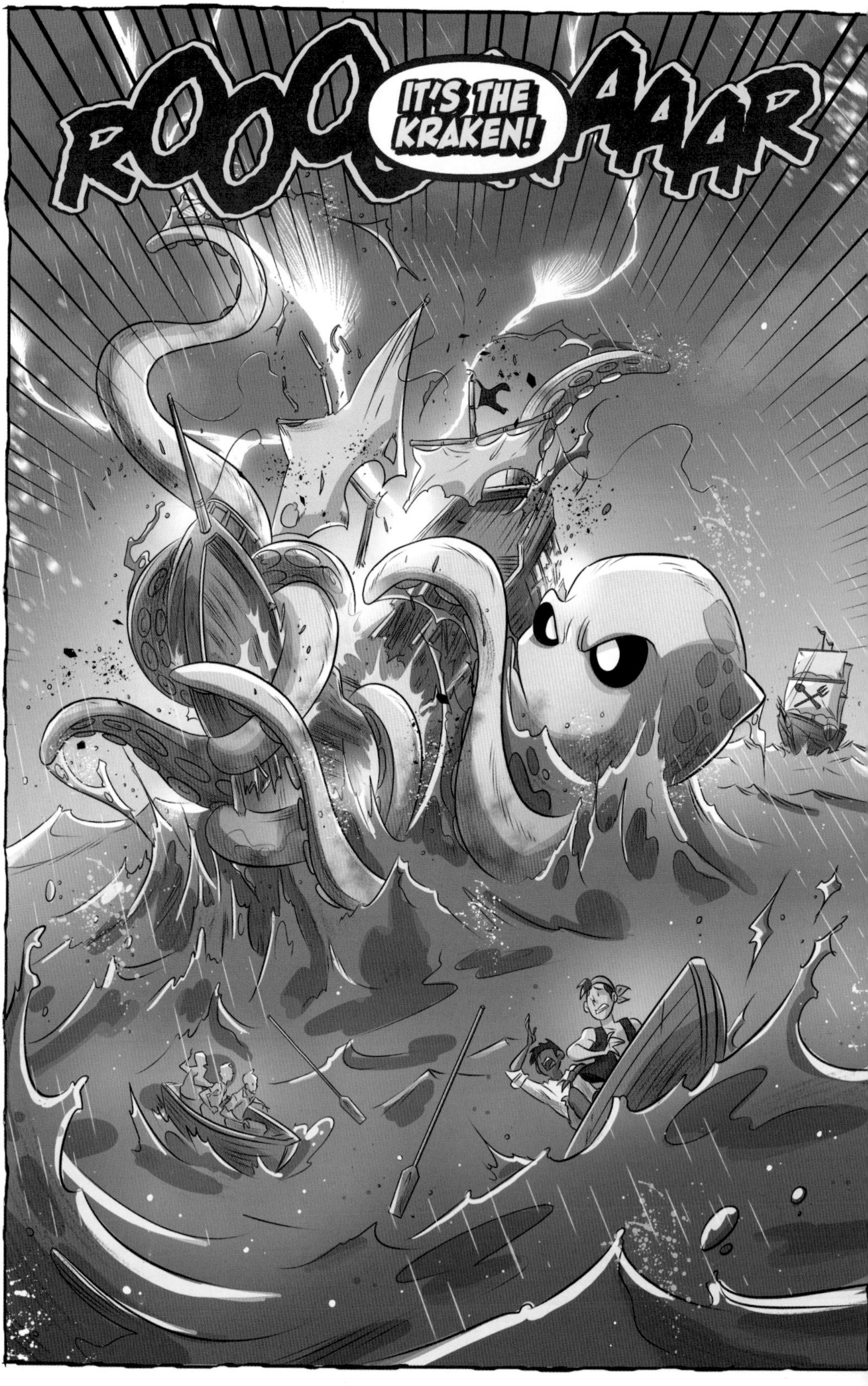
ROOO
IT'S THE KRAKEN!
AAAR

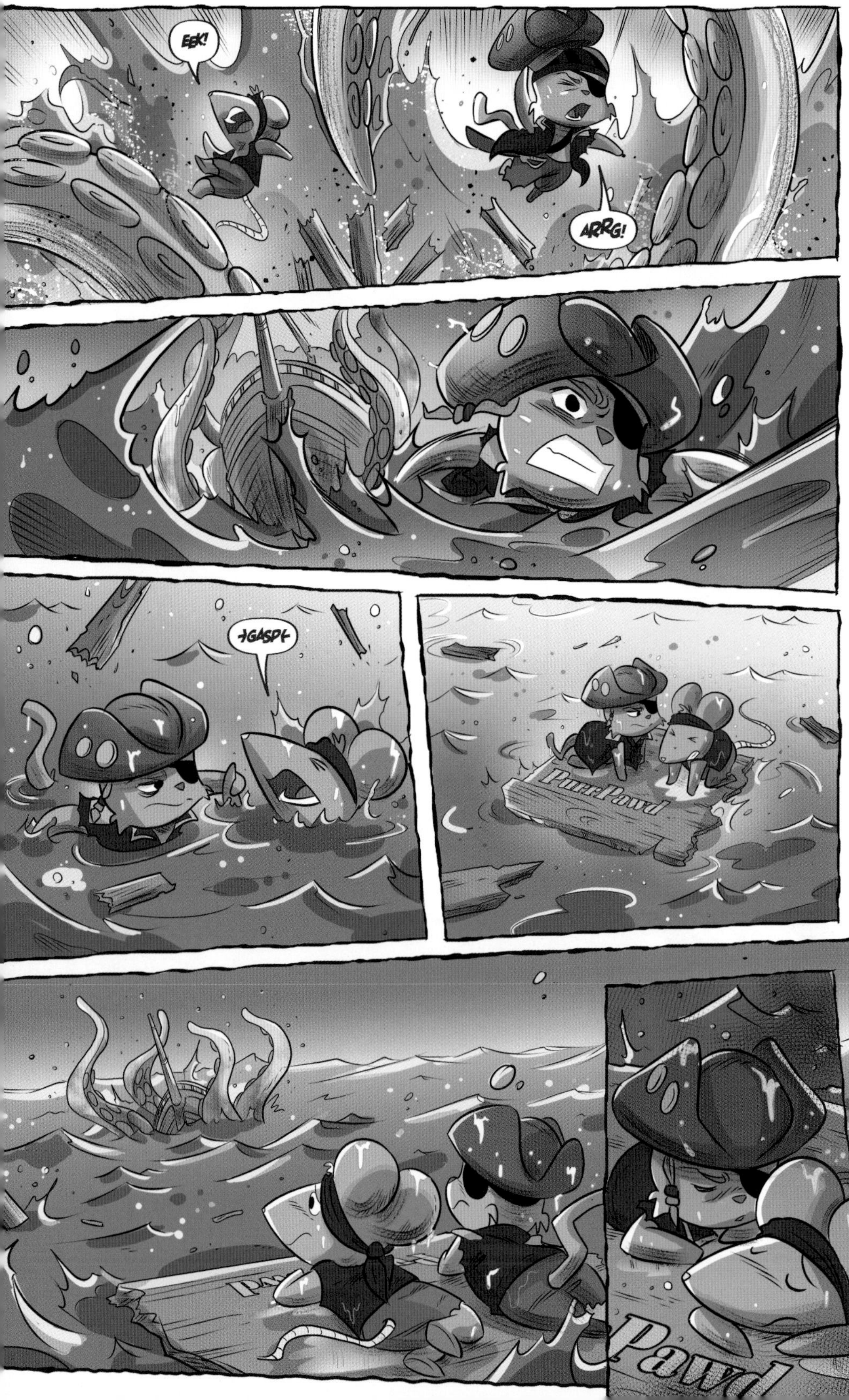
EEK!
ARRG!
-GASP-
PurrPawd
Pawd

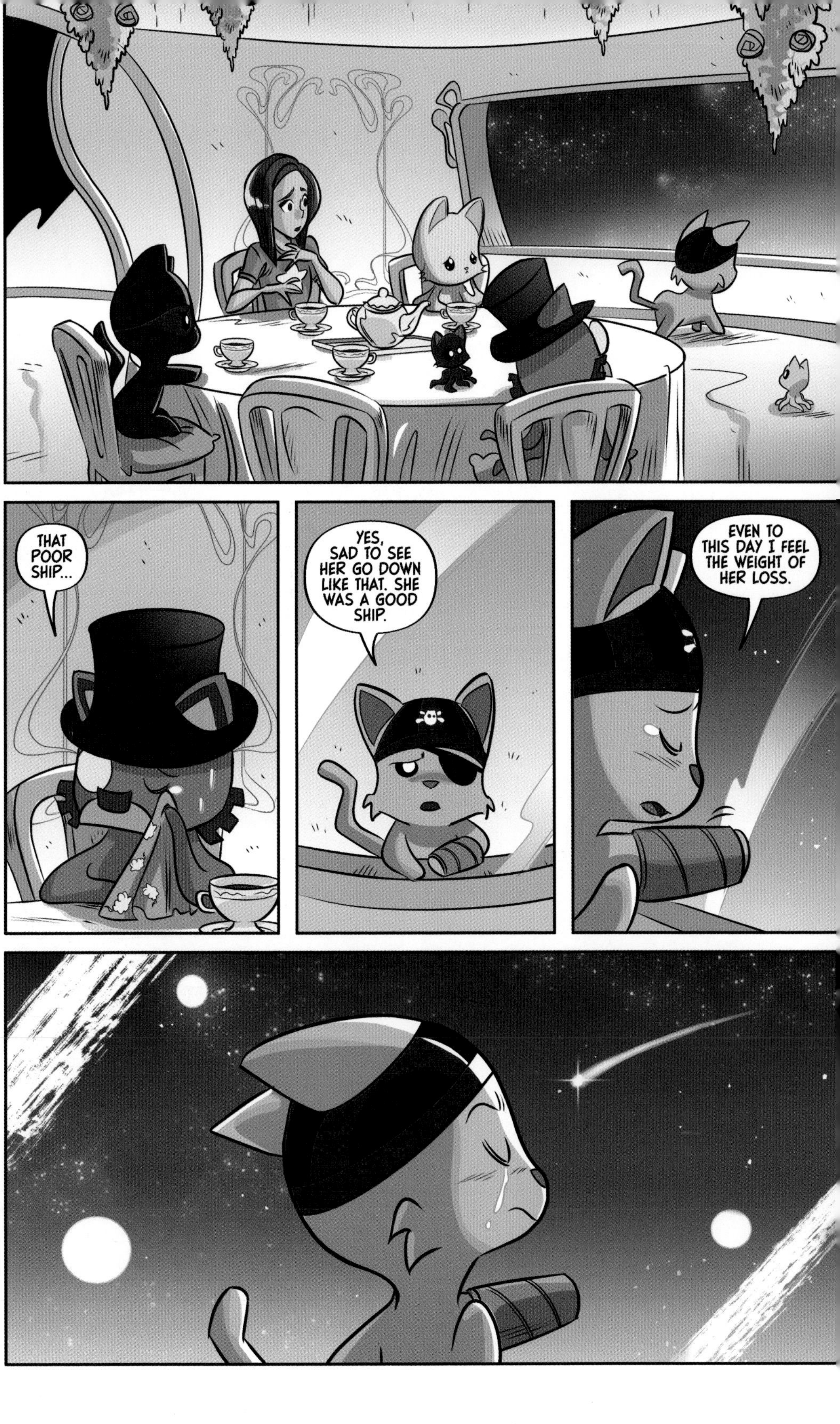
THAT POOR SHIP...
YES, SAD TO SEE HER GO DOWN LIKE THAT. SHE WAS A GOOD SHIP.
EVEN TO THIS DAY I FEEL THE WEIGHT OF HER LOSS.

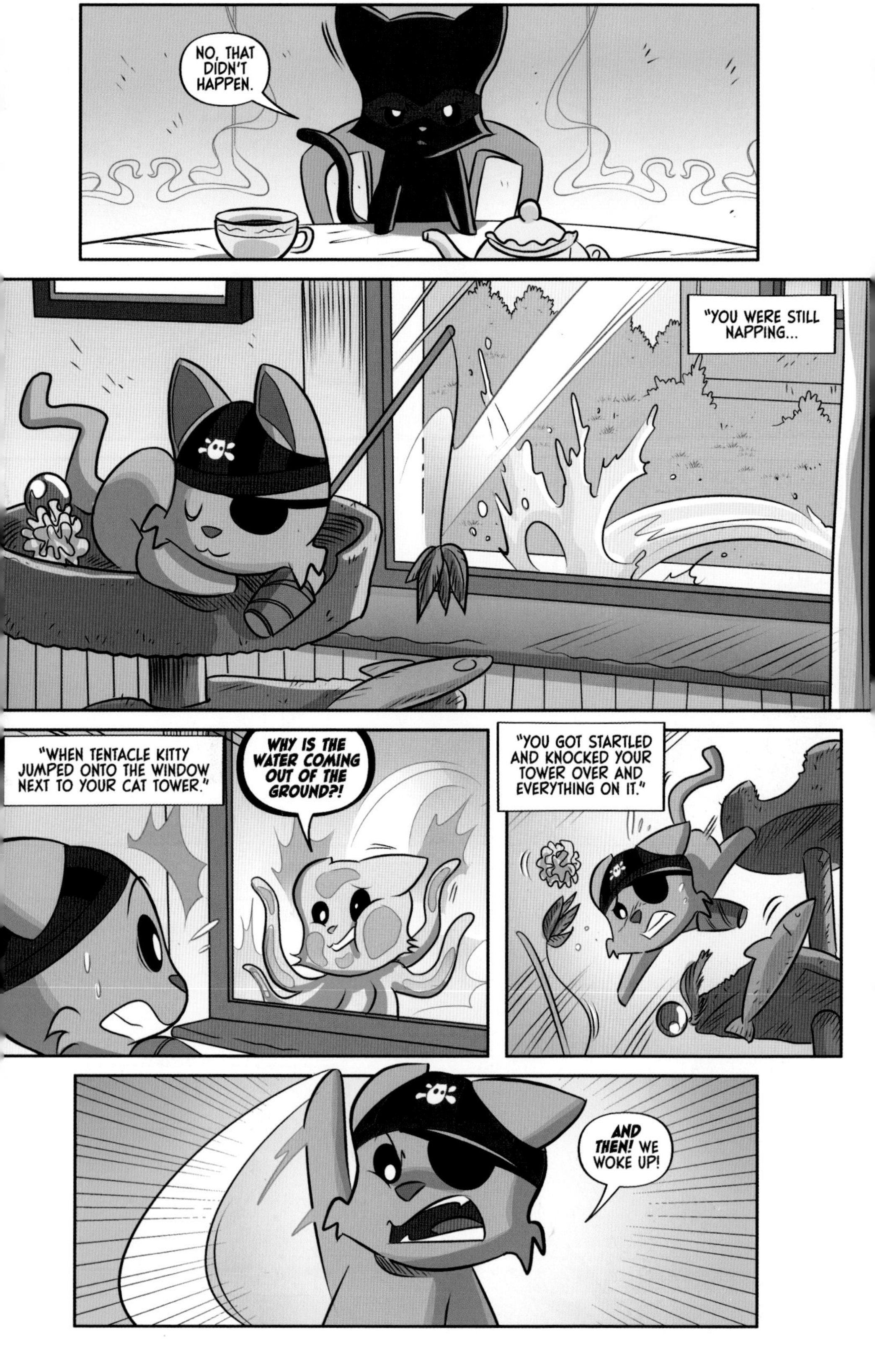
NO, THAT DIDN'T HAPPEN.
"YOU WERE STILL NAPPING...
"WHEN TENTACLE KITTY JUMPED ONTO THE WINDOW NEXT TO YOUR CAT TOWER."
WHY IS THE WATER COMING OUT OF THE GROUND?!
"YOU GOT STARTLED AND KNOCKED YOUR TOWER OVER AND EVERYTHING ON IT."
AND THEN! WE WOKE UP!

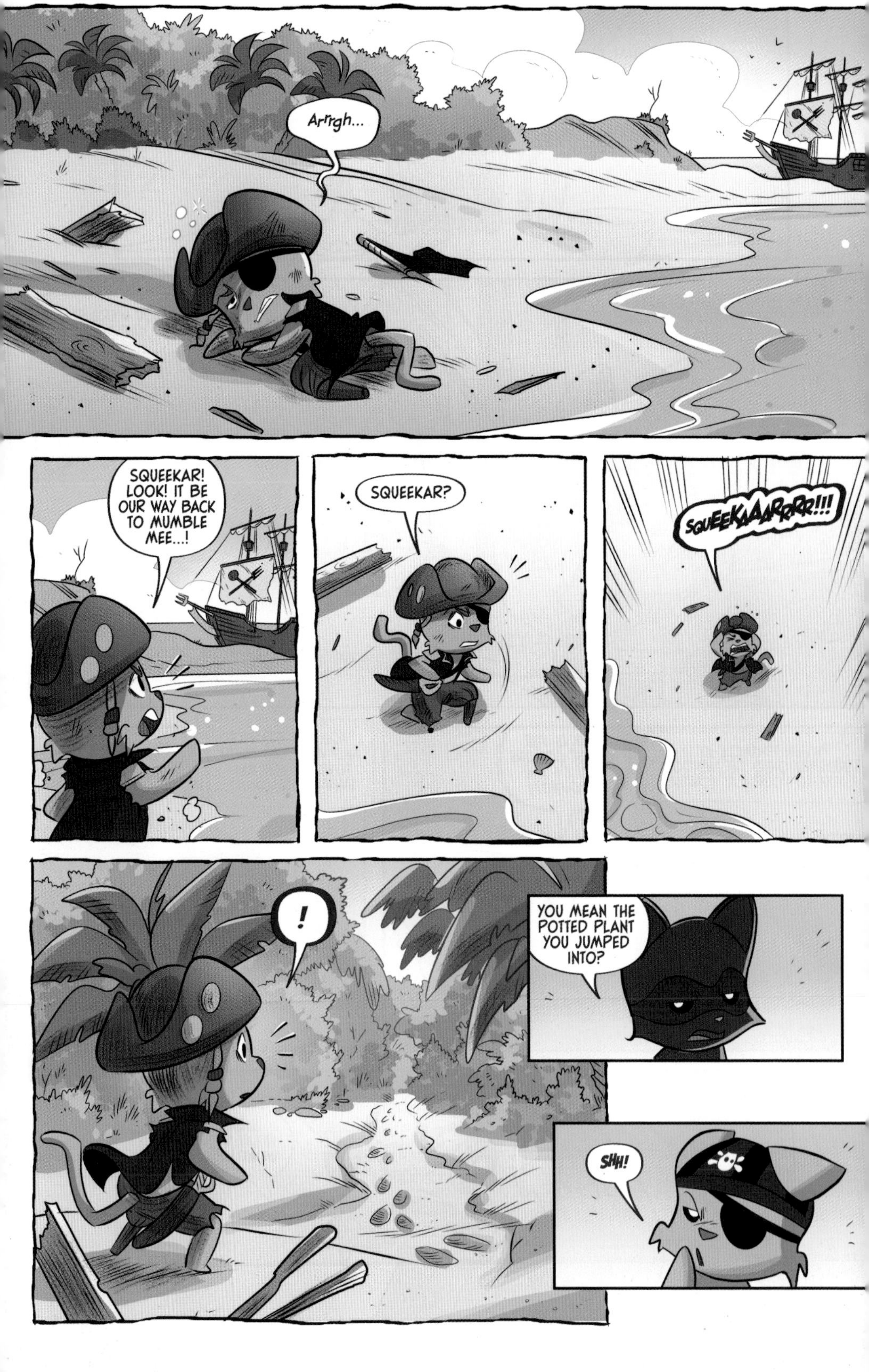
Arrrgh...
SQUEEKAR! LOOK! IT BE OUR WAY BACK TO MUMBLE MEE...!
SQUEEKAR?
SQUEEKAARRRR!!!
!
YOU MEAN THE POTTED PLANT YOU JUMPED INTO?
SHH!

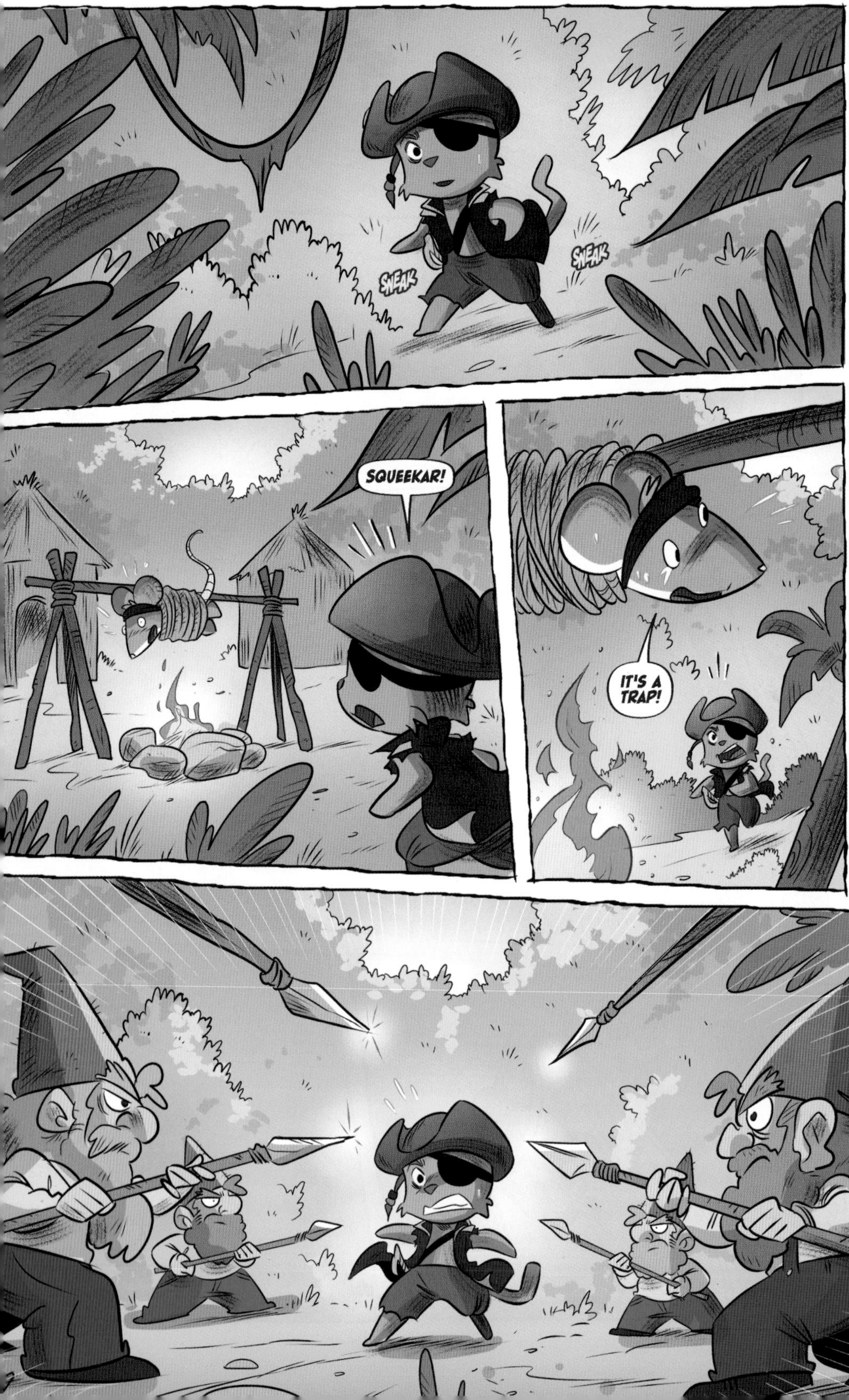
SNEAK
SNEAK
SQUEEKAR!
IT'S A TRAP!

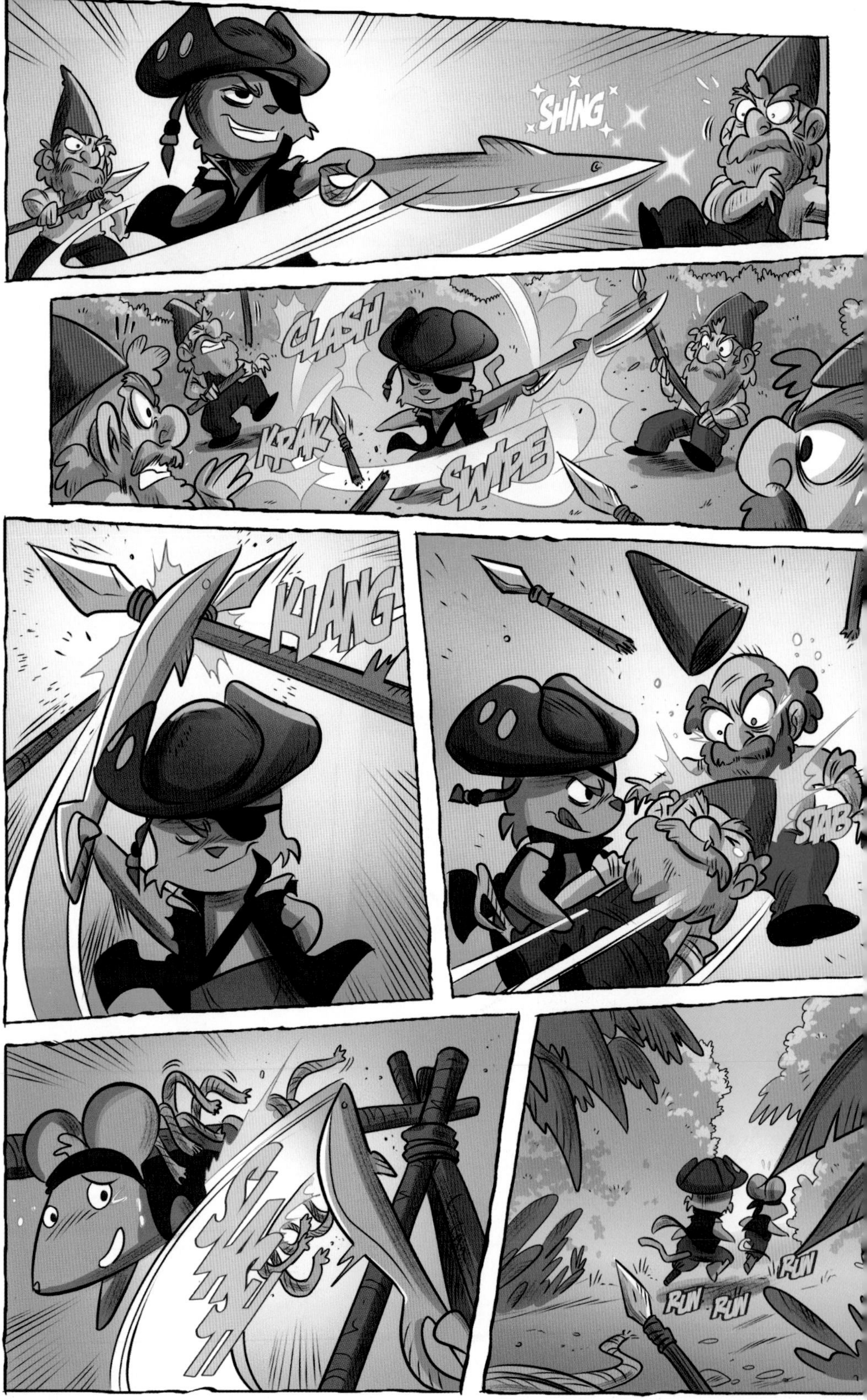
SHING
CLASH
KRAK
SWIPE
KLANG
STAB
RUN
RUN
RUN

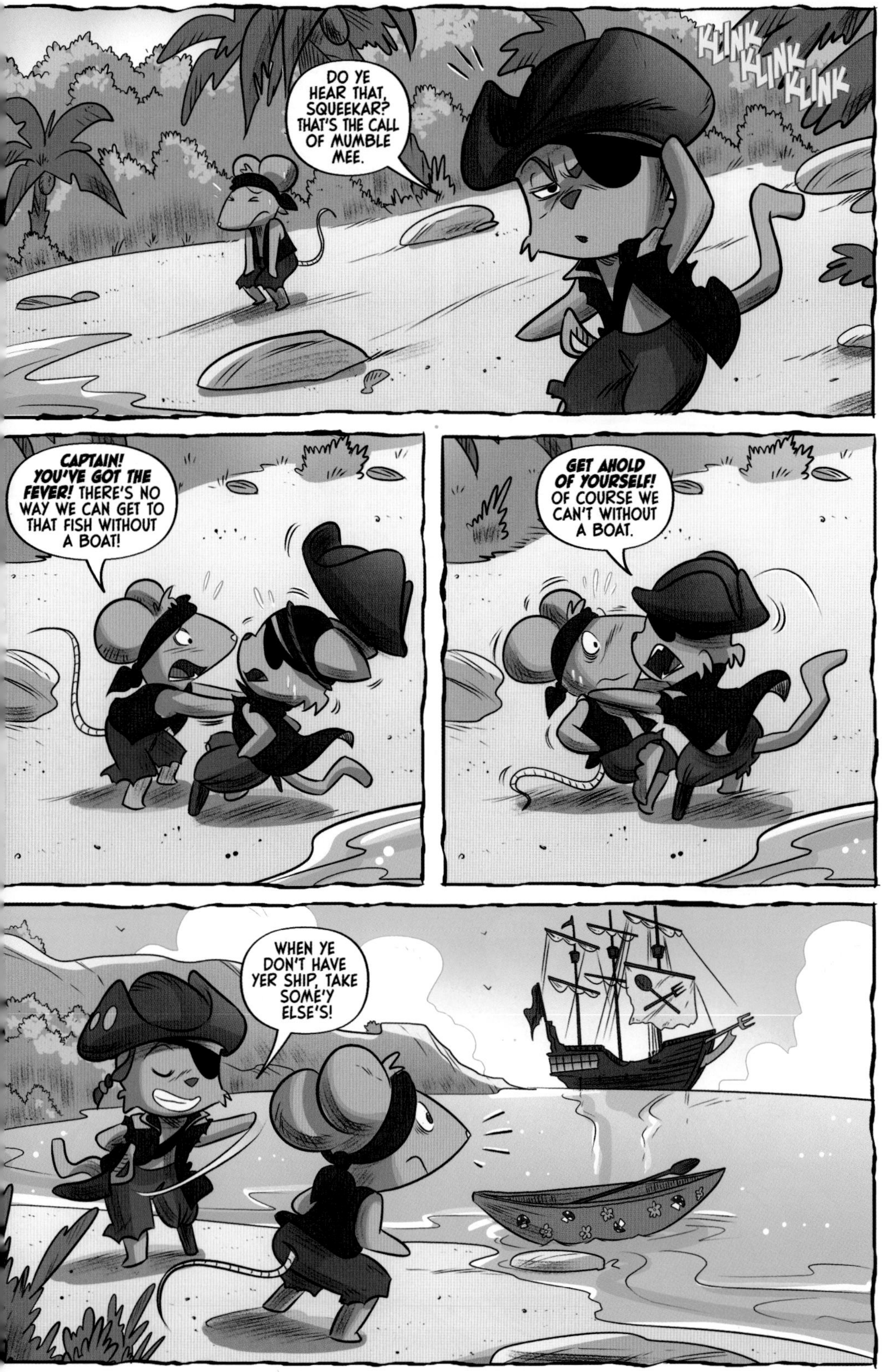
KLINK KLINK KLINK
DO YE HEAR THAT, SQUEEKAR? THAT'S THE CALL OF MUMBLE MEE.
CAPTAIN! YOU'VE GOT THE FEVER! THERE'S NO WAY WE CAN GET TO THAT FISH WITHOUT A BOAT!
GET AHOLD OF YOURSELF! OF COURSE WE CAN'T WITHOUT A BOAT.
WHEN YE DON'T HAVE YER SHIP, TAKE SOME'Y ELSE'S!

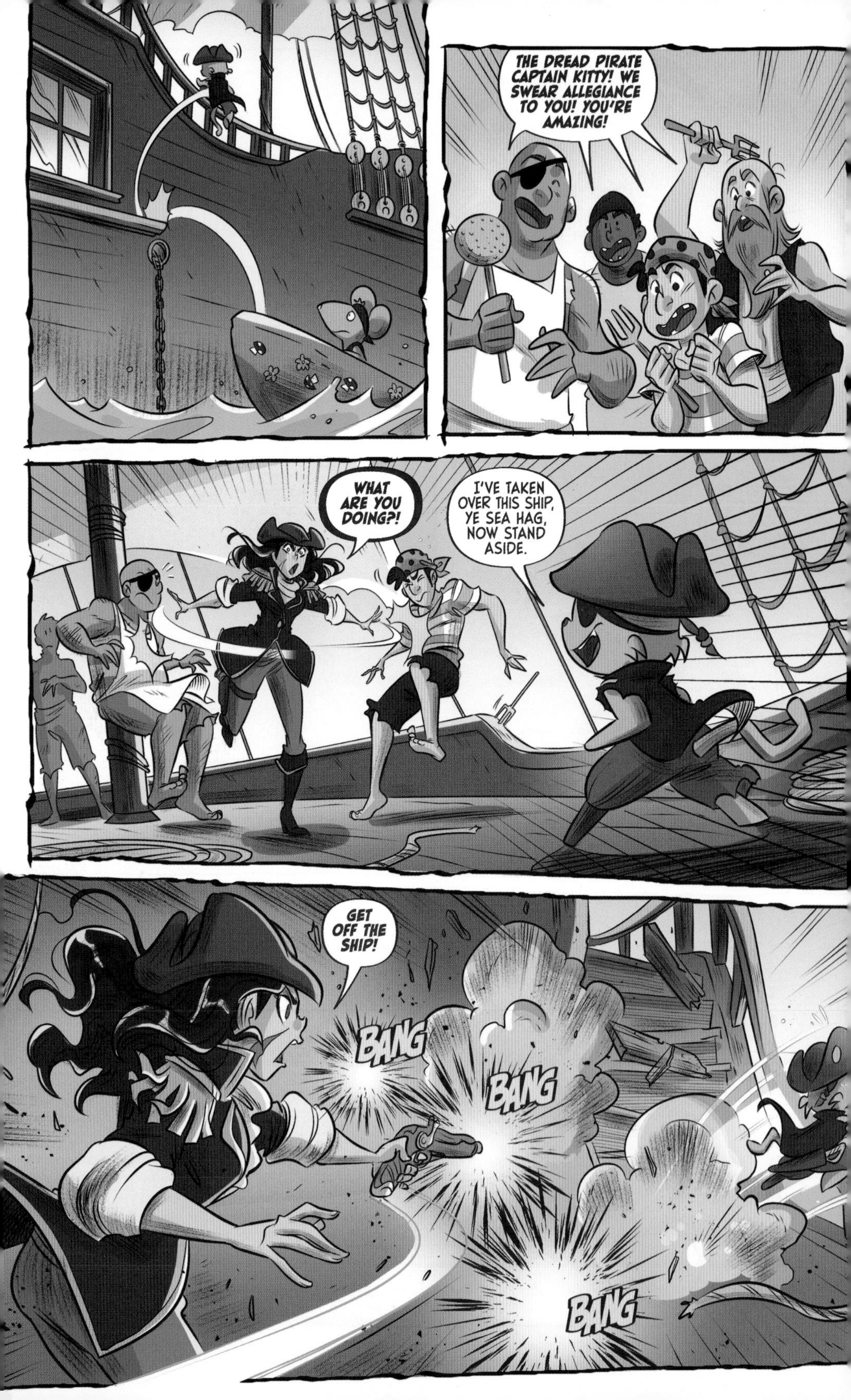
THE DREAD PIRATE CAPTAIN KITTY! WE SWEAR ALLEGIANCE TO YOU! YOU'RE AMAZING!
WHAT ARE YOU DOING?!
I'VE TAKEN OVER THIS SHIP, YE SEA HAG, NOW STAND ASIDE.
GET OFF THE SHIP!
BANG
BANG
BANG

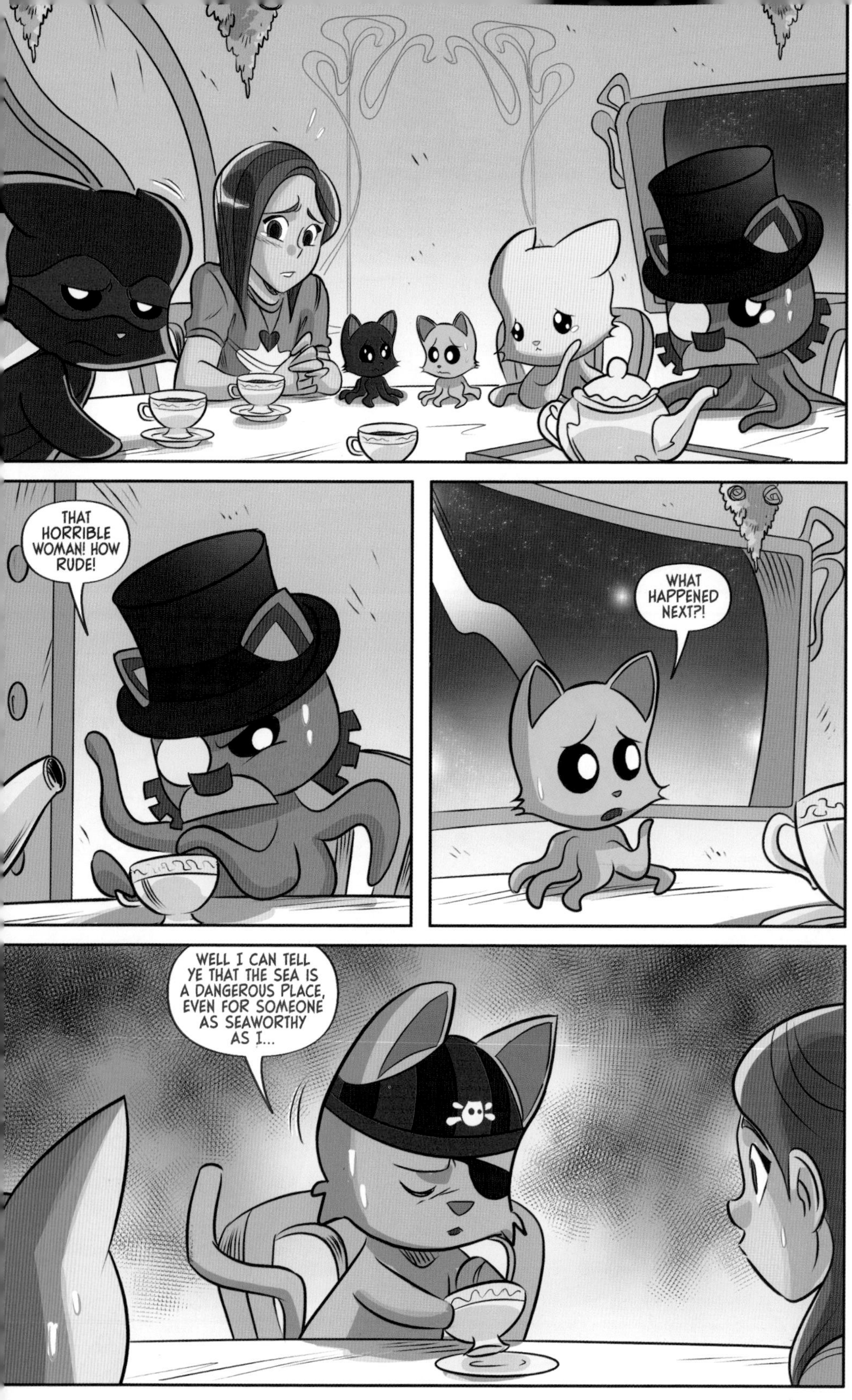
THAT HORRIBLE WOMAN! HOW RUDE!
WHAT HAPPENED NEXT?!
WELL I CAN TELL YE THAT THE SEA IS A DANGEROUS PLACE, EVEN FOR SOMEONE AS SEAWORTHY AS I...

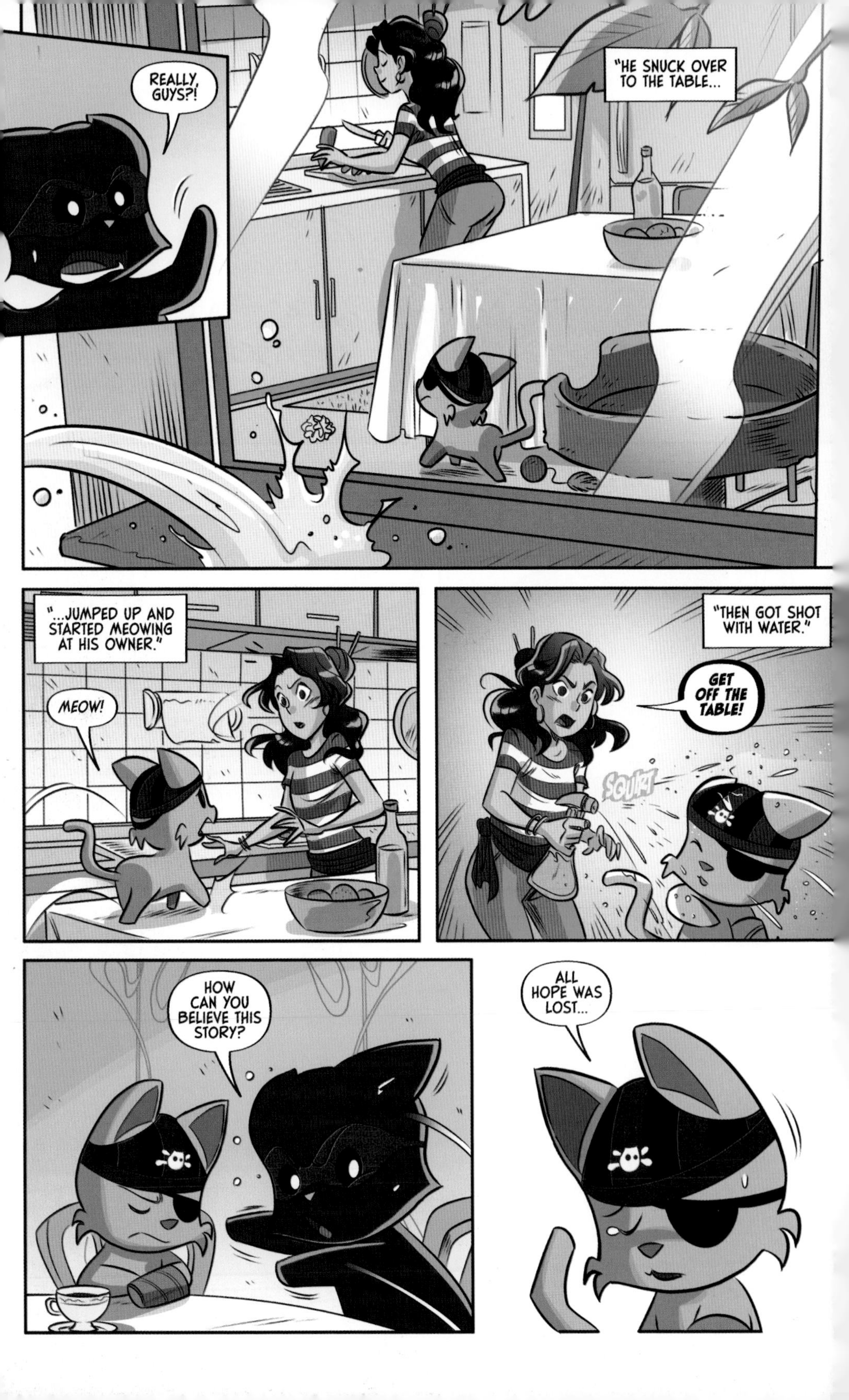
"HE SNUCK OVER TO THE TABLE...
REALLY, GUYS?!
"...JUMPED UP AND STARTED MEOWING AT HIS OWNER."
MEOW!
"THEN GOT SHOT WITH WATER."
GET OFF THE TABLE!
SQUIRT
HOW CAN YOU BELIEVE THIS STORY?
ALL HOPE WAS LOST...

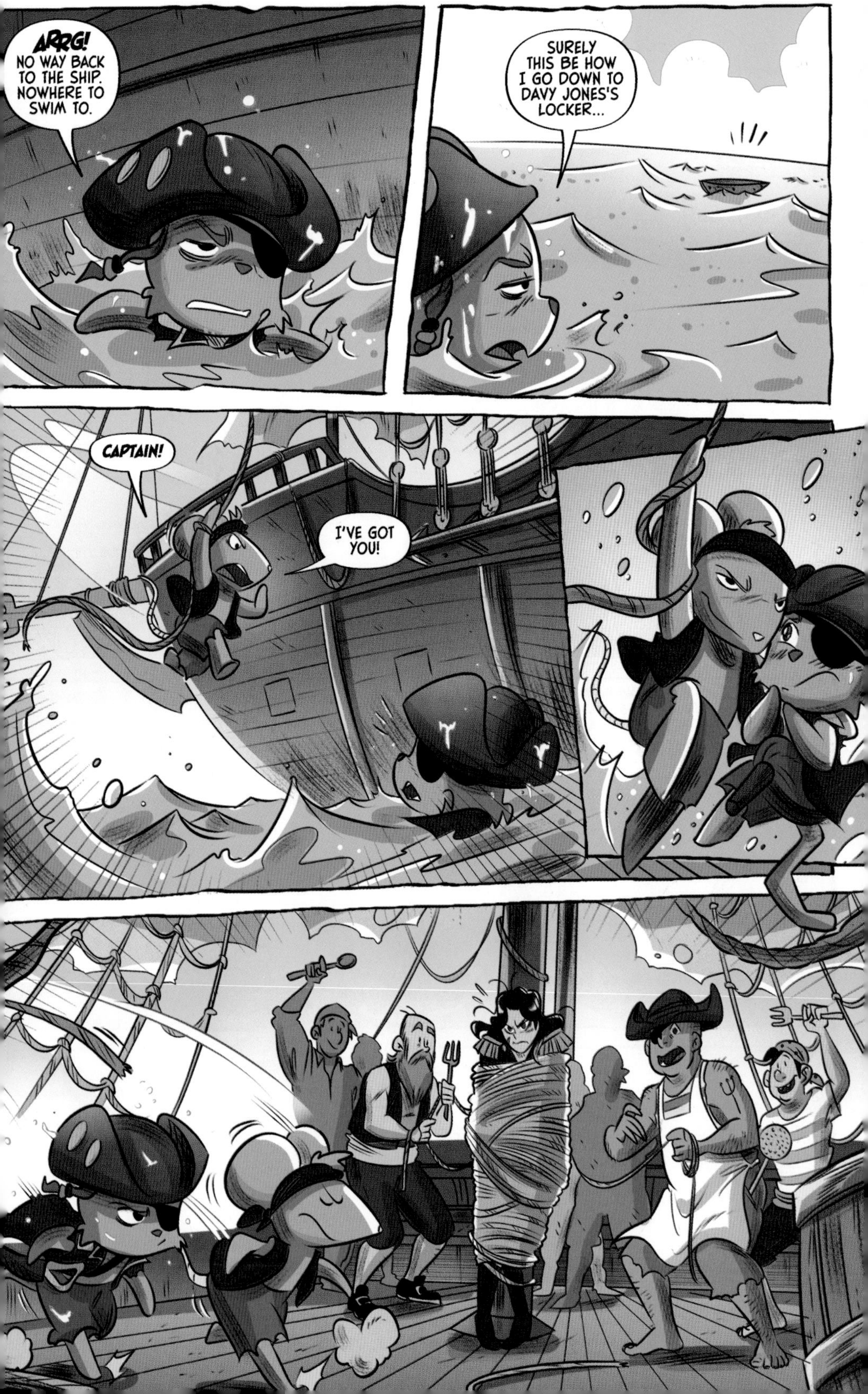
ARRG!
NO WAY BACK TO THE SHIP. NOWHERE TO SWIM TO.
SURELY THIS BE HOW I GO DOWN TO DAVY JONES'S LOCKER...
CAPTAIN!
I'VE GOT YOU!

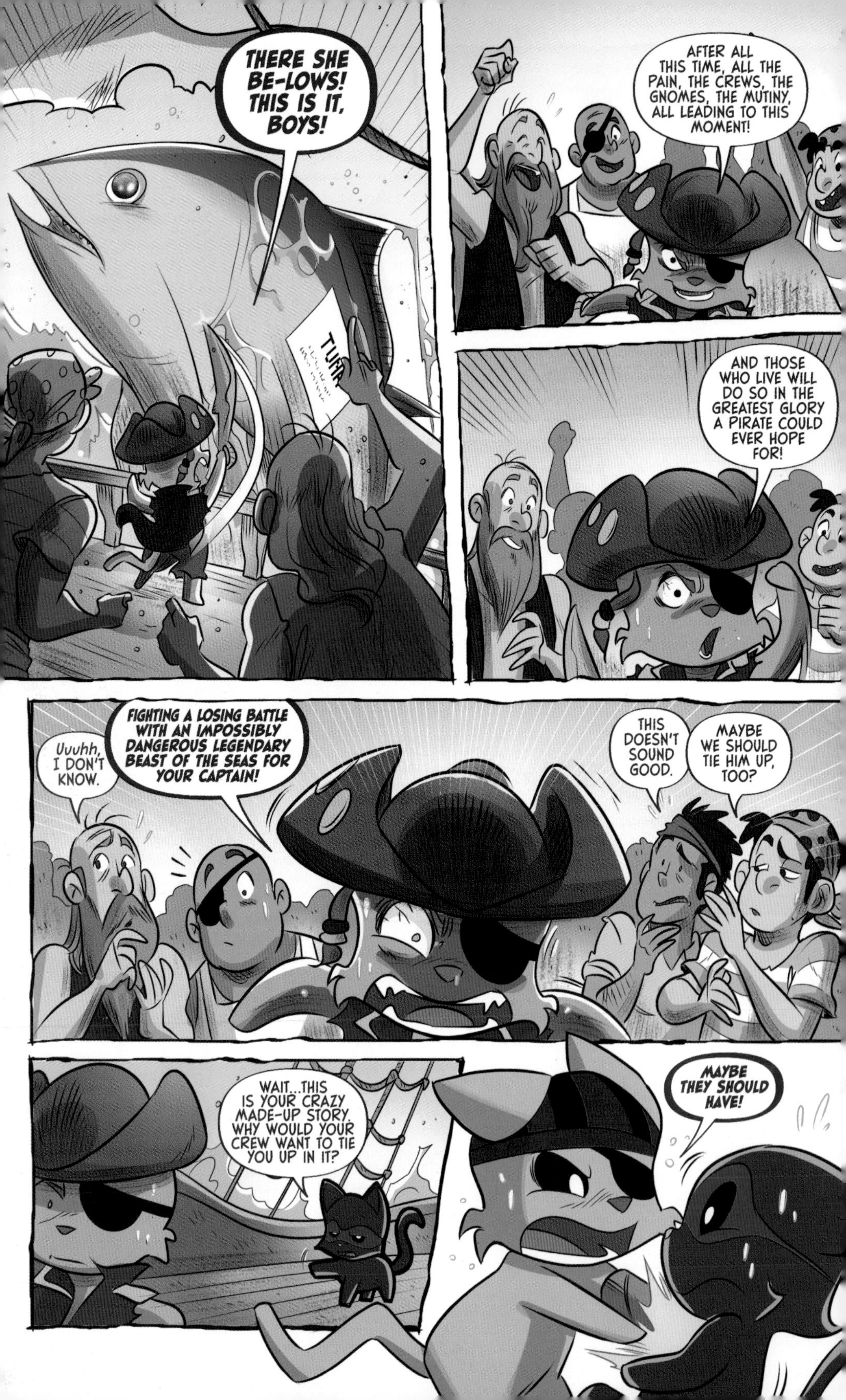

THERE SHE BE-LOWS! THIS IS IT, BOYS!
AFTER ALL THIS TIME, ALL THE PAIN, THE CREWS, THE GNOMES, THE MUTINY, ALL LEADING TO THIS MOMENT!
AND THOSE WHO LIVE WILL DO SO IN THE GREATEST GLORY A PIRATE COULD EVER HOPE FOR!
FIGHTING A LOSING BATTLE WITH AN IMPOSSIBLY DANGEROUS LEGENDARY BEAST OF THE SEAS FOR YOUR CAPTAIN!
Uuuhh, I DON'T KNOW.
THIS DOESN'T SOUND GOOD.
MAYBE WE SHOULD TIE HIM UP, TOO?
WAIT...THIS IS YOUR CRAZY MADE-UP STORY. WHY WOULD YOUR CREW WANT TO TIE YOU UP IN IT?
MAYBE THEY SHOULD HAVE!

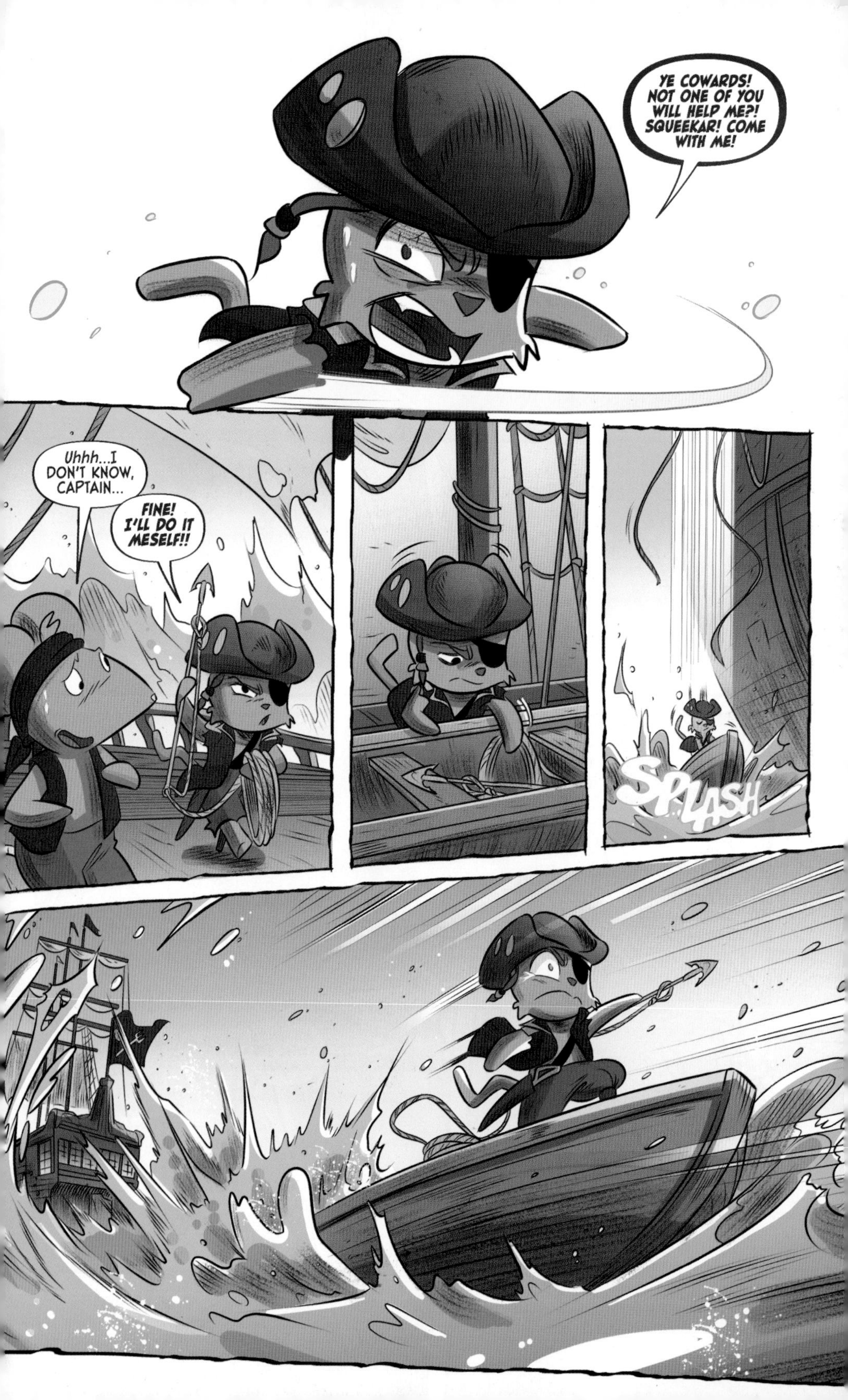
YE COWARDS! NOT ONE OF YOU WILL HELP ME?! SQUEEKAR! COME WITH ME!
Uhhh...I DON'T KNOW, CAPTAIN...
FINE! I'LL DO IT MESELF!!
SPLASH

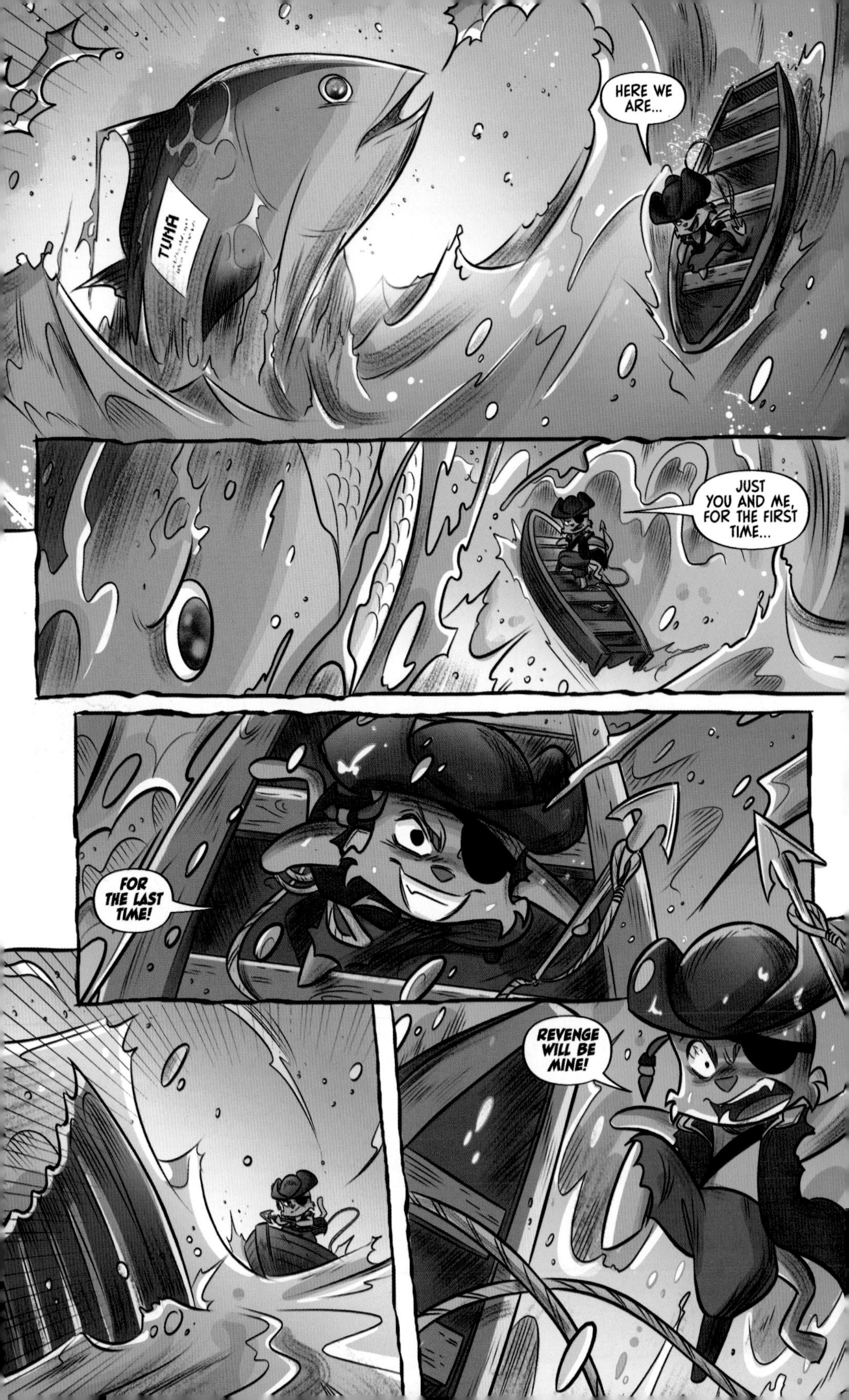
TUNA
HERE WE ARE...
JUST YOU AND ME, FOR THE FIRST TIME...
FOR THE LAST TIME!
REVENGE WILL BE MINE!

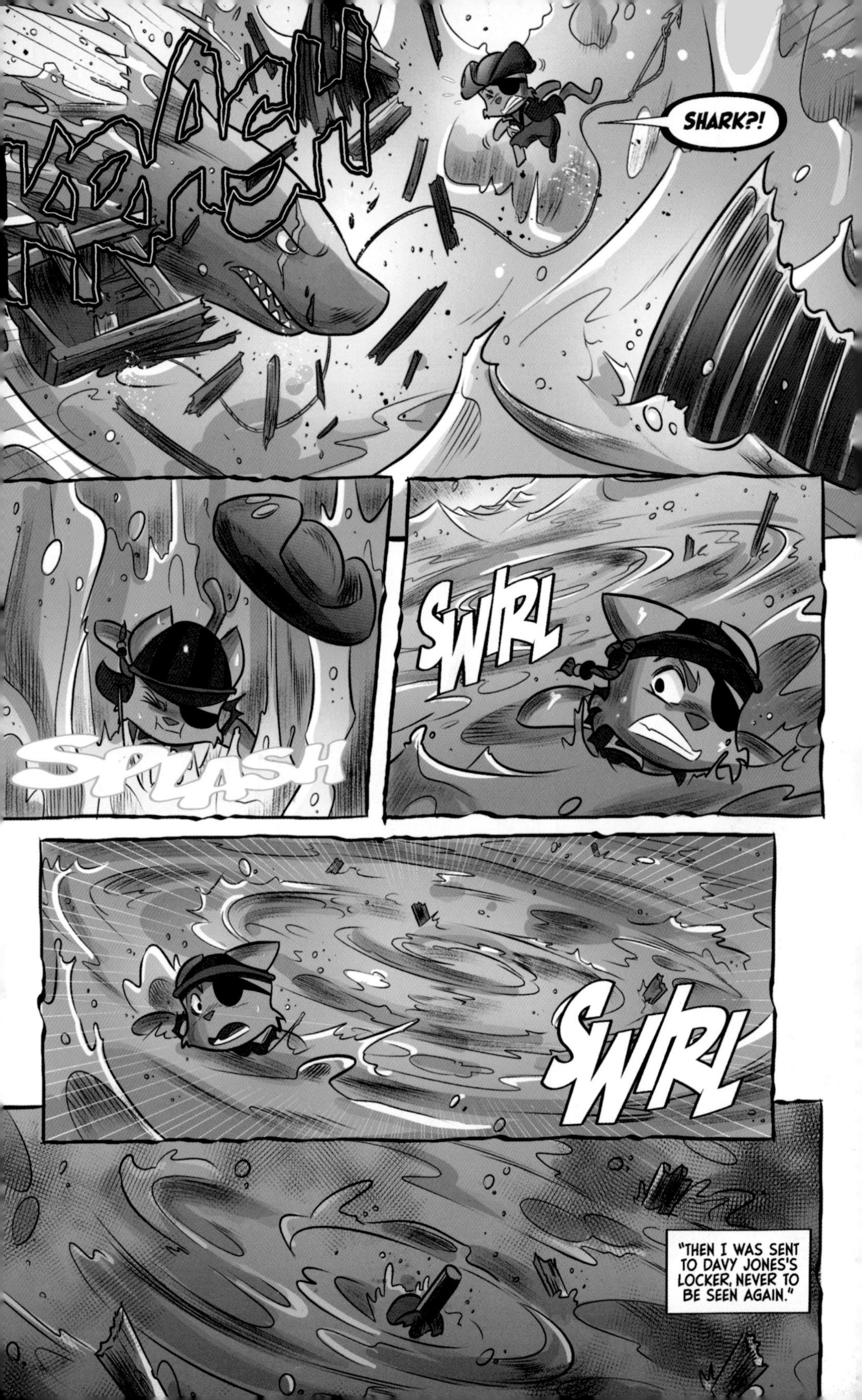
SHARK?!
SPLASH
SWIRL
SWIRL
"THEN I WAS SENT TO DAVY JONES'S LOCKER, NEVER TO BE SEEN AGAIN."

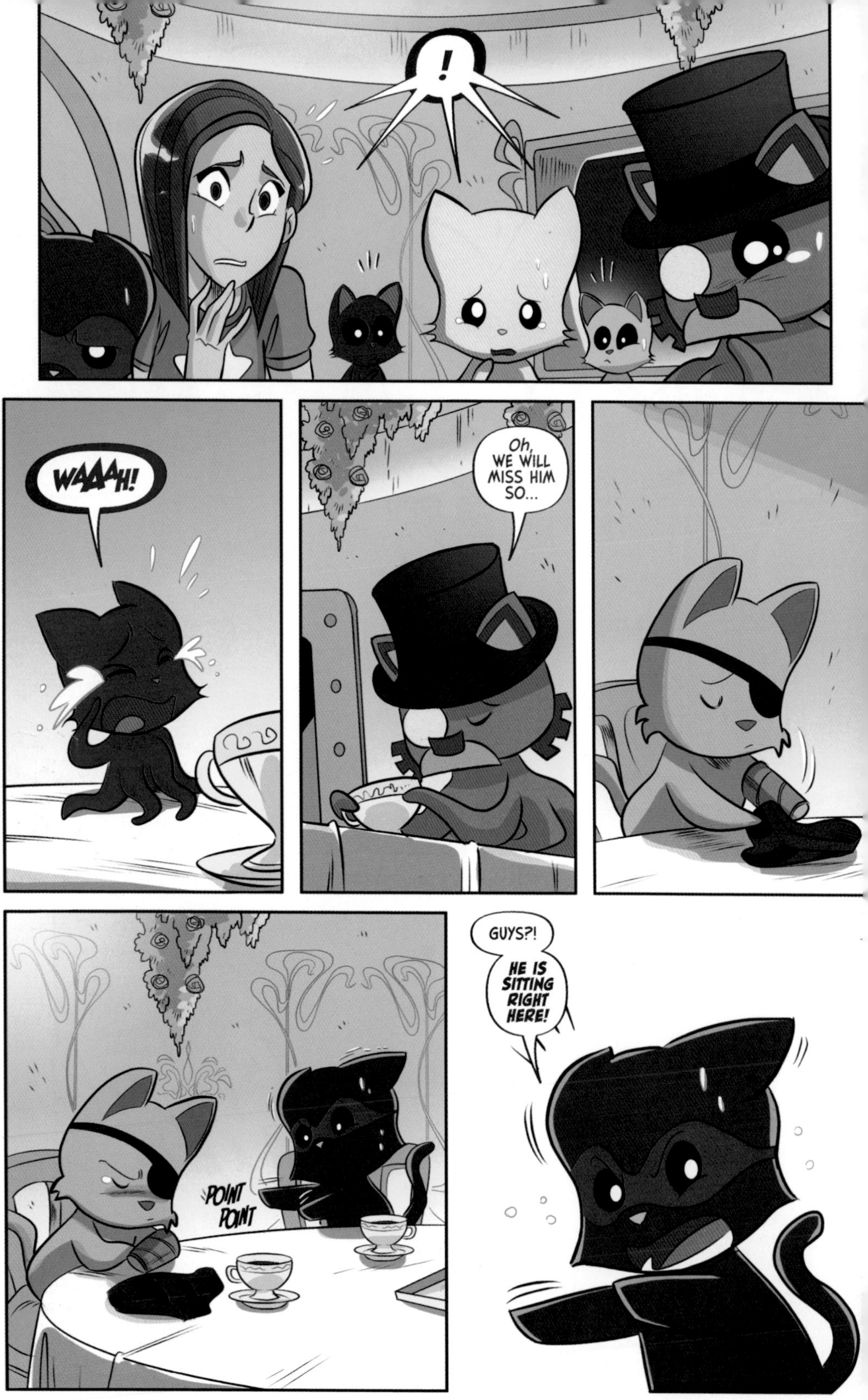
!
WAAAH!
Oh, WE WILL MISS HIM SO...
POINT POINT
GUYS?!
HE IS SITTING RIGHT HERE!

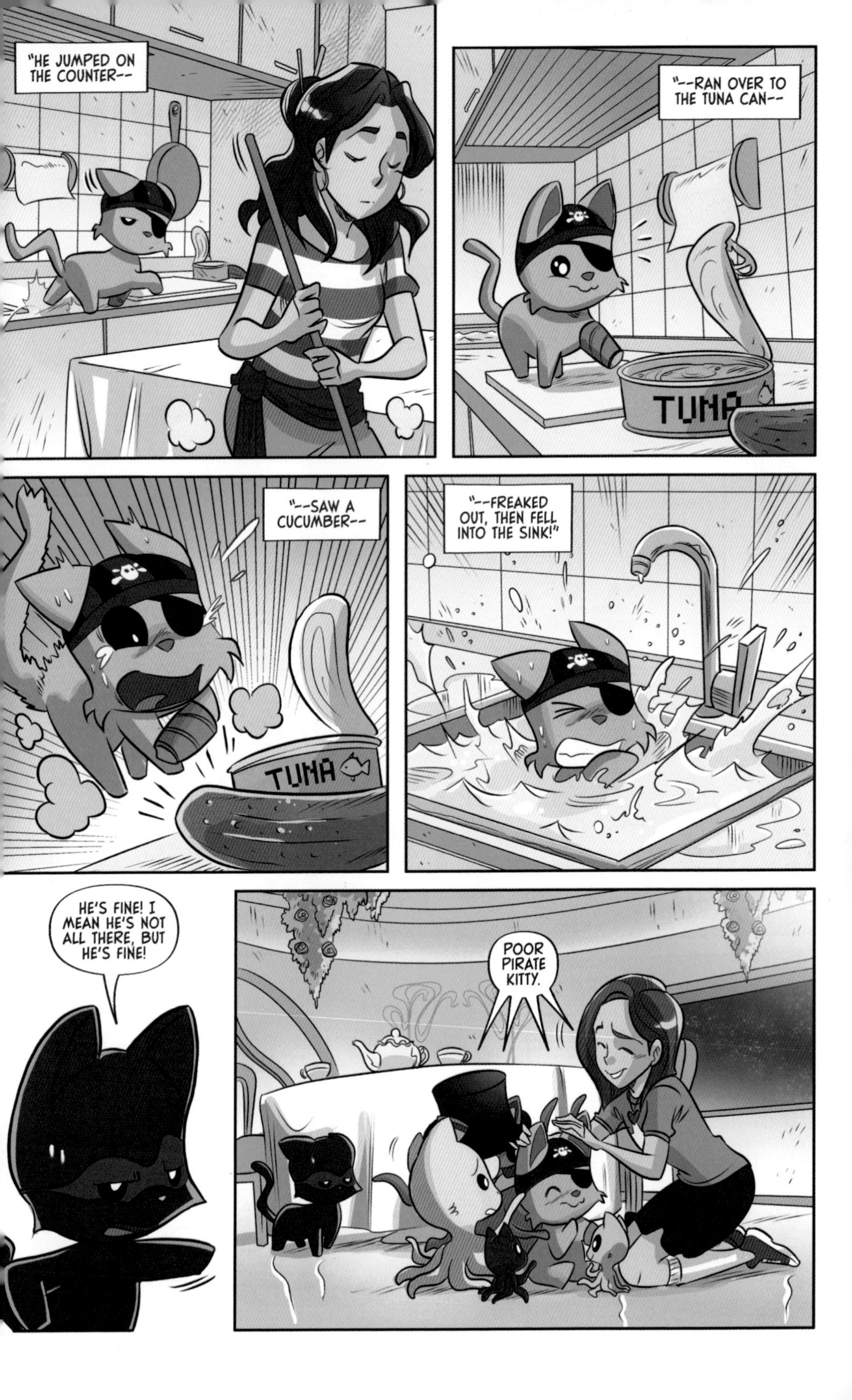
"HE JUMPED ON THE COUNTER--
"--RAN OVER TO THE TUNA CAN--
TUNA
"--SAW A CUCUMBER--
TUNA
"--FREAKED OUT, THEN FELL INTO THE SINK!"
HE'S FINE! I MEAN HE'S NOT ALL THERE, BUT HE'S FINE!
POOR PIRATE KITTY.

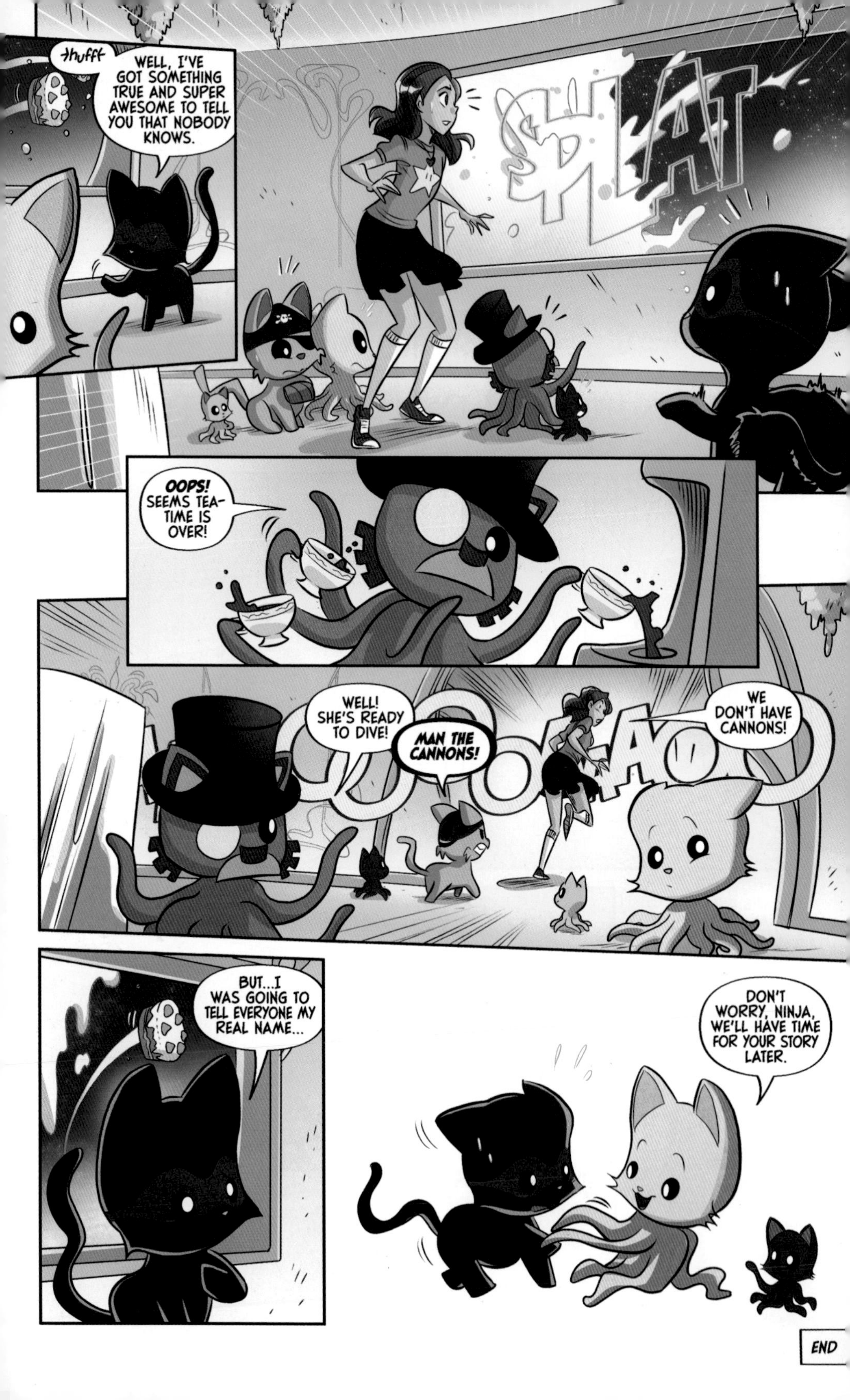
thufff
WELL, I'VE GOT SOMETHING TRUE AND SUPER AWESOME TO TELL YOU THAT NOBODY KNOWS.
SPLAT
OOPS! SEEMS TEA-TIME IS OVER!
WELL! SHE'S READY TO DIVE!
MAN THE CANNONS!
WE DON'T HAVE CANNONS!
BUT...I WAS GOING TO TELL EVERYONE MY REAL NAME...
DON'T WORRY, NINJA, WE'LL HAVE TIME FOR YOUR STORY LATER.
END

Space
Boy

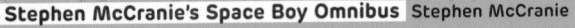

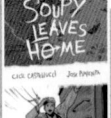

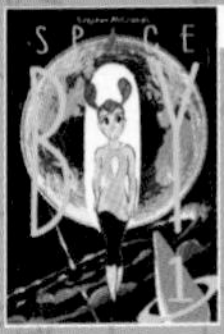

Stephen McCranie's Space Boy Omnibus **Stephen McCranie**

To Amy, everyone has a flavor. When her dad loses his job on their remote deep space colony, Amy and her family are forced to start a new life back on Earth. Emerging from a cryotube after a thirty-year voyage, Amy awakes to find herself in a strange land of heavy gravity, weird people, and an endless blue sky.

Volume 1: $19.99 • 978-1-50672-643-4
Volume 2: $19.99 • 978-1-50672-644-1
Volume 3: $19.99 • 978-1-50672-645-8—Available September 2022

Soupy Leaves Home
Cecil Castellucci
Jose Pimienta

Soupy Leaves Home **Cecil Castellucci, Jose Pimienta**

Pearl ran away from home to escape an abusive father and unhappy future. Disguised and reborn as a boy named Soupy, she hitches her star to an unlikely hobo and they begin their journey from the cold heartbreak of their eastern homes toward the sunny promise of California in this train-hopping, Depression-era coming-of-age tale.

$17.99 • 978-1-50672-205-4

Bandette
Presto!
Tobin
Coover

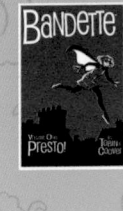

Bandette **Paul Tobin, Colleen Coover**

The world's greatest thief is a costumed teen burglar by the *nome d'arte* of Bandette! Gleefully plying her skills on either side of the law alongside her network of street urchins, Bandette is a thorn in the side of both Police Inspector Belgique and the criminal underworld. But it's not all breaking hearts and purloining masterpieces when a rival thief makes a startling discovery. Can even Bandette laugh off a plot against her life?

Volume 1 TPB: $14.99 • 978-1-50671-923-8
Volume 2 TPB: $14.99 • 978-1-50671-924-5
Volume 3 TPB: $14.99 • 978-1-50671-925-2
Volume 4 HC: $17.99 • 978-1-50671-926-9

Goblin

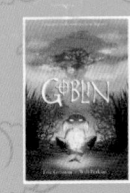

Goblin **Eric Grissom, Will Perkins**

A young, headstrong goblin embarks on a wild journey of danger, loss, self-discovery, and sacrifice! One fateful night, a sinister human warrior raids the home of the young goblin Rikt and leaves him orphaned. Angry and alone, Rikt vows to avenge the death of his parents and seeks a way to destroy the man who did this. He finds aid from unlikely allies throughout his journey and learns of a secret power hidden in the heart of the First Tree. Will Rikt survive the trials that await him on his perilous journey to the First Tree? And is Rikt truly prepared for what he may find there?

$14.99 • 978-1-50672-472-0

Steam

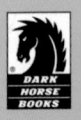

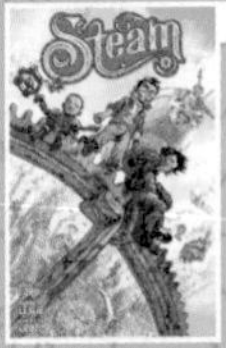

Steam **Drew Ford, Duane Leslie, Eva de la Cruz**

A young boy named Arlo escapes his abusive guardians on Earth, through an intergalactic portal to the steam-powered planet of Pother. While there he discovers that his long-lost father inadvertently helped a powerful corporation from Earth, in their efforts to deplete the planet's resources. In an attempt to set things right, Arlo joins a small group of resisters from Pother, as they work to both remove this dangerous organization from their world and protect the planet's indigenous beings. Through this epic adventure, Arlo discovers his own self-worth, and perhaps even his life's ultimate destiny.

$14.99 • 978-1-50671-726-5

AVAILABLE AT YOUR LOCAL COMICS SHOP OR BOOKSTORE! To find a comics shop in your area, visit comicshoplocator.com. For more information or to order direct, visit DarkHorse.com.

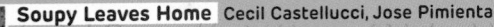